ACCIDENT... OR MURDER?

Amanda Hazard towed Officer Nick Thorn down the cellar steps to examine the body she'd discovered during the devastating storm that struck Vamoose an hour earlier.

"He's gone!" Amanda howled in disbelief.

"Are you sure he was dead?"

Amanda scowled. "Give me a little credit, Thorn. I know dead when I see it. This is my second murder victim, after all."

"*Murder,* Hazard? Let's not jump to conclusions." Nick surveyed the scene before him. "From the look of things, Elmer Jolly fell on his way to the storm shelter. The old man wasn't sure of foot and he was undoubtedly in a hurry. He tripped on these rickety steps, latched onto the shelves for support, and pulled them down on top of him. Somebody else must've found him and called an ambulance while you were trying to track me down. I'll check with the medical examiner."

"No, you won't," Amanda grumbled. "You don't believe me, but I intend to prove Elmer was murdered."

"And what, I'd like to know, has convinced you of that?"

"Elmer was wearing his false teeth when I found him," Amanda said, as if it explained everything.

Nick groaned. "Damn it to hell. Here we go again . . ."

DEAD IN THE CELLAR

CONNIE FEDDERSEN

ZEBRA BOOKS
KENSINGTON PUBLISHING CORP.

*This book is dedicated to my husband Ed
and our children, Christine, Jill and Kurt,
with much love.*

ZEBRA BOOKS are published by

Kensington Publishing Corp.
475 Park Avenue South
New York, NY 10016

First Printing: May, 1994

Printed in the United States of America

Chapter One

The jingling phone shattered the silence. Amanda Hazard stuck a well-manicured forefinger on the piece of paper in front of her to keep her place and reached for the receiver.

"Hazard Accounting Agency."

"Missy? Elmer Jolly here."

"Hi, Elmer. What can I do for you?"

"I need to see you PDQ."

That was Elmer Jolly through and through. The old man never had the time or inclination for social amenities. He said what he wanted to say and then he got off the phone. Some of Amanda's elderly clients had a tendency to ramble incessantly about their families or most recent ailments, but not Elmer. He was a plain-spoken recluse who lived several miles northwest of Vamoose. Elmer ventured into town twice a month to purchase supplies and then returned home having made as little contact with the outside world as possible. But for some reason he had taken an instant liking to Amanda. Perhaps it was because she was also a no-nonsense kind of individual who did not mince words.

Whatever the case, Elmer had handed his accounts and tax forms over to Amanda with a decisive nod of approval, declaring she was "the best damned accountant" he had ever met.

"Do you want me to come see you tomorrow morning, Elmer?"

"Not good enough, missy." Elmer's gravely voice boomed back at her. "Those sons-a-bitches are trying to have me committed, damn their sorry hides! I won't stand for it, I tell you! When I depart from this earth, I'm leaving my money and property to whomever I want to leave it to, and *nobody* is going to try to change my mind!"

"Who is trying to have you committed?"

Apparently Elmer didn't hear the question. Either that or he was too frustrated to listen. It was also obvious to Amanda that Elmer wasn't wearing his false teeth. He was gumming the words and smacking his lips each time he paused for breath.

"They're trying to have me declared incompetent so they can steal me blind. But I fixed 'em good! I wrote up my will and had the banker witness it. I named you the executor of my estate, and no matter what, don't you believe a word of the lies!"

Elmer had worked himself into a lather, and he wheezed as he tried to catch his breath. After a moment of sputtering and coughing, he plowed on. "I'm leaving you my critters, missy. I know you'll take care of them the same way I would. And all the cash that I have stashed in the house in canning jars is yours to pay the critters' expenses."

When Elmer sputtered again, Amanda leaped at the chance to interject a comment. "I'm flattered that you'd trust me to oversee your estate, Elmer, but I think a lawyer would—"

"Lawyer? Lawyer!" Elmer crowed like a rooster. "I ain't messing with no damn lawyer, and that's final! The first and last lawyer I dealt with tried to swipe the mineral rights to my land in exchange for conducting a legal transaction. I refuse to deal with them. They ain't getting a penny from me, either!"

At seventy-three, Elmer Jolly was a hot-tempered eccentric, and his mind was encased in cement. Amanda knew it was a waste of breath to argue the virtues and benefits of attorneys or anything else. Elmer also harbored trepidations about computers, newfangled electronic devices, and the tortures of retirement homes. Amanda knew better than to get Elmer started on those sensitive subjects. What he did not completely understand, he didn't trust. He believed what he believed, and no one could change his mind.

"All right, Elmer, if you want me to handle your estate when the time comes—"

"You're damn tootin' that's the way I want it! You hightail it out here after lunch so I can get things squared away. I'm putting my will in your hands."

"But—"

"I won't be able to rest until you've seen the will. I don't want anybody stealing my notes and my money. By God, I'll find a way to take them with me first!"

Elmer had worked himself into such a tizzy that Amanda was willing to say anything to reassure him. "Don't worry about a thing, Elmer. I promise you that I'll see your wishes carried out to the letter."

"I knew I could count on you, missy. I'll simmer

down, eat my lunch, catch the farmers' market report on TV, and then we'll talk."

The line went dead and Amanda frowned at the receiver. My, but Elmer was in a fine temper this morning. She was beginning to wonder if he hadn't developed symptoms of paranoia as well as senility. But then, who was she to criticize? If she lived to be seventy-three, she might have a few eccentric tendencies herself.

Up to this point, Elmer had possessed a sharp, alert mind, but he had definitely been raving like a madman this morning. Something had upset him. Hopefully, he would calm down after he had lunch and listened to the farmers' market reports, as he did faithfully each day. Then perhaps Amanda could get the details on exactly who "they" were.

Tucking the conversation in the back of her mind, she returned to the papers on her desk and completed her calculations. When thunder rumbled, she glanced out the window of her new office on the main street of Vamoose to see cumulonimbus clouds piling up.

It was springtime in Oklahoma, and this region of the country wasn't called Tornado Alley for nothing. Amanda had developed a wary respect for thunderstorms over the years; so had the citizens of this farming community. When lightning streaked across the sky, tractors and implements ground to a halt; cattlemen gathered their fencing tools and headed for shelter. Too many folks had been struck down trying to repair barbed-wire fences or zapped while their plows were half-buried in farm ground.

No one took tornadoes and severe storms lightly in Vamoose. Weather was a serious determining factor in farming and ranching. Mother Nature had a way of dipping her hand in the pocket of profit, just when everything was coming up roses, or rather, coming up cotton, wheat, and alfalfa, as the case happened to be in Vamoose. Amanda had become as conscious of weather conditions as her rural clientele. When storms approached, all eyes turned skyward. Televisions and radios were tuned into the meteorologists' forecasts. Storm alert teams from Oklahoma City swarmed the countryside to dramatize disaster.

Another crack of thunder rattled the windowpane and brought Amanda straight out of her chair. A quick glance at her watch indicated that she had just enough time to grab a greasy hamburger and fries at the Last Chance Cafe before she drove out to Elmer Jolly's farm. Amanda intended to be within running distance of a storm shelter if severe weather threatened. From the look of the blackening sky, hell was going to break loose somewhere in Tornado Alley before the day was out.

Amanda dashed across the street to Vamoose's one and only restaurant just as the church bell chimed high noon. As usual, the cafe was packed with farmers and cattlemen. Speculations on how the weather would affect crops and livestock were buzzing around it. One stubble-faced farmer in OshKosh overalls was comparing this year's weather patterns to the 40's, while his companion was contradicting his every word. Faye Bernard, the harried waitress, was scurrying from one table to another, delivering hamburgers and refilling coffee cups.

Amanda caught a glimpse of Officer Nick Thorn, Vamoose's chief of police, in the corner booth, surrounded by three cattlemen. When Thorn noticed Amanda's arrival, his dark eyes flicked over her business suit. He nodded a greeting before turning his attention back to his companions. Without a second glance in Thorn's direction, Amanda headed for the counter to order a hamburger to go.

Since she had cracked her first murder case a few months earlier, she and Thorn had become acquainted—intimately, in fact. Their . . . relationship . . . was one of the best-kept secrets in a town where everybody liked to keep abreast of everybody else's business.

Velma's Beauty Boutique and the Last Chance Cafe were hot beds of, and breeding grounds for, gossip. Amanda had used that fact to her advantage in solving her first murder case. Of course, Nick Thorn had scoffed at her techniques for gleaning information about a murder he'd refused to believe had even been committed. But he had come around to Amanda's way of thinking eventually. In the end, they had made a fine detective team. Their . . . relationship . . . might have progressed at an accelerated rate if Amanda had not been so swamped during tax season and Thorn had not been busy making his appointed rounds and keeping abreast of his part-time farming and cattle operation. In short, their promising romance had been put on the back burner because their professions took precedence.

After solving her first murder case, Amanda had gained so much notoriety that new clients had flocked to her in droves, forcing her to rent office space in town and spend only one day a week with her previous Oklahoma City employers: Nelson, Blake, and Cosmos Accounting. Seeing Thorn reminded her that these days, the *only* thing she got her hands on was her calculator.

Suddenly Amanda felt a presence beside her, and she knew instantly who had approached the cash register to pay for his meal. She would have recognized that tantalizing masculine scent anywhere, even if it *had* been a long time since she'd been even closer to it. There were some things a woman did not forget. Nick Thorn was one of them.

"Hello, Hazard. It looks as if we're in for a stretch of rough weather, doesn't it?"

Nick leaned leisurely against the counter, his uniform straining against the expanse of his broad, male chest. Amanda had a most outrageous urge to reach out and touch him. Damn, it really *had* been too long since she and Thorn blew off a little steam . . .

She cleared her throat and silently cursed herself for emulating her mother's annoying habit. "Um . . . yes . . . rough weather, Thorn," she agreed while her hormones rioted inside her.

"How's the accounting business coming along? Any relief in your work load?"

Nick Thorn wanted to grab this sexy blonde and disappear with her for a couple of hours. One look at Hazard and his temperature rose ten degrees. If he'd had his way, their affair would have been common knowledge long before now. Unfortunately, Miss Propriety had been leery about making a public commitment after her unpleasant divorce seven years earlier.

Since Hazard had only resided in the small town of Vamoose for a year, and now handled almost everyone's accounts except his, she had a fanatic desire to ensure that her high-profile image remained unblemished. She cringed at the idea of being the subject of juicy gossip. Nick, however, had no qualms about letting folks know she was his woman. He liked Hazard, and she claimed to like him—in private. In public, Hazard expected him to play the role of casual acquaintance.

Nick reminded himself that they'd both been so busy there hadn't been time lately for anything except work. But that didn't alter the fact that he was about to blow a fuse for want of this woman.

"Hazard, I need a little relief," Nick murmured just as Faye Bernard scuttled over to bring Amanda her hamburger to go.

Amanda nearly dropped the paper sack she'd received in a handoff. "Keep your voice down, Thorn," she hissed.

"I can keep my voice down, but that's about all I can keep down." He leaned over to hand Faye a five-dollar bill to pay for his lunch. Straight-faced, he whispered, "A man can stand only so many cold showers. I've reached my limit. Your place or mine?"

Amanda darted a discreet glance in every direction. "Yours. But if you grin and strut on your way out of the cafe, I'll hold it over your head for the rest of your life."

No cold shower tonight! thought Nick. But with the nonchalance and reserve befitting an officer of the law, he stuffed his change in his pocket and ambled toward the door. He paused to make small talk with Chester Korn who was lounging in a booth with his son. The tactical maneuver provided time for Hazard to catch up with him without the crowd at the Last Chance Cafe knowing they were planning a long-awaited tête-é-tête.

When Amanda stepped outside, she cast Thorn an aggravated glance. "Confound it, Thorn, she could have overheard you."

"Who? Faye? She was too busy counting change and

serving meals to give a thought to anything else. Besides, I think it's time Vamoose knows we're an item," he said, flashing Amanda a heart-melting smile. "I gave up clandestine work when I resigned from the narcotics squad of the Oklahoma City police force."

"Well, I don't want to wind up as news on the bulletin board at the Last Chance Cafe, or the hottest gossip at Velma's Beauty Boutique," Amanda huffed as she moved toward her compact Toyota.

"If you had any pride in the fact that we are more than casual acquaintances, you wouldn't mind letting Vamoosians know we're having an affair."

Amanda winced at the *A* word and clutched her paper bag in a tight fist. "I believe in being discreet," she muttered. "One does not publicize one's private life."

"Then I suppose you want me to pick you up at your place and drive you to my place so nobody will suspect anything is going on." Nick tossed her a goading grin. He had always derived excessive pleasure from ruffling Hazard's feathers. "Are you going to duck down in the seat of my truck like you did the time Velma Hertzog met us on the road?"

Amanda blushed beet red and flounced into her car. She supposed Nick had a legitimate point. Maybe she was carrying this secrecy thing a bit too far. But she had never been worth a damn at casual ... relationships. Her old-fashioned midwestern ideals nagged her to death. What she and Thorn had was good, especially in the bedroom. Okay, better than good, Amanda amended. *Aw, come on, Hazard, tell it like it is.* Oh, all right, she and Thorn were dynamite together, Amanda admitted. Thorn was the first man who had gotten past her bedroom door since her divorce. However, that did not signify that she had lost all sense of logic. She had made one mistake. She was *not* going to blunder blindly into another.

Stabbing her hand into the grasy sack, she grabbed her hamburger and ate as she drove. She and Thorn would hash out the terms of their . . . relationship . . . tonight. The thought sent a tingle of anticipation down her spine. Thorn was right. Cold showers were for the birds. It had been too long since they had enjoyed any privacy.

A naughty little grin curved her mouth upward as she bit into her hamburger. Nick Thorn in uniform had always been a sight to see. His good looks were impossible to ignore. But out of uniform, Thorn was something else again . . .

Amanda switched the air conditioner onto MAX to cool off. The last thing she needed was to get hot and bothered before consulting with Elmer Jolly.

Discarding the lingering vision of Nick Thorn naked, Amanda switched on the radio and concentrated on the problem at hand. The fact that she was living in Tornado Alley struck her when the meteorologist interrupted regular programming to issue a special bulletin. Vamoose and the nearby town of Pronto were under a tornado warning. A strong low-pressure air mass had plunged across the Great Plains to collide with the warm, moist air that had been sucked up from the gulf. A dry line had formed over Oklahoma, and conditions were ripe for tornadic activity.

Great. Just great.

To emphasize the grim report, lighting flashed and thunder exploded overhead. Amanda instinctively ducked and lost her grip on her hamburger. Her high

cholesterol lunch kerplopped onto her lap, leaving a noticeable stain on her linen skirt.

Before she could pick up the half-eaten sandwich, her
Toyota sideswiped the gargantuan clump of weeds and
gravel that lined the country road.

"I swear Commissioner Brown and his road-grading
crews screw up these roads on purpose!"

The insufferable condition of the country roads had
always been one of Amanda's pet peeves. In winter, the
rural byways were frozen into deep ruts that could, and
did, wreack havoc on her compact car. In spring, the
ditches boasted such an array of weeds that the roads
were reminiscent of the paths carved out by covered
wagons in the pioneer days. Grass grew in the middle of
the road, and huge mounds of downed weeds, gravel,
and dirt lined both sides like guard rails. Meeting another vehicle on a one-lane path was treacherous business. A driver could get high center in no time at all on
the piles of graded weeds.

Still muttering about the road conditions, Amanda
opted for the middle and prayed she didn't meet oncoming traffic when she topped the hill. She cringed
to think what would happen to these roads when the
torrential rains came. On her return trip from Elmer
Jolly's farm, she might wind up in a ditch, up to her
axles in goo.

She forgot her irritation with County Commissioner
Brown and his road brigade when another weather
alert blared over the radio. A wall cloud had been
sighted. The projected path of the storm put the communities of Vamoose and Pronto in jeopardy. Worse,
Amanda was heading directly into the path of the ap-

proaching storm in her crackerbox car. What else could go wrong?

She craned her neck to get a better view of the swirling clouds that hung from the sky like vaporous stalactites. "Holy hell!" Amanda floored the accelerator and created her own cloud of dust, hoping to reach Elmer Jolly's farm before disaster descended. From the look of things, she and Thorn might not have a choice of her place or his. One or both might be blown to smithereens before the sun went down.

Huge raindrops pelted the Toyota, and Amanda switched on the windshield wipers. As lightning illuminated the darkening sky, the meteorologist urged everyone in the path of the storm to seek shelter—immediately.

"I'm trying, for God's sake!" Amanda yelled at the radio. She still had a mile to go before she reached Jolly's farm. If she didn't kill herself first driving at seventy miles an hour on impassable roads, the storm would probably swallow her alive.

She gritted her teeth and zoomed toward the farm, serenaded by thumps as gravel put dents in her Toyota. Up ahead, Amanda spotted another cloud of dust left by a speeding vehicle . . . or was it the makings of a tornado?

Amanda stamped on the brake to make the turn on two wheels. The Toyota skidded sideways in the loose gravel and scraped the corner fence post that marked Elmer's driveway. She cursed and plowed on ahead. In the distance she could see the cloud of dust swirling off in the raging wind, assuring her that it was definitely another speeding vehicle, not a tornado, that caused the billowing brown fog.

Just as Amanda stuck a pantyhose-clad leg out the

door, the clouds opened. Rain hammered against the tin granary and barn, amplifying the feeling of oncoming disaster. The fierce wind that had been blowing from the southeast switched directions, practically ripping the door off the car and succeeding in tossing Amanda off balance. The Toyota wobbled on its wheels when another blast of wind pummeled it.

Amanda inhaled a fortifying breath and dashed toward the porch. It was then she saw what she hadn't wanted to see. Black clouds churned counterclockwise, sucking up debris from the ground below. She and Elmer Jolly were in serious trouble! If the tornado touched down within the next few minutes, she and Elmer would be goners. She had seen homes and buildings wiped off their foundations by F5 tornados. Hiding in a hole was the only sure way to ride out a destructive twister. She had to get Elmer into the outdated storm cellar that sat behind the house, and she had to do it *now!*

"Elmer!" Without awaiting an invitation, Amanda barreled through the front door. The small black and white television in Elmer's front room was blaring to accommodate the elderly farmer who was hard of hearing and refused to wear auditory devices. The meteorologist was indicating the dark patches on radar, pinpointing the strongest cells in the storm. And of course Amanda was in one of the dreaded dark patches!

She glanced anxiously around the house. Elmer's half-empty plate sat on the table. One corner of the square tablecloth which was draped over the round table nearly touched the floor. And Elmer's chair had been left sitting at an angle instead of being pushed into its normal position. The pudgy tomcat—Hank was his

name—was prowling the confines of the room, looking
every bit as uneasy as Amanda felt.

"Elmer? Where are you?" Amanda scurried down the
hall, scooping up Hank to cuddle him protectively
against her.

Elmer's bedroom stood empty, but several drawers in
his antique walnut dresser were gaping open. The un-
made bed looked as if a tornado had already struck. The
sheets had been pulled away from the mattress and lay
in a pile. Wherever Elmer was, he was not in bed.

When hail pounded against the roof, Amanda whirled
around and dashed to the kitchen. In her mind's eye, she
could see her shiny Toyota being beaten by golfball-
sized chunks of ice. She also pictured herself buried
beneath falling debris.

"Elmer!" she howled while Hank squirmed and caterwauled in her crushing grasp.

The electrical power shut down. Lights and television
flickered off as the snapping of tree branches mingled
with the steady thump of hailstones. Amanda was running out of time. If Elmer had already taken the precau-
tion of huddling in his storm shelter, she was likely to
be the one blown away while trying to rescue the elderly farmer from disaster.

Yielding to a sense of panic, Amanda plunged out the
back door with Hank clutched to her bosom. Hank sank
in his claws and squirmed when rain and hail descended
on him, but Amanda held onto him and darted toward
the cellar.

The warped cellar door lay open, the hatchway lined
with rotting wooden steps slick with rain. Amanda
tossed Hank inside and made a grab for the door, but the
howling gale prevented her from shutting them in. Mut-

tering unladylike curses, she stumbled down the steps, steadying herself against the damp walls of the underground shelter that looked as if it should have been bulldozed in long ago. A musty smell saturated her as she descended into the darkness.

"Elmer?" Amanda squinted into the shadows to see remains of wooden shelving which had tumbled to the floor. Broken glass jars littered a floor three inches under water. Green beans, beets, peaches and pickles were strewn about like casualties of war, but there was no sign of Elmer.

When Amanda realized a deadly calm had settled over the cellar, she pivoted on the slimy step and scrambled up the stairs. She made a frantic grab for the rope that served as a handle on the inside of the door, and the wooden portal clanked into place a split second before a roar, like that of a locomotive, rumbled overhead.

Amanda clamped both hands on the rope to secure the door and prayed for all she was worth. Visions of the dilapidated cellar caving in around her danced in her head. The cement walls and arched ceiling were already cracked and bulging. Streams of mud and water seeped inside the cellar and dribbled down the walls. The violent force of a tornado could leave this flimsy structure a pile of rubble.

A yelp burst from Amanda's lips when the door was sucked upward, drawing her up too. She clung to the rope as if it were her salvation, and the door dropped back. Minutes passed, and the storm raged on. Hail pounded like fists on the wood above her, the and unseen objects banged into it. She wondered if Thorn had had time to seek cover before the storm struck. She hoped his streak of machismo hadn't gotten the best of him. She liked him—too much for her own good, if the truth be known. Even if she had been discreet and wary of gossip, their . . . relationship . . . had promise. Indeed, if it were not for Amanda's excessive work load and Thorn's career and farming obligations, this might be a romance in full blossom. It would definitely bloom tonight, Amanda promised herself. If they both survived this calamity . . .

A deafening crash shook the wooden door and Amanda squealed. With her luck a tree had been uprooted above her, trapping her inside this outdated cellar. No one knew where she was. She would die of starvation before somebody thought to look for her.

No, Amanda assured herself shakily. She wouldn't starve. She could munch on the fruits and vegetables that floated in the rising ground water. Yummy. She could pry the air vent off the ceiling and stuff Hank through it with a note tied around his neck. She might be rescued . . . in a couple of years.

Depression closed in on her as the howling storm had. "Ah, Thorn. I guess I shouldn't have made such a big deal of keeping our . . . relationship . . . a secret. Maybe we could have seen more of each other, if only from two to six in the morning."

The wind wailed; hail pounded on the wooden door. Amanda wondered if she would emerge from the inky darkness to find herself surrounded by Munchkins, viewing the Land of Oz in living color. Elmer Jolly would be the great and wonderful wizard who . . .

Where the hell was Elmer anyway? If he had made it to the cellar, why hadn't she heard a peep out of him?

"Elmer? Are you down there? It's me, Amanda," she yelled over the storm.

Hank meowed.

Another few minutes elapsed before the second eerie calm settled over the black hole Amanda had shut herself into. Deeming it safe to emerge, she shoved her shoulder against the door and pushed. It wouldn't budge.

Climbing a step higher, Amanda crouched under the door to use the strength in her legs. The door creaked, but only opened a few inches. Cursing loudly, she fumbled down the steps to locate a piece of wood to prop the door open wide enough to wriggle out.

Once she had lifted the weight of the door, she shoved the board into place, snagging her pantyhose and jacket sleeve in the process. Another expensive ensemble torn to hell. Of course she *was* overdressed for coping with the destruction left by a tornado.

Worming through the narrow opening, Amanda emerged like a turtle poking its head from its shell. The scene before her did nothing to improve her bleak mood. Fallen tree branches testified to the intensity of the storm which had cut a swath across the countryside. Wood from the barn and tin from the sheds were scattered hither and yon. The screen door on the back of Elmer's house sagged on its hinges, and shingles littered a lawn covered with a white glaze of egg-sized hailstones.

A whine from the barn demanded Amanda's attention. Still lying prone in the mud, she swiveled around to see Pete, the three-legged dog, hobbling toward her. With a wag of his soggy tail, Pete licked the cobwebs and goo from Amanda's face.

"Hello, Toto. Did the storm blow us all the way to Kansas?"

Pete limped off to join Elmer's other critters. Lucky, the duck, was having a field day digging roots from water holes. The chickens were on a worm hunt, and Amanda could hear Elmer's pigs squealing in their pen beside the barn, carrying on as if they were trying to tell her something. Now, if only she could locate Elmer, all would be present and accounted for.

Amanda scraped her muddy self off the ground and surveyed the tree limb that had crashed onto the cellar door. Bracing her legs, she tugged on the branch. One shoe was sucked off her foot as she struggled with it. The other red pump fell by the wayside on her second step backward. Shoeless, Amanda nonetheless managed to dislodge the branch that blocked the cellar door.

Glancing around, she tried to locate a rag to wipe the mud and sap from her hands. Then, with a hopeless shrug, she grabbed the hem of her silk blouse. The costly ensemble had suffered irreparable damage already. What did a little more mud and sap matter?

A groan came from Amanda when she caught a glimpse of her Toyota. The car looked as if it had sprouted leaves. She didn't even want to imagine the size of the dents in the top and hood, not to mention the damage the hail had done.

"Elmer, come out. Come out wherever you are," Amanda yelled at the top of her lungs.

No answer. Where was that old man?

After pulling the branches from her car to determine whether the damage was as extensive as she suspected—it was—she propelled herself toward the house, which had managed to survive the storm relatively intact. A thorough search of it turned up nothing. Elmer was simply nowhere to be found. Maybe he had been in the speeding car she had seen topping the hill when she'd arrived at the farm.

Amanda ventured back outside to free the tomcat from the cellar. Two kitty, kittys later, Hank still refused to slink out. Muttering, Amanda descended the stairs. Her foot slipped on the broken bottom step, and she plummeted over the fallen shelves that had once held Elmer's supply of canned goods. Hank meowed from somewhere in the shadows.

"Come here, you stupid cat," she snapped.

Hank caterwauled, but he didn't come.

Crawling on hands and knees, Amanda inched over the shelves until her foot connected with what felt suspiciously like a body. Amanda glanced sideways and automatically recoiled as if she had been snakebit. Now she knew what had become of Elmer Jolly. She had touched his bony body with her foot, and the thin shaft of light that fell into the cellar spotlighted the outstretched arm that protruded from the overturned shelving. A hand, resembling a bird's scaly claw, was barely visible in the water. Amanda looked down into a pair of glassy eyes and swallowed hard.

Obviously Hank had found Elmer a half-hour earlier, but Amanda had not been able to understand his feline call for assistance.

Elmer Jolly, Amanda was sad to report, had weathered his last storm. The "they" who'd threatened to have him locked away were no longer of any consequence. Elmer was headed to that Great Barnyard in the Sky, and now Amanda was responsible for the critters he had bequeathed to her. The recluse of Vamoose would never again have to worry about humanity crowding in on him. Elmer would have all the space he wanted in the netherworld far, far way . . .

Chapter Two

This was the second time Amanda Hazard had stumbled onto a dead body in the vicinity of Vamoose. Having watched her fair share of *Magnum P.I.* reruns, while drooling over Tom Selleck, Amanda had learned to survey the scene for important details. From what she could ascertain, Elmer had hobbled into the outdated cellar and tried to grab the warped shelving for balance. The shelves must have come crashing down on him. He had either broken his neck or suffered a fatal blow. Whatever the case, Elmer had departed from this life and Amanda had been named executor of his estate.

Amanda knew enough from watching detective shows and reading mysteries—in what little spare time she had—that it was a no-no to disturb the scene of an accident. Besides, she would need assistance to lever the shelving off Elmer. The shelves, constructed of one-by-twelves and two-by-fours, spanned the full length of the twelve-foot wall—from ceiling to floor. There was no way Amanda could lift the shelving by herself. Her only recourse was to contact Thorn.

Hoisting herself to her feet, Amanda stared down at

Elmer Jolly. His bald head was framed by warped shelving and his wire-rimmed spectacles dangled off the one half of a submerged earlobe. A lump formed in her throat when she focused on the glassy eyes that stared up at her. It was as if Elmer were issuing a silent command to take charge of the situation . . .

It was at that moment, while Amanda stood in the gloomy silence of the cellar, staring down at the man who had demanded that she come to his isolated farm home PDQ, that she knew what *looked* to be an accident was *no* accident at all. Someone had snuffed out Elmer Jolly at the spry age of seventy-three. He had not flown off to the pearl gates by accident, no matter what the scene implied. Amanda was certain Elmer had been a victim of foul play.

How did she know? It was simple actually. Elmer was wearing his store-bought teeth. They were visible in his sagging jaw.

Amanda slogged through the water, her mind reeling with questions. A pained hiss burst loose when her hose-clad foot connected with broken glass, taking a chunk out of her heel. With a noticeable limp, she ascended the steps to find four chickens, a rooster, a three-legged dog, and a quacking duck awaiting her. Two pigs squealed in the distance.

Amanda scrutinized her newly adopted family—Elmer's precious critters. Responsibility had been thrust upon her. The size of her household had increased and she was about to embark on another crusade for truth and justice.

Elmer Jolly had been murdered. The dismal thought stuck in Amanda's mind like a porcupine quill. Unfortunately, given the sketchy details at the scene of the crime, proving a murder had been committed and apprehending the killer would take some doing. And enlisting Nick Thorn's assistance would be no easy task. Thorn had been highly skeptical the first time Amanda cried murder because she had few clues to reinforce her suspicions. Thorn was definitely not going to cooperate this time, either.

Leaving blood puddles on the porch, Amanda hobbled to the house to call for assistance. The phone was as dead as Elmer. Curse it, Amanda would have to physically track Thorn down. Wrapping a dish towel around her injured foot, Amanda limped toward her Toyota and drove off.

Just as Amanda had predicted, the country roads were as slick as ice. All that prevented her from sliding into the bar ditch were the clumps of tangled weeds that lined the roads. Progress was further impeded when she had to stop to remove tree branches from her path.

The countryside lay in devastation. The hail had shredded vegetation and hay barns had become twisted masses of steel and tin. Amanda sympathized with the farmers whose wheat crops had begun to ripen in the fields. The economy in Vamoose had taken a direct hit.

The closer Amanda came to town, the more depressed her mood became. Downed trees, strewn shingles, broken windows, and scattered debris greeted her. Half of Vamoose had suffered wind damage; the other half had been pelted by hail. Families were emerging from shelters to evaluate the damage and take head counts of friends and neighbors.

It was impressive how Vamoosians banded together when disaster struck. Rural communities were noted for being close-knit groups who rushed to each other's rescue when times were hard. Amanda remembered the previous fall when one aging farmer had been injured in an accident. Family and neighbors climbed on their tractors, hitched up their drills, and planted the injured man's wheat crop for him. That was the kind of cooperation that existed in small-town America, and it made Amanda proud to be a Vamoosian.

Amanda cruised past the school where some of the citizens had congregated to seek shelter in the underground athletic dressing rooms. But there was no sign of Officer Thorn's squad car anywhere. Amanda was becoming frantic. What if Thorn had attempted to save some unfortunate victim from disaster and had succumbed to the storm? He could have been crushed beneath a fallen tree limb, slashed by flying tin . . .

An enormous sigh of relief gushed from Amanda's lips when the black and white patrol car squealed around the corner with lights flashing like a Christmas tree.

Nick pulled up beside the dented Toyota and stared at Amanda in concern. Her blond hair was plastered against the sides of her muddy face. The condition of her expensive clothes suggested she had been wallowing in a pigsty.

"Where in the hell have you been, Hazard? I turned this town upside down looking for you?"

Amanda glanced around her. "*You* did all this damage, Thorn? I thought it was the work of an F2 tornado."

Nick refused to be amused. "Are you all right? You look like hammered hell."

Before Amanda could reply, Deputy Sykes' voice blared over the two-way radio.

"Nick, I've got an 11-79. Chester Korn has been pinned in his overturned truck a half mile north of town. He's got a gash on his head and he's cursing the air blue. If we don't get him out quick, the old goat will go berserk. You know how Chester is about enclosed places."

"I'm on my way," Nick confirmed.

Hurriedly, Nick leaned over to open the passenger door and gestured for Amanda to climb inside. Amanda glanced at the congregation of citizens on the school grounds and hesitated.

Nick scowled sourly. "I'm sure all of Vamoose thinks this is innocent and above board, so don't get tangled in all your hang-ups. Quit worrying about your damned reputation and get the hell in the car."

"I wasn't—"

"Yes, you were," Nick muttered resentfully.

Amanda barely had time to seat herself before Nick took off with his siren screaming.

"The whole town has sustained some kind of damage or another," Nick declared as he cut a sharp corner. "God, would you look at this place? It's a mess."

"Thorn, I—"

"I haven't even had time to check my own farm and livestock." Nick whipped around another corner, causing Amanda to clank her head on the side window. "It will take weeks to clean the place up."

"Thorn, there's something—"

"Christ, wouldn't you know it? The mobile unit news team has already arrived on the scene. Just what we need."

Amanda knew exactly what Nick implied by that comment. No sooner had disaster struck than news-hungry reporters and cameramen arrived to interview the bewildered victims. When the squad car screeched to a halt, Amanda climbed out to find a pushy reporter shoving a microphone up her nostrils. No doubt, in her battered clothes and a dish towel wrapped around her injured foot, she looked like a prime target for an up-to-the-minute interview.

"Ma'am, can you tell us how it feels to survive the worst storm to hit Vamoose in twenty-five years?"

Amanda did what she wished more disaster victims would do when unwelcome interviews were thrust upon them. If the reporter and cameramen were expecting her to burst into tears and add to the melodrama of their fast-breaking story, they were in for one helluva surprise!

"You wanna know what it's like, mister hot-shot, on-the-spot reporter? Well, I'll tell you. It's the most fun I've ever had," Amanda said sarcastically. "I just love digging myself out from under a pile of rubble and running around barefoot, soaked to the bone, and wounded. In fact, when I saw the storm coming, I drove straight toward it so I could get my car hammered by hail and dented by falling tree limbs." She gave the reporter her best snarl. "Any more stupid questions?"

The reporter's jaw fell off its hinges.

"I—a member of your television viewing audience— would like to say that I am sick and tired of having you chase down victims to shove microphones up their snouts and film close-ups of teary-eyed survivors who have lost family or worldly possessions." Amanda waved her arms in expansive gestures. "Now put down that damned mike and camera and go help Office Thorn upright that truck so Chester can get free. For once, be of some help instead of standing in the way!"

The reporter gathered his wits and wheeled toward the camera. "We will have more details later. This is David Hicks reporting live in Vamoose for news team six—"

Amanda snatched the microphone up and shook it in his face. "Snap to it, David Hicks from news team six, or else you are going to eat this mike for a between-meal snack!"

"Lady, you can't talk to *me* like that!" David Hicks from news team six huffed.

"Oh yeah? Well, you and your camera-happy friend better haul ass or—"

"Um, Hazard?"

With blue eyes snapping and nostrils flared, Amanda wheeled around on her good foot to find the six-feet-two body of Officer Thorn towering behind her.

Nick's lips twitched as he stared down at the human firecracker. If there was one thing to be said about Hazard it was that she never fell short on nerve. She would take on the devil himself, cut his legs off with her rapier tongue, and send him crawling back to hell.

"Do me a favor and radio the dispatcher," Nick requested. "We need to send word for Opal Korn to meet her husband at the county hospital. Chester's injuries require medical attention."

Amanda lurched back around, lifted her chin, and looked down her nose at Hicks and his sidekick. "At least *I* will be doing something constructive while you two buzzards are hovering around, waiting to catch a bereaved victim on the verge of tears!"

"You two men help us upright the truck," Nick ordered the reporters.

To Amanda's complete and utter satisfaction, she saw both men's freshly starched shirts receive a dousing of mud when Chester's truck splashed down on its wheels in the ditch. After Amanda did as Thorn requested, she hobbled over to watch Chester Korn stagger out of his pickup to wilt on the ground. Within moments, the ambulance's shrill siren blasted the air. The crowd that had gathered to lend assistance parted to allow the paramedics to scurry forth, examine Chester, load him up, and haul him away.

After casting Amanda mutinous glowers, the newsmen stamped back to their car and zoomed off. Amanda childishly stuck out her tongue at the departing car. She had watched too many offensive interviews on television to feel not even the slightest twinge of regret for her outrageous tirade. In her opinion—and she was never without one on any subject—the media had gotten carried away with themselves, all in the name of reporting the news, whether the rest of the world wanted or needed to hear it or not!

Amanda slumped against the passenger door of the squad car while Nick folded his tall frame beneath the steering wheel. She could see the amusement dancing in those onyx eyes as he shifted the car into drive.

"We are a little testy this afternoon, aren't we, Hazard?"

"No, Thorn, we are righting wrongs," Amanda clarified. "I have had it with obnoxious reporters who practice irresponsible journalism and who believe they have been sent to earth to inform the *ignorant* masses. And so have you. Don't bother denying it. I said what you wanted to say, but you couldn't because the media would have been all over you like grease on bacon. Of course, they won't bother with a no-account accountant like me."

"No-account? You, Hazard? Not hardly." Nick outstretched an arm to brush the glob of mud from the tip of her nose. "I value your worth, even if David Hicks from news team six thinks you're a certified lunatic."

"Thanks, Thorn. I like you, too, but we have a bit of a problem."

"I know. I believe I made mention of that fact at lunch today."

"Not *that* problem," Amanda muttered, noting his rakish grin.

Nick took his eyes off the road long enough to scrutinize her grim expression. "What's wrong, Hazard?"

"Elmer Jolly was murdered this afternoon."

"What?" Nick crowed.

"I was on my way out to his farm in response to a phone call he made before lunch. When I got there, the storm struck and I headed for the cellar. Elmer was lying under the overturned shelves. Somebody killed him."

Amanda recognized that skeptical look on Thorn's handsome face at a single glance. She had seen it one too many times before, thank you very much.

"It's true, Thorn," she said with unwavering conviction.

"Now, Hazard . . ." he said warningly.

"Don't *now Hazard* me. There's no question in my mind—"

"Ah, yes, the mind which contains an imagination that is ten sizes too big."

"Damn it, Thorn. I know what I saw." Amanda's arm shot northwest. "Take me out to Jolly Farm."

Nick flicked on the siren and mashed on the accelerator.

"Watch your driving," Amanda advised. "These country roads are slick as glass, and slamming into those wads of mud and weeds is worse than bouncing around in bumper cars."

The proverbial back seat driver was sitting right beside him. How nice. "I've been driving for years without your assistance, Hazard," Nick said with a scowl.

Nick's mood was deteriorating by the second. He knew exactly what the next few weeks would entail. Whether or not a crime had actually been committed, Hazard would feel compelled to investigate. This crusading accountant had a curious and suspicious mind. She envisioned herself as the female version of Sherlock Holmes. If there wasn't a murder, she would invent one.

True, not too long ago Hazard had stumbled onto a murder victim who looked as if he had suffered a fatal farming accident. And true, she had cracked a case that Nick wasn't sure existed. But every death in Vamoose was not a murder. Accidents did happen and some folks simply expired from natural causes. Nonetheless, Nick was doomed to deal with Hazard's suspicious notions— again.

Damnation, if Hazard took their turtle-paced affair as seriously as she did possible murder cases, he would not be such a sexually frustrated man. Two weekends of fooling around with Hazard in the past three months did not a sizzling affair make! This gorgeous blonde was the one thing Nick was *not* getting enough of. And the worst part was that he had come to realize what a wonderfully passionate woman Hazard could be when she did manage to work him into her busy schedule. It offended his male ego to be put on hold—like a "call waiting". Hell, sometimes Nick found himself wondering if this hot-shot accountant whose praises had been sung by Vamoosians one and all, was *ashamed* of her attraction to a country cop in this rinky-dink little town. Maybe she thought she was just a little too good for the likes of him. She had all the diplomas while he had only graduated from the school of hard knocks.

Nick set his personal problems aside as he parked beside Elmer Jolly's dilapidated storm shelter. Before Nick could order Amanda to stay put, she was up and gone. She scuttled halfway down the cellar steps and gasped in disbelief.

"He's gone!"

"Are you sure he was dead?"

Amanda scowled. "Give me a little credit, Thorn. I know dead when I see it. This is my second murder victim after all."

"*Murder*, Hazard? Let's not leap to ill-founded conclusions," Nick requested. "Did you call an ambulance?"

"No, the phone was dead."

Nick strode over to study the tracks left by another vehicle. "Somebody must have found Elmer after you left. It looks as if an ambulance was here. The county sheriff's department might have sent an officer to investigate. The medical examiner will have a report. I'll check on it."

"No, you won't," Amanda grumbled. "You don't believe me."

Nick peered down at the bedraggled female whose head protruded from the cellar. "I believe Elmer Jolly is dead," he conceded. "I expect he accidentally fell on his way to the storm shelter. A man his age is not as sure of foot as he should be and he was undoubtedly in a hurry. He must have latched onto the shelves and pulled them down on top of him." Nick pivoted on his heels. "Let's go, Hazard. I want to check on my farm to see how much damage was done."

Climbing up to stand beside Nick, Amanda lifted her chin in her characteristic manner that indicated she was going to be stubborn and persistent. "With or without your help, Thorn, I intend to investigate and to prove that Elmer was murdered."

"And what, I'd like to know, has so thoroughly convinced you that Elmer was murdered, Hazard?" Nick slopped toward the squad car, pausing only when he saw two red pumps stuck in the mud. He plucked up Hazard's missing shoes. "These belong to the Wicked Witch of the West, I presume."

"Very funny, Thorn." Amanda snatched her mud-caked pumps from his fingertips and contemplated throwing them at him.

"I thought you liked my sense of humor, among other things. My magnificent body, for one." He flashed her an ornery grin. "I believe that is a direct quote, if memory serves after such a long abstinence."

Amanda glared at Thorn as she climbed in the car. "You can forget about tonight."

"Withholding sexual favors to control me, are you?" Nick questioned. "I suppose if I agree that Elmer was murdered, without even seeing his body at the scene of this so-called crime or reading the coroner's report, to-night will be back on again."

Amanda really was tempted to slug him. Admirably, she restrained herself. "No, tonight would still be off because I am no longer in the mood for love, and I might not be for another year or so!"

"Are you saying that you want to call it quits just be-cause I am not convinced that a murder was commit-ted?"

"See, Thorn, you just said *murder.*"

"Elmer's *unexpected death,*" Nick corrected gruffly.

"Murder!" she argued, rather loudly.

"Accidental death!"

"Murder!"

"Then prove it, Hazard!"

"I damn well intend to, Thorn. So there!"

Amanda lapsed into silence while Nick navigated over the treacherous roads. Honestly, there were times when she wondered what she saw in this pig-headed man. Thorn could be so infuriatingly unreasonable sometimes. He didn't trust her instincts or intuition. She had literally dragged him through the first murder inves-tigation, and it wasn't until she almost got herself killed that Thorn finally realized she was on to something.

Obviously, Nick Thorn was in this ... relationship ... just for the sex and nothing more. He had no faith in her convictions and no respect for her intelligence. To him, she was just an amateur sleuth sticking her snout in places it didn't belong. When she dared to tread on his private territory, he always got huffy. Come to think of it, the only time she and Thorn were completely com-patible was in the privacy of her bedroom—or his. He didn't care which as long as he got what he wanted.

Here was the shining example of Neanderthal Man mentality, thought Amanda. Nick Thorn wanted food, shelter, and sex, and not necessarily in that order.

Shortly thereafter, Amanda found herself deposited beside her dented Toyota. With offended dignity, she climbed out of the squad car—eyes straight ahead, chin up.

"Careful, Hazard," Nick said to her departing back. "If it rains again, you'll drown."

After climbing into her own car, Amanda cranked the engine and ignored the snide remark.

"Oh, and Hazard, just for the record, what convinced you that Elmer Jolly was murdered?"

Ever so slowly, Amanda turned her head to glare out the open window at the annoying country-bumpkin cop. "Because, Officer Thorn, Elmer was still wearing his false teeth long after he finished his noon meal."

Nick stared at Amanda as if she had mattress springs protruding from her head. He was still staring after her when she zoomed off.

"Jesus H. Christ." Nick slumped in the seat and shook his disheveled raven head. "I'm attracted to a blond-haired loon!"

On that dismal note of realization, Nick headed for his farm to see how well his home, his wheat crop, and his livestock had survived the force of the F2 tornado.

Amanda sped down the highway, noting that the sign posted on the edge of the city limits, welcoming travelers with the words—*If you like it country style, then Vamoose*—was dangling by one bolt on its metal post. The upturned sign was symbolic of the havoc wrought by the violent storm. It also represented Amanda's emotional state. Enduring the storm and finding Elmer Jolly dead had thrown her for a loop. Learning that Thorn still had no respect for her analytical deductions and intuition set fuse to her temper.

True, her suspicions were founded on a phone call from her irate client and the fact that Elmer was a creature of ritualistic habit. Elmer only wore his false teeth while eating—period. Each time Amanda ventured to Jolly Farm, she had noticed Elmer's absolute refusal to keep his ill-fitting teeth in his mouth. According to Elmer, dentures were a damned nuisance. More often than not, the store-bought teeth clamped down on his tongue while he tried to talk. Consequently, he kept them in his shirt pocket unless he needed them for chewing.

Happy to arrive home and find the house still standing, Amanda trashed her muddy red pumps and soiled business suit and headed for the showers. Dressed in country attire of galoshes, jeans, and western shirt, Amanda tromped back outside to renovate the pens beside the barn to accommodate her new family. Amanda was sorry to say she knew absolutely nothing about pigs, having spent her youth and adult life in the city. Did one really slop one's hogs? And what exactly did slop consist of?

Despite Amanda's grievances with Thorn, she needed his expertise and assistance in the livestock department. The part-time policeman/farmer/stockman was well-informed and knowledgeable, having lived on a farm most of his life.

Amanda snatched up pliers and baling wire to secure the metal panels that would serve as the pig pen. She was sure her newly inherited hogs would approve of their new residence. The pen was full of grass and mud holes to wallow in. The place looked like hog heaven—minus feeding troughs brimming with this mysterious concoction called slop.

The dilapidated henhouse that had been standing empty for years required hammer and nails. There were not nests of straw to accommodate the forthcoming chickens, Amanda noted. Employing her imagination, Amanda slogged back to her house to gather several shoe boxes from the closet and situated them on the shelf she had nailed up in the coop. Well, that took care of the hens and rooster, but what about the duck? Amanda made a mental note to ask Thorn what sort of accommodations a duck needed to live a comfortable life.

After thoroughly assessing the farmhouse and its out-buildings, Amanda realized she had been more fortunate than other Vamoosians. True, she was going to need a new roof after the hail storm, and the tin on the barn and sheds would have to be battened down. But all in all, her rented home had sustained only minimal damage. Her landlady, Emma Carter—aunt of the rising country singing, Billie Jane Baxter—was responsible for hiring someone to replace the shingles and repair the outbuildings. Amanda's responsibilities entailed retrieving her family of critters from Jolly Farm and opening her own private investigation to prove to muleheaded Nick Thorn that Elmer had met with foul play!

Determined of purpose, Amanda piled into the gas-guzzling jalopy of a pickup she had purchased earlier in the year and aimed herself toward Thorn's ranch. In spite of their recent conflict, she needed Thorn's help and she was not allowing their personal problems to stand in her way.

From his position high atop the barn, Nick saw and heard Hazard's red jalopy coming a mile away. He really hadn't expected to see her so soon after their disagreement. A wry smile pursed his lips as he braced a knee on the loose tin and hammered it back onto place. Perhaps Hazard had gone home to collect her thoughts and composure and realized she had leaped to ridiculous conclusions about Elmer Jolly. Maybe she had come to make amends and keep the appointed rendezvous scheduled for this evening.

Nick could use some consolation and physical distraction right about now. Part of his wheat crop had been shredded by hail, the outbuildings were in need of repair because of wind damage, and he had lost one of his pure bred Salers cows that had been standing too close to a metal fence post when lightning struck. He had not had a good day. He would very much like to enjoy a satisfying night.

"Thorn?"

Nick glanced down to see Hazard's curvaceous jean-clad body perched on the top wrung of the ladder. He hammered the ring shank nail into place before responding. "Yes, Hazard?"

"I came for information."

Nick yelped and shook his thumb when he hammered the wrong nail—his fingernail. Damn, so much for his erotic visions of naked bodies tumbling around in bed. This was not a social call. No doubt, Hazard intended to drill him with questions about Elmer Jolly and his relationships with other Vamoosians who might have had some mysterious motive for doing the old man in.

Well, fine, if Hazard was going to give him the third degree, she could haul her fabulous fanny on the roof of the barn and be of some assistance to him.

"Grab that extra hammer and a handful of ring shank nails and come up here so we can talk while I work."

Amanda wrapped the leather nail-and-tool pouch around her waist and stuffed the extra hammer in its loop. When she tried to pull herself onto the roof, she discovered—to her shock and dismay—that she had an unnerving fear of heights. Her body was frozen to the spot and her heart was pounding like a tom-tom.

"Um . . . Thorn?"

"Now what, Hazard?" Rat-tat-tat.

Wide blue eyes soared up the incredibly steep pitch of the roof to where Nick was hammering industriously. "I don't think I can climb up there."

Nick ceased hammering and twisted around to stare at her. "Why the hell not?"

"I just discovered that I'm acrophobic."

Nick knew he probably should have taken pity on the citified female, but he wasn't feeling that charitable toward Hazard at the moment. No sex, no sympathy, that was his present motto. He wasn't letting her off the hook—or off the ladder, as this case happened to be.

Setting his hammer aside, Nick sidestepped down the steep incline and hoisted Hazard onto the roof. She instinctively clung to him like a cat sinking its claws into tree bark. Mmm . . . this was as close as he and Hazard had been in weeks. It felt pretty damned good.

"Gee, Hazard, I never dreamed you'd get so intimate right up here, for God and all of Vamoose to see."

"Knock it off, Thorn," Amanda muttered into the front of his shirt, afraid to move an inch for fear she would fall to her death and no one would ever learn the truth about Elmer Jolly's murder. "I'm scared as hell and you know it."

He inhaled the scent of her fresh, clean hair and wished he and Hazard were lying flat on their backs in bed. Resigning himself to wishes that wouldn't come true, Nick propelled Hazard over the loose flaps of tin to the peak of the barn.

"Good Lord!" Amanda made the mistake of glancing down at the flock of sheep that grazed behind the barn. From where she stood, the flock resembled mobile cotton balls. The thought of falling and confronting Atilla, the cantankerous ram, sent a shiver of panic undulating through her.

"Yeah, I know," Nick said with a devilish grin. "I really need to get those sheep sheared. It's getting too hot for them to be tramping around in their thick wool coats. You can help me with that chore this weekend in exchange for whatever information you think I can supply."

When Nick plunked Amanda down, straddling the peak of the roof, he swore she was hyperventilating. "Get a grip, Hazard. This isn't skydiving or bunji jumping. Don't be such a wimp. It's out of character, especially after you put the royal hatchet job on the reporter and cameraman." With those words Nick leaned down to unclamp one of Amanda's hands from the tin and shoved the hammer at her. "Start nailing and fire away with your questions. It will take your mind off your acrophobia."

While Nick resumed his position twenty feet away,

Amanda inhaled several shaky breaths and battled for
hard-won composure. "What"—gasp, gasp—"entails
slopping hogs, Thorn?"

With hammer poised in midair, Nick peered bewilderedly at Hazard. Of all the questions he expected her
to ask, that wasn't even on the list! "Hogs?" he repeated
stupidly.

"Yes, you know, those hairy, four-legged, mud-loving
creatures with pointed ears and long schnozzles," she
prompted caustically.

"I know what pigs are. I just haven't figured out what
you and hogs have in common," Nick snorted.

Amanda hammered a nail into place and shifted
position—carefully. "I inherited two hogs from Elmer,
along with a menagerie of other critters. I want to know
how to care for them properly."

"You're going to raise hogs?" His voice was incred-
ulous.

"And chickens, a duck named Lucky, a tomcat called
Hank, and a three-legged dog called Pete," she informed
him.

"Well, I'll be damned."

"Yes, Thorn, I suspect you surely shall." Amanda
glanced up at Tom Selleck's clone—minus the mustache. "But I want to know how to slop a hog."

"That is an antiquated custom of using house scraps,
curds, and whey to feed pigs. These days, farmers either
grind their own wheat, corn, and maize or purchase
sacks of pig feed at the grain elevator. You didn't inherit
a milk cow, too, did you, Hazard?"

"I don't think so." Rat-tat-tat. "I'll know for certain
this evening when I borrow your stock racks so I can
collect my inheritance."

Nick stared somberly at Hazard. "You're serious about this, aren't you?"

Blue eyes, fringed with long lashes, peeked up at him. "As serious as I am about investigating Elmer's murder, with or without your cooperation. I have only resided in Vamoose for a year and you have lived here all your life. You can provide plenty of background information about Elmer, if only you would."

"You are going to be as determined about probing into Jolly's death as you were about your previous murder case, I assume?" Thump, thump.

"Every bit, Thorn." Rat-tat-tat.

"I knew you would say something like that," he muttered, disgruntled. "Okay, Hazard, I'll tell you what I know about the Jolly clan, but do *not*, for one minute, assume that because I am providing information that I agree with your conclusions of murder."

"The fact is duly noted." Amanda grabbed another ring shank nail and hammered away.

"First of all, Elmer Jolly has been a recluse since I have known him. He was a bachelor all of his life and he dabbled with perfecting a variety of wheat seed that was specifically adapted to the Oklahoma climate. He spent years developing grazing wheat that could also provide high production at harvest. Elmer crossed grains of high test weights and harvest yield with seeds that showed strong resistance to diseases such as septoria, leaf blotch, stem rust, and mildew."

My, but Thorn did know his wheat seeds and crop diseases intimately, didn't he? Amanda was impressed.

"Elmer designed his own thrasher to collect the hybrid seeds in his various test plots and he kept detailed data on his findings."

That must have been the sacred notes Elmer had mentioned on the phone, Amanda decided. She had been befuddled by Elmer's comment, but he hadn't given her the chance to question him on that, or any other subject.

"Elmer was breeding a new variety of wheat that could be planted deeper and much closer to subsoil moisture, one with a stalk that was not too tall or brittle to be affected by strong winds, and one with a head that didn't shrivel when harvest was delayed by rains."

"The perfect wheat seed with bountiful yields for harvest and also the maximum winter grazing forage for cattle," Amanda summarized.

"Exactly."

"And do you think Elmer did perfect this magical variety of wheat?"

"According to local gossip, yes." Nick inched down to secure another piece of loose tin. "But as far as I know, he never registered his findings with the agronomists in the agricultural department at Oklahoma State University. I have read nothing in the literature from the extension office that indicates Jolly wheat has been certified and packaged for sale. Some of Elmer's neighbors were hassling him to plant his hybrid seeds in their fields as test plots. When Elmer refused, I heard that somebody had hoisted a few bushels of seed wheat from Elmer's granary and he was livid about it."

"Wheat piracy, I assume? A farmer gathers some of the super-duper seed, plants it the following year, and, presto, he has stolen Jolly wheat."

"That's about the size of it, Hazard."

"Do you think such an occurrence did take place?"

Nick glanced up and smiled wryly. "Are we groping for a murder motive, Hazard?"

She returned the phony smile. "My curious mind wants to know."

"Your *suspicious* mind, you mean."

"Just answer the question, Thorn. Are there probable wheat-seed pirates around Vamoose?"

"Greed is a foible of humanity," Nick replied philosophically, sidestepping toward Hazard. "And yes, in the past, Elmer did get into shouting matches with some of his neighbors who wanted to get their hands on his hybrids and sell the formula for certification."

When Nick outstretched his arm to assist her to her feet, Amanda clamped hold of him and told herself not to look down. She also told herself not to become distracted by the tantalizing scent of this man. Thorn had always had a dizzying effect on her brain, not to mention the heat that was released from the internal chemical combustion in her body. In simple laymen terms, Thorn turned her on, though not as often as he would have preferred.

When Nick choked for breath, Amanda lifted her head which—to her surprise—had been mashed against his chest. Her arms were fastened so tightly around his neck that his face was turning blue. She had latched onto Thorn as if he were her life support system. She couldn't seem to loosen her grasp on his solid masculine form.

"Sorry, Thorn," she apologized as he half carried her down the steep slope. "This height thing really seems to get to me."

"Too bad it isn't *me* who gets to you, Hazard," he

murmured against that ultrasensitive point beneath her ear.

Amanda chose to ignore the comment, and the erotic sensations. This was not the time for an amorous distraction. She had pigs to chase down and chickens to catch before sunset. Her newly adopted critters needed her now that Elmer had soared off to that Great Barnyard in the Sky.

Chapter Three

Nick situated the metal stock racks in the back of Amanda's jalopy truck and climbed inside. "I'll help you collect your livestock."

She cast him a cynical glance as she navigated around the water holes. "Does your generosity come with strings attached, Thorn?"

"You know what I want, Hazard," he said, simply but directly.

"My body?"

"That, too." Nick stared out the mud-splattered windshield. "I also want a little respect."

Amanda applied the brake and stopped in the middle of the road to gape at him. "What the devil are you talking about?"

"I am tired of the secretive affair we're having, *when* you can fit me into your allocated time slots," he told her bluntly. "Maybe I'm just a small-town cop and a part-time rancher in your eyes, but I do have my pride. I think you're ashamed of me."

Amanda expelled a rush of breath. "Thorn, you have it all wrong."

"I'm beginning to think I've got it exactly right," he concluded.

Up went the chin. "I do not wish to have this discussion." As she stepped down on the gas pedal, her hands were gripped so tightly around the wheel that her knuckles turned white. "You were the one who said the only rule to be observed in this ... relationship ... is that there are no rules."

"Then I can tell anyone who cares to listen that we are an official item?"

"No," she burst out before she could stop herself.

Nick regarded her for a long, pensive moment. "Why not, Hazard?"

"Because ... I'm not sure what kind of commitment we expect from each other." Amanda braced herself when the truck plunged into the deep ruts in the road.

"You like me and I like you. How much more commitment do you want? I always knew you had hang-ups because of your divorce, but geezus, we are both mature, consenting adults, not teenagers with hormone imbalances—"

"Ah, here we are, Thorn," Amanda interrupted as she steered through Elmer's gate. "And while we're here, maybe you should investigate the scene of the crime, just in case my assumption proves correct and you discover, much to your surprise, that Elmer's death was no accident."

Nick groaned. "Damn it to hell, here we go again."

While Amanda collected the wire cages she had brought along to confine the cat, duck, and chickens, Nick half-heartedly tramped down into the cellar to survey the broken shelves. With the aid of his flashlight, he surveyed the holes left in the concrete where the screws had dislodged from the wall. Then he inspected the rotten wooden step that had apparently cracked under Elmer's weight, forcing the old man to grab onto the first anchor within reach—the row of warped shelving. Despite Hazard's harebrained assumptions, Nick could only draw one sensible conclusion. Elmer Jolly had fled the house during the storm. He had descended into the outdated cellar on his wobbly seventy-three-year-old legs. The rotten step gave way and he grabbed for support. Elmer had fallen and accidentally pulled the shelving down on him. End of story.

"Well?" came an insistent voice from above.

It wasn't God. It was Hazard.

Nick marched up the steps to confront Hazard's belligerent stare. "Accidental death. Sorry, Hazard. There is no murder weapon, except dozens of broken canning jars. Your own testimony indicates that Elmer was not stabbed through the chest with a piece of jagged glass. But to pacify you, I will call the coroner first thing in the morning for the results of his preliminary examination."

To pacify you? Amanda clinched her teeth and resigned herself to the fact that she was going to have to show conclusive cause and motive before she gained Thorn's willing assistance. And in the meantime, he was going to get an earful of her suspicions, whether he wanted to hear them or not.

"If you would accompany me into the house, I would appreciate it. Since Elmer named me administrator of his estate, I need to locate his will and gather the data you claim he made on his variety of disease-resistant wheat."

When she entered the house, she found the television

blaring, just as it had been earlier in the day. The electricity had obviously been restored after the storm.

"Elmer always ate his lunch while he watched the news and farm market report," Amanda informed Thorn. "Elmer had very little regard for the rest of television programming, hence the outdated black and white TV set. He was also hard of hearing and the volume was always on roar—"

"Hazard—"

"Note that the television was not turned off, as Elmer was in the habit of doing after catching the agricultural market reports. That in itself is highly irregular—"

"Oh, for God's sake, there was a storm brewing. Maybe he—"

"And Elmer's dinner plate is still sitting—" Her voice evaporated. The plate, knife, fork, and glass had disappeared and the checkered tablecloth that had been dangling off the side of the table was gone.

Nick strolled over to survey the antique oak round table that had nary a speck of food on it. "Don't tell me, let me guess, Hazard. The knife and fork got up and danced off while the dish ran away with the spoon . . . and the ac*cow*tant and her suspicions jumped over the moon."

"You are a regular laugh a minute, Thorn-in-the-side," she sneered at him. "I swear to you that the plate and silverware were on the table when I arrived shortly after one o'clock. It is obvious that the murderer returned to the scene of the crime to double check him- or herself, or themselves. That suggests the work of amateur assassins."

"Lord, Hazard, you have been watching too damned many detective shows."

"And you remind me of Tom Selleck."

"I do?" He brightened considerably and grinned at the unexpected compliment.

"Yeah, except Magnum P.I. never met a case he didn't investigate, unlike *some* people I know."

"Come off it, Hazard. Just because you stumbled onto one murder case and accidentally solved it—at the risk of your own life—doesn't mean *this* is murder. You're going to become a nuisance to yourself and to everybody else if you pursue this farce of an investigation. Just gather your legal documents like a good little executor of the estate, collect your inherited critters, and forget about it. Elmer was a crazy old coot who never adapted to society. He was a throwback to the pioneer days when folks had little contact with civilization in this part of the country."

"I happened to be fond of Elmer," Amanda said on the dead man's behalf.

"Well, you were one of the few who got along with him. I guess strange ducks of a feather always flock together," he taunted, though he wasn't sure why. Probably because sexual frustration had begun to decay his brain. Before Amanda could respond in like manner, Nick hurried on. "Two weeks ago, I answered a call from Lenny Roscoe, the local electrician and plumber who runs a business out of his home."

"I know him. He's one of my clients. But then, many a Vamoosian has become my client after I solved my first *murder* case. Except for you, of course. *You* don't think I respect you, and *I* don't believe you trust me since you don't allow me to handle your tax forms. Do you think I'll blab your gross income all over town, Thorn?"

Although the well-aimed jibe scored a bull's eye, Nick plowed on, "Lenny was hired to repair the plumbing under the kitchen sink after Elmer tried to do it himself and flooded the floor. When Lenny handed Elmer the bill, the old curmudgeon went after him with a pipe wrench, swearing the plumber was trying to rob him blind. Elmer refused to pay for services rendered and Lenny wound up with a knot the size of a wrench on his thigh. Elmer had a shiner the size of Lenny's fist."

"Revenge . . ." Amanda murmured.

Nick flung up a hand in a deterring gesture. "Now hold on, Hazard. I didn't tell you that to incriminate Lenny. I can name several other Vamoosians who have clashed with Elmer the past few years."

"Fine, name four," she challenged.

"The entire Jolly family for starters. Elmer also has three renters who plant crops and graze cattle on his farm ground. Elmer went several rounds with his renters because he objected to spending a penny to repair fences or replace posts. Elmer refused to pay his share for fertilizer when the soil tests indicated a nitrogen deficiency. Low soil pH affects yields, and Elmer wouldn't part with any money when his renters requested he help them pay. He also raised the rent on his tenants when they didn't mow the roadside ditches the minute he demanded it."

"That is only one side of the story. I imagine Elmer's version would have been different, if only he were alive to tell it," Amanda inserted. "Perhaps you should check out those accusations."

"Your loyalty is admirable, but Elmer was no saint. He raised all sorts of hell when he *suspected* his neighbors of stealing his hybrid wheat seed from the granary." Nick gestured toward the shotgun that hung above the dining room door. "That was the weapon Elmer used when he tried to shoot Clive Barnstall's head off. Clive swears he was nowhere near the granary and had nothing to do with the missing wheat, though how Elmer could detect the loss of a few bushels in a bin the size of the Empire State building I have no idea."

"So those are the arguments used in an effort to have Elmer declared incompetent," Amanda mused aloud.

"Who was trying to have Elmer committed?"

Amanda sighed audibly. "Elmer was too upset when I spoke to him on the phone to name any names. He just kept ranting about *they.*"

Nick strode over to shut the front door and switched off the television. "Come on, Hazard. It's almost dark. We better load your hogs and get them back to your farm."

Amanda allowed Nick to usher her out the back door while she cursed the fact that there weren't enough hours in the day to pursue her one-woman investigation and keep up with her clients. She had yet to locate the will or research notes Elmer mentioned. It looked as if she was going to have to close down her office and spend the following day at Jolly Farm. She would have to bring home her accounting files to work at night. She was also going to schedule an appointment at Velma's Beauty Boutique in hopes of gleaning information from Vamoose's most dependable gossip. A visit to Last Chance Cafe to eavesdrop on conversations about Elmer wouldn't hurt, either. Before Amanda was through, she would know the life story of the Jolly family and every citizen connected with them. Someone had purposely disposed of Elmer, and Amanda would not rest until she knew why.

"Well, don't just stand there, Hazard, help me round up these pigs." Nick grinned mischievously. "Wallowing in the mud should get your goat."

"I don't have a goat, or were you referring to the billy goat of a man I am dating?" she questioned snidely. When she noticed that Thorn was standing ankle deep in mud while two one-hundred-pound hogs tried to stare him down, Amanda frowned. "Can't we just holler 'Here, piggy, piggy,' and let them follow us to the truck?"

Nick flung her a withering glance. "The first thing you have to learn about pigs is that they are smart enough to be contrary. You might train them to come when you call, *after* you have waved food under their snouts a couple dozen times. But you can bet money these hogs are going to put up a stink—and I mean literally—when we try to catch them."

With her mouth set in grim determination, Amanda swung a leg over the fence and advanced on the hogs. Nick glanced at her in amusement. The city slicker didn't have a clue how difficult this chore was going to be—yet. "Ever play tackle football, Hazard?"

"No."

"Ever mud wrestle?"

"Certainly not."

Nick broke into a grin. "Go grab a pig."

Amanda stalked her prey. To Nick's astonishment, she sprang forward to latch onto the hog's hind leg, just as she had done when she snatched up the squawking chickens and stuffed them in a cage. Hazard had quick hands. Nick had made that discovery in a most enjoyable way. Too bad those hands were wasted on hogs.

The squealing hog slopped mud all over Amanda, but she didn't shy away. She put the grimy creature in a hog-hug and carted it—kicking and snorting—toward the gate. Nick made a diving catch when the other pig romped around the corner of the shed. He jerked up his prey and followed two steps behind Hazard. By the time both hogs were locked in the stock racks and the tail gate of the truck was secured, Nick and Amanda shared the noxious fumes of pigs.

While Amanda drove away with her newly inherited livestock, Nick cast her a discreet glance. The woman, despite her annoying flaws and infuriating hang-ups, never ceased to surprise him. He had expected her to become squeamish about wallowing with hogs and chasing chickens. She did nothing of the kind. Hazard handled herself like any self-respecting livestock owner. She had even battled down her acrophobia to pound a few nails on the steep-sloped barn. And Hazard, he knew for sure and certain, was going to pursue this investigation of Elmer's death with the same unswerving determination. Of course, this time Hazard would be doomed to disappointment. Elmer Jolly had suffered a fatal accident. Sooner or later, Hazard was going to have to accept that conclusion. Her suspicious mind had overreacted. She was on a wild goose-chase.

When they arrived back at Amanda's house, Nick burst out laughing when he freed the chickens and rooster and noticed the shoe box nests. But to his astounded amazement, the hens strutted up the lopsided ladder Amanda had constructed for them and settled themselves in the straw-filled boxes.

"And they'll probably lay golden eggs," Nick said to himself before he strode back outside.

When the hogs put up the same fuss at being toted to their new pen as they had when they were hauled from the old one, Nick was reminded of why he no longer raised hogs.

Pensively, Nick surveyed the farmyard of newly acquired critters. "You realize, of course, that with the exception of your hens, you have surrounded yourself with males. That unsettling fact will probably keep you up nights, won't it, Hazard?"

Amanda filled the hog trough with fresh water and glared at Thorn. "You have been deliberately provoking me for the better part of the evening. Would you mind telling me why?"

"No, I don't mind one bit," Nick accommodated her. "I don't know if there are substantiated cases of men dying from sexual deprivation, but I don't want to be the first. Surliness and sarcasm are common symptoms."

"And I am supposed to provide the cure?"

He waggled his eyebrows. "I thought you would never offer."

When sinewy arms fastened around her, Amanda felt that old familiar attraction setting fire to the hormones she had tried to keep in cold storage. It was no use, not when this human torch was within touching distance.

"Okay, Thorn, you win. But if you gloat, I'll toss you and your toothbrush out of my house for good."

"Not the toothbrush that is engraved with: *Brush with the fuzzy end?*" he gasped in mock horror.

Amanda nodded affirmatively, trying to keep a straight face and failing miserably. "You can kiss your private stock of dental floss goodbye, too."

"You're a hardhearted woman, Hazard, but I'll over-look it."

Nick practically dragged Amanda into the house, and while he headed to the shower, Amanda put supper on the stove. The scratching at the front door caught her attention. She found Hank the tomcat waiting impatiently to be invited inside. Amanda had never been allowed to have pets in the house as a child. Mother wouldn't stand for it. But Hank was accustomed to having the run of Elmer's house. Amanda could just imagine the stricken look on Mother's face when she arrived for a visit and found a pet in the house. That in itself was enough incentive for Amanda to let Hank inside.

When Amanda closed the door and turned around, Nick was standing in the hall, wearing a towel and a seductive smile. She remembered the first time she had seen this Adonis in a bath towel. It had caused her feminine senses to short circuit. The man oozed sex appeal from his pores. It was a wonder Amanda had managed to keep this gorgeous hunk at arm's length as often as she had.

Clearing her throat, and peeved at herself for again adopting her mother's unconscious mannerism, Amanda headed for the showers. "Check on supper, Thorn. Don't let it burn."

Nick stirred the creamed tuna and stuffed the bread in the toaster. Shit on a shingle. Yummy, yummy. He was more of a meat and potato man, but Hazard didn't waste her valuable time preparing fine cuisine. She had never been worth a damn in the kitchen. Such were the habits of the modern woman. Give her a microwave or a meal in a pouch that required nothing more than boiled water and she was as happy as a clam.

Wandering back to the front room, Nick grabbed the remote control and switched through the channels in his customary manner. Hazard had accused him of suffering from Remote Control Syndrome often enough for him to know better than to flick through the stations while she was in the same room. It drove her crazier than she was by nature. She didn't approve of his machismo tendencies, either. The picky woman. Honestly, there were times when Nick wondered why he found her so damned appealing . . . except, of course, when they were in bed.

"Ouch!" Nick yowled when the tomcat pounced on his lap and sank in his claws, puncturing vital parts of his male anatomy. Nick tolerated cats if they were good mousers, but he refused to let the creatures in his home. What he faced here was a tomcat with an attitude.

Clutching Hank by the hair on his neck, Nick tossed the offending feline none too gently against the wall. The cat, Nick noted with spiteful satisfaction, did not land on his paws. That should give Hank a clear understanding of who was boss. The cat had better not crowd Nick's space—or else.

Having satisfied his daily craving for channel switching, Nick padded back to the kitchen to stir supper. He set the table, awaiting Hazard's return. Looking like a sea goddess, she emerged with damp hair and a fresh scent that tempted Nick to toss the main course to the cat and dive straight into dessert. God, he had been deprived for more weeks than he cared to count!

"Thorn, were there ill feelings between Elmer Jolly and his family?" Amanda questioned out of the blue as she sat down at the table.

Nick sighed heavily. He should have known they

couldn't make it through the night without a few dozen questions. "I really don't know all that much about Elmer's life history, other than the fact that there were four Jolly brothers. Now there are only two left. Elmer was the oldest. The youngest one passed on about eight years ago. The Jolly brothers married three sisters, two of which were twins."

"How interesting," Amanda said between bites of creamed tuna. "That sounds like some sort of contracted marriage from days gone by."

"It was more than a coincidence," Nick informed her. God, he hated creamed tuna with a passion. It was all he could do to choke it down. "The Jollys and the Mopopes farmed in the same area northwest of Vamoose. As you know, that is a rather isolated sector. And in those days, there wasn't much time for traveling far and wide to select a bride. Society wasn't nearly as mobile as it is now. Farming was a full-time endeavor without modern inventions, and neighbors often helped neighbors sow crops, swath hay, and thrash wheat. John Mopope had three daughters and the Jollys had four sons. I imagine both families encouraged the practical marriages. Odie Mae Mopope married Melvin Jolly and her twin sister, Eula Bell, married Claud. The youngest sister, Bertie Ann Mopope, married the youngest Jolly, Leroy. Since the two families were closely entwined, I'm sure they had their differences over the years. What families don't?"

"Someone wanted Elmer declared incompetent," Amanda put in. "I want to know who and why and for whose benefit."

"You'll have to search elsewhere for that information, Hazard. I can't supply it. That's all I know about the various branches of the Jolly family tree."

Amanda knew where to go for more information. Velma Hertzog—the town's only beautician—was the caretaker of Vamoose family trees. And if there were skeletons rattling around, Velma would know which closets to search.

"Then tell me the names of the renters who clashed with Elmer," she requested over her second helping of creamed tuna.

"Harry Ogelbee, Abner Hendershot, and Clive Barnstall were his renters. All three men butted heads with Elmer from time to time." Nick scraped off the tuna and ate the toast.

"And who would benefit most from Elmer's death?" she quizzed him.

"I haven't seen the will," Nick muttered, tiring of the topic and the meal. "Can we turn our minds to more pleasant matters? I waded through mud and wrestled hogs for you. Cut me a little slack here. I've been as charitable and gallant as I can stand for one day."

Impulsively, Nick reached over to pull Hazard out of her chair and into his arms. "I've been wanting to do this for weeks on end."

When his full lips slanted over hers, Amanda realized she had wanted him to do this for weeks on end, too. She had simply refused to acknowledge that she was vulnerable to this tall, dark, handsome hunk of a country cop.

Amanda wrapped her arms around Thorn's neck and kissed the lips off him. They were halfway down the hall when the blaring phone broke the mood like a rock shattering a windowpane.

"Damn!" Nick groaned in torment. He didn't switch directions. There was a phone beside the bed. That was the only one he would allow Hazard to use. This, after all, was as close as they had been to a bed in weeks!

When Nick sank onto the satin bedspread with Amanda clutched possessively in his arms, she made a grab for the phone.

"Hello?"

"Hi, doll. Are you all right? I've been trying to call since your dad saw the report on television about Vamoose being hit by a tornado. I couldn't get through for hours."

It was Mother. Amanda had been expecting the call. "I'm fine, Mother. The roof will have to be replaced and my car needs body work to beat out the dents left by falling tree limbs."

"My God!" Mother yowled.

Amanda held the receiver away when her eardrum was very nearly shattered. "I wasn't in the car at the time."

"Well, you contact your insurance representative right away, doll. You'll need to speak to the adjustor."

"I know the procedure, Mother."

"And call your landlady immediately so she can get *her* insurance company to replace your roof. Those leaks will ruin your expensive furniture if you aren't careful." Mother cleared her throat. "Did I tell you what your brother did last week?"

Nick counted the cracks in the ceiling while Mother briefed Amanda on the family news. Though Nick had never met Mother, he had heard her blaring voice on the phone on several occasions. Mother, Nick had the unshakable feeling, was a bit of a strange duck herself.

"Now, doll, I know I told you about our family reunion," Mother yammered on. "I'll be so disappointed if you don't come. Your cousins always ask about you."

"Right," Amanda mumbled sardonically. "They want me to figure their taxes for free."

"Now, doll, don't be so cynical. We are family, you know."

"My misfortune," Amanda muttered under her breath.

"Come again?"

"Nothing, Mother."

"Well, we'll expect you at the reunion Friday night. And bring that man you're dating with you." That sounded like a direct order from headquarters.

Amanda glanced warily at Thorn. She wasn't sure that was such a good idea. Mother could grind on one's nerves. Thorn objected to Amanda's questions about Elmer Jolly. But nobody could fire questions with the rapidity of Mother! She would demand an extensive account of Thorn's life from age two until present, omitting no obscure details in between.

"I'll let you know about the reunion later," Amanda hedged. Surely she could dream up a reasonable excuse before Friday. "Talk to you soon, Mother. I'm kind of in the middle of something at the moment."

"Middle of?" Nick snorted in disgust. "We were just getting started. All these interruptions are spoiling the romantic mood." He glanced down his torso. Too late. The *mood* was diminishing in intensity by the minute.

"Shh . . . shh . . . !" Amanda hissed as she clamped her hand over the mouthpiece.

"What was that, doll?" Mother inquired.

"I punched the wrong button on the remote control," Amanda lied through clenched teeth. "I accidentally turned on the volume."

"That's about all that's getting turned on around here." This from the disgruntled Thorn.

"Well, we'll see you Friday night. And don't forget to buckle up. It's the law, you know. Oh, and make sure you don't forget to—"

"Goodbye, Mother." Amanda dropped the receiver in the cradle.

Nick propped up on an elbow and stared solemnly at Amanda. "Too ashamed to be seen at the family reunion with me, Hazard?"

"No, Thorn, I'm only saving you from the family dragons." Her voice altered noticeably when skillful hands flooded over intimate places that had long been neglected.

His head moved steadily toward hers, his onyx eyes focused on the inviting curve of her lips, his body beginning to throb with renewed anticipation. The *mood,* Nick was pleased to report, was back. "So you do have my best interest at heart, after all."

"No." An implish smile tugged at her mouth when she heard Thorn swallow his breath. "I have your best interest *in hand* . . ."

The phone blared at the worst of all possible moments. Amanda groaned and Nick sent up a foul curse that hung over the room like a fog.

"Hello?"

"Amanda? This is Deputy Sykes. Do you know where Nick is? The last time I saw him was this afternoon when he was with you."

Amanda glanced sideways. "I think I know where to find him. Do you want me to deliver a message?"

"Yes. I've got a Code 20 two miles south on the cut-off to Pronto. And tell him it's a Code 2."

"A Code 20, 2," Amanda repeated.

"No, not *Code 22,*" Benny corrected, or so he thought. "I've got a Code 2, and Code 20."

My, Benny really enjoyed flinging police jargon around, thought Amanda. He could have saved time if he would have explained it in simple terms.

"I'll get in touch with Thorn as quickly as possible and give him your message."

"10-4."

"10-4 to you, too, Benny," Amanda managed to say without snickering.

By the time Amanda hung up the phone, Thorn was already on his feet, looking for his clothes and heading for the door. He was wearing a dark scowl that did his handsome features no justice whatsoever.

"Good night, Hazard," he muttered over his shoulder. "Don't worry. I'll make up some story to explain my whereabouts. We have to protect your sterling character and flawless reputation, after all. Heaven forbid that anyone should learn about the two of us."

"Thorn, I was just trying to—"

The bedroom door slammed in midsentence. Thorn, Amanda guessed, was not a happy man.

Amanda guessed right . . .

Chapter Four

Amanda jotted down her list of errands and proceeded in her customary, methodical manner. She called the insurance representative—not because Mother had instructed her to do so, but because that was standard procedure. Her insurance representative requested an estimate of damage to her Toyota. Amanda promptly drove to Cleatus Watt's Auto Body Shop which sat beside his brother's Auto Repair Shop in Vamoose. It seemed Cleatus bore many of the Watt's family characteristics that brother Cecil possessed. Both men rarely spoke in complete sentences and both moved at a pace that only a snail could appreciate. Amanda predicted the body work needed on her car would take weeks. It looked as if she would be driving her gas-guzzling jalopy for quite some time.

When Cleatus offered to drive Amanda back home to retrieve her alternate mode of transportation, she scooted over to the passenger side and fastened her seat belt. Cleatus had the dazed look of a deer blinded by headlights. In Amanda's estimation, Cleatus had been inhaling way too many paint fumes. It was a good thing

Amanda only lived a few miles from town. A lengthy road trip with Cleatus Watt behind the wheel could prove disastrous.

"I suppose you heard about Elmer Jolly," Amanda baited in her neverending search for information. "Did you know Elmer?"

"Yeah. Did some body work for him a couple years back. Wrecked his truck."

"Oh? Was Elmer injured?"

"Nope. Tried to run Chester Korn's cattle off the road in a fit of temper. Hit one. Smashed up his hood and caved in the door." Cleatus flicked his Bic and lit up a cigarette. "That steer was dead as a doornail. Chester wouldn't pay the truck damages. Elmer took after him and plowed through a fence. Ornery old cuss, Elmer was."

"Did Elmer balk at paying you for the repairs?" Amanda questioned her frizzy-haired companion.

"Paid half." Cleatus took a long draw on his cigarette and exhaled.

Amanda bit back a cough when smoke fogged the inside of the car.

"Said it took twice as long as it should've to make repairs. I gave Elmer a cussin'. He climbed in his truck and practically ran me down. Ain't seen him since."

Cleatus flicked his ashes toward the open window, but they caught in the wind and whipped around the interior of the car settling on Amanda's shoulders. Mr. Paint-Fumes-for-Brains didn't seem to notice.

"You hear about the robbery south of town last night?" Cleatus questioned between drags on his cigarette.

"No, I didn't." Amanda brushed the ashes off her clothes and held her tongue—for once.

"Somebody broke into the Korn's house while Chester and Opal were at the hospital. Stole some cash, a TV, microwave oven, and radio."

Now Amanda knew what Benny Sykes' call was all about. It sounded as if someone was looking to make a little spending money by selling stolen goods at the city pawn shops.

When Cleatus rolled to a stop, Amanda stepped out to stare at her battered Toyota one last time. She didn't expect to see her car for several weeks. Time was of no consequence to Cleatus.

Resigned to her newest mode of transport, Amanda piled into her pickup and headed for Jolly Farm. She was anxious to locate Elmer's will and determine who had the most to gain from his death. Since Elmer had no wife or children, Amanda assumed the property and savings accounts would be bequeathed to his surviving brothers, nieces, and nephews. She, of course, already knew who had inherited Elmer's critters.

When she finally got to the farm, Amanda stared at the run-down farmhouse and outbuildings. She knew Elmer had a sizable fund of cash in his savings and received royalty checks from gas and oil wells that had been drilled on his property. He also collected rent on his farm land, but he lived like a pauper. His fifteen-year-old green Chevrolet pickup was parked on the hill because the worn-out battery couldn't crank the engine. Elmer gave the vehicle a push, popped the clutch, and started the engine on the run when making his bi-monthly jaunts to Vamoose. He was too tightfisted to replace the battery and he left his motor running while he made his stops in town. For a man who had scads of money, Elmer had never learned how to enjoy it.

One glance around the living room of Elmer's home testified that he refused to spend money on modernization. He had piped in running water, but that was his only luxury.

"Quit dawdling, Hazard." Amanda gave herself a mental shove and strode off in search of Elmer's important documents—a will, research notes, land titles, etcetera. After an hour of rummaging through the cabinets and drawers, all Amanda had turned up was a stack of junk mail on which Elmer had jotted research data on wheat seeds with which he had experimented in 1947. Notes on junk mail, of all things! The old man was even too chinchy to purchase a journal.

Now where in the world had Elmer stashed his will? Amanda wondered. Since Elmer had demanded to see her the previous day, one would conclude that the will would have been lying out in plain sight. Or had the murderer confiscated the will? Did person or persons unknown think he, she, or they could forge a new will? Surely the banker had a copy of the document. Elmer had told Amanda over the phone that the banker had witnessed the will. Amanda could have the original copy or a duplicate in her hands in two shakes. So what would the murderer have to gain by swiping the document? Damned if she knew.

Amanda halted at Elmer's bedroom door and frowned in bewilderment. The previous day she had found the room in disarray. Now the dresser drawers were closed and the bed was made. Somebody around here had a penchant for tidiness and it damned sure wasn't the deceased! Elmer Jolly was anything but organized—a fact

Amanda could attest to after pilfering through his closets and cabinets. Elmer was a pack rat whose method was to cram objects in every nook and cranny. He was an older version of Nick Thorn.

A half-remembered thought struck Amanda. She marched toward the walnut dresser to remove the top drawer. She recalled what Elmer had said about stashing money throughout his house—funds to be used to feed his critters. Sure enough, a junk mail envelope was taped to the back side of the dresser. Amanda tore the envelope loose and counted out fifty one-dollar bills and five silver dollars. The second envelop she found contained five twenty dollar bills.

Amanda continued her treasure hunt to find five canning jars—crammed full of quarters—stashed behind the bottom drawer. Elmer *pinched* pennies but he *saved* dollars and quarters. Two more envelopes from Time-Life Books had been taped on the bottom of the flour and sugar canisters in the kitchen. Elmer's "critter fund" was increasing by the minute!

Although Amanda had gathered several hundred dollars, she had no way of knowing if she had located all of Elmer's stashes. Whoever had returned to the house in her absence could have confiscated the obvious collections of cash.

Amanda wondered if the burglar who had hit the Korn's house had also heard about Elmer's death and stolen whatever could be found. But didn't thieves usually *make* messes instead of *cleaning* them up . . . ?

A muted sound caught Amanda's attention and she wheeled toward the front door. She had the unnerving feeling that someone had been spying on her. It couldn't have been one of Elmer's critters since she had loaded them up and taken them home.

Amanda took off like a cannon and zoomed out the door. She found traces of mud that looked as if someone had been walking tiptoe across the porch. Someone had definitely been keeping surveillance on her—the same someone, she guessed, who had tidied up Elmer's bedroom and dining room. It made her wonder if the ransacked condition of the bedroom the previous afternoon had been a search for the will and research papers, or if Elmer had been looking for something himself and couldn't remember where he had stashed it.

With determined strides, Amanda propelled herself toward the barn that looked as if it had been built at the turn of the century. When she stepped into the shadowed building, she halted in her tracks and strained her ears, hoping to detect the sound of footsteps. Cautiously, she inched toward the ladder that ascended into the hay loft.

Her hand settled on a rung containing more mud. Somebody had definitely been prowling around the farm. Thief or murderer? She wasn't sure which.

"I know you're up there. You may as well show yourself—"

Amanda yelped when she saw the square bale of hay fill the opening above her. Before Amanda could scramble down the ladder, the hay bale plunged toward her. Another bale followed shortly thereafter. The first bale collided with her shoulder. The second bale konked her on the head. Amanda thrust out her arms when the straw-covered barn floor flew up at her with startling speed. Hitting the ground hard, dirt burned her eyes until they welled with tears. Her breath came out in a whoosh when another dusty bale landed squarely on her spine.

Cursing colorfully, Amanda bucked off the bale and bounded to her feet. She was halfway up the ladder when she heard the whine of rusty hinges and a thunking sound. Fighting her inconvenient fear of height, Amanda battled her way to the loft.

Light from the opened loft door speared across the straw-lined floor. Gathering her courage, Amanda pulled herself into the loft and inched toward the door. She made the mistake of looking out to see if someone had shinnied down the rope that hung on the iron block and tackle above the opening. Her stomach lurched and she retreated two quick steps. Just as she gathered the courage to inch back toward the opening in hopes of getting a bird's eye view of whoever had pelted her with hay bales, an unseen object rammed her broadside.

Amanda screamed bloody murder and flailed her arms in an attempt to regain her balance. The hay bale that had been heaved at her cartwheeled through the five-foot wide loft door and plunged to the ground. Meanwhile, Amanda was hanging onto the barn rope by her fingernails, draped half in and half out of the barn.

Behind the stacks of hay that formed a semi-circle in the loft, Amanda heard scuffling noises. Whoever had attempted to knock her out of the loft was scurrying toward the ladder to make a fast getaway. In sheer determination, Amanda slung a jean-clad leg into the opening and tried to claw her way back to solid ground. Unfortunately, there was so much loose straw on the floor that she slid out the opening, held aloft by the frayed rope. No doubt about it, she was going to fall!

No, you aren't, you wimp. Haul your butt back up

here and quit acting like some helpless female, she said to herself. Come on, Hazard. Move!

Amanda gritted her teeth, prayed fervently, and scrambled back into the loft. She granted herself a full minute of heavy breathing before gathering her noodly legs beneath her. She had come dangerously close to suffering a nasty accident. Indubitably, by the time her mangled body had been found on the ground below, the unidentified intruder would have been long gone.

When Amanda emerged from the barn, she had the feeling she was completely alone. A quick survey of the area left her wondering if her attacker had fled to the tree-lined creek in the pasture. She also wondered if she would meet with another harrowing accident if she went in search of the intruder.

Inhaling a deep, cleansing breath, Amanda took inventory of her injuries. Other than a few splinters, scratches, and a bruised shoulder, she was in reasonably good condition. She was lucky to be alive.

Muttering, Amanda stamped back to the house to gather the money she had collected from her treasure hunt. She was tempted to report the incident to Thorn, but she knew he was skeptical of her suspicions. Amanda had gone running to Thorn during her first murder investigation and he had called her a lunatic with paranoid tendencies.

No, this time she would keep her trap shut. This incident may not have had anything to do with Elmer's demise, she told herself reasonably. There was a thief running around loose in Vamoose. . . .

Amanda pulled the straw from her hair and thought of Velma Hertzog. It was time to pay the gossipy beautician a call. Velma could give a detailed account of everyone connected to Elmer Jolly. Within a few days, Amanda would have a list of probable suspects. And then she would contact Thorn with concrete evidence and believable motive.

"Well, hi, hon. I haven't seen you for a spell." Chomp, chomp, crack. Velma, proprietor of Beauty Boutique, chewed vigorously on her wad of bubble gum and motioned for Amanda to take a seat after Millicent Patch vacated "The Chair." "I guess you were snowed under during tax season. And now we'll all be busy with clean-up duty after the tornado. I've got leaks like you wouldn't believe."

Amanda approached The Chair like a prisoner trudging to the gallows. She knew Velma was scissor-happy. The only reason Amanda put herself at Velma's mercy was to acquire information. Velma gave haircuts that had gone out of style twenty years earlier. And obviously Velma had not heard that aerosol hair spray damaged the atmosphere. The fog in the beauty parlor could have shattered the ozone layer in ten minutes flat.

"Trim or cut, hon?" Smack, crack.

"Just trim the dead ends, Velma."

Velma raised her scissors and gave a quick snip. Amanda cringed and mustered her courage. The Amazon beautician loomed behind her like Edward Scissorhands. Amanda began to fear she was in danger of being scalped.

"I heard Elmer Jolly bit the dust." Crack, pop.

Of course, Velma had. That was why Amanda was here. "Poor Elmer. He was such a nice old man."

"Nice?" Chomp, snap. "Are you kidding? He was a

cantankerous, tightfisted old buzzard who didn't get along with much of anybody. He came in here a few times after he got too old to slap a bowl on his head and trim around his ears. He left that green truck of his running and told me to make it snappy because he was burning expensive gas. The old goat tossed me a fifty-cent piece and went on his way."

Millicent Patch, another pruner of the Vamoose grapevine, looked up from her magazine and added, "The old rascal shooed me off his porch with a broom after I was nice enough to take him a dozen home-canned fruits and pickles, compliments of the Methodist Women's Society. He thought I was trying to come on to him!" Millie sniffed in offended dignity as she tugged her wash-and-wear polyester skirt around her knees. "And I can tell you for sure that door-to-door salesmen left Elmer's place with their hair standing on end more than once. Elmer took after unwanted visitors with a twelve-gauge shotgun. He was the most unsociable individual I ever met."

Amanda glanced sideways when one of the high school cheerleaders bounced into the shop as if she had springs in her sneakers. She wore a crowd-pleasing smile and an ultraskimpy pleated skirt.

"How are things at school, Deidra?" Chomp, snip, snip.

"Great! It's less than a month before I graduate."

Ah, the irrepressible enthusiasm of youth. It was disgusting, thought Amanda. It was also getting more difficult to even remember being that young.

Amanda shot a glance in the mirror to monitor Velma's wild whacking. "Not too much off the sides, please."

"Got it, hon." Thump, snip.

"Bobby Sherman made all-state in basketball, you know," Deidra imparted with her usual enthusiasm. "He plays in the conference all-star game tonight. We're all going over to the city to watch him."

Before the conversation went too far off track, Amanda quickly changed the subject. She needed information about Elmer and she had better get it quickly or Velma would have Amanda's shoulder-length blond hair cropped above her ears.

"Are you sure everybody in Vamoose had trouble with Elmer? He and I always got along fine," Amanda said as casually as she knew how, considering her hair was dropping to the floor in clumps.

"Well, you're about the only one, hon." Snap, crackle, pop. "Elmer had the crazed notion that anybody who tried to befriend him was after his money. You know how some folks butter up lonely widows, widowers, and old bachelors, hoping to be included in the will. Elmer would have none of that. You couldn't even get a glass of water to wet your whistle at his house because he wouldn't let anybody stay long enough to get thirsty. He tried to sic that three-legged dog on visitors, but ole Pete would just wag his tail."

Millicent leaned out from under the dryer to check the rollers and added her two cent's worth. "Why, Elmer wouldn't even have much of anything to do with his own brothers and sisters-in-law. He wouldn't let them borrow his tools or machinery if they were in a pinch. Odie Mae and Eula Bell tried to do some matchmaking with their younger sister after Leroy Jolly passed on, but nothing ever came of it. Elmer must have decided he was too old to marry, but who knows for sure what he thought? All I know is that those Mopopes and Jollys always were an odd bunch. My dear Henry, God rest his sweet soul, always said the whole lot of them preferred to isolate themselves and stick to old traditions."

"I'd like to know who's going to inherit all that property, mineral rights, and cash." Velma stepped back apace to survey her masterpiece before hunkering over to snip an errant strand of hair. She popped a bubble inches from Amanda's ear, causing her to flinch as if she had been shot.

"I'm dying to find out what's in Elmer's will," Millie seconded.

Amanda would dearly like to know what was in that will, too. As of yet, she hadn't located the damned thing. To her dismay, she discovered that the banker had not been permitted to make a copy of the document which—Amanda learned to her astounded disbelief—had been written on the inside of a junk mail envelope and signed by two witnesses—the banker and his private secretary. Amanda had been assured, however, that the will would be accepted in court since it was in Elmer's handwriting and had been signed by two credible witnesses. But Elmer had not allowed the banker to read the paragraphs that bequeathed his worldly possessions to thus-named beneficiaries. It was all kept very secretive.

Elmer's eccentric behavior confirmed that he insisted on his privacy. Amanda could not begin to imagine who had inherited Elmer's fortune, if not the family. But Velma insisted the elder Jolly wasn't close to his brothers. Good Lord, he hadn't left his inheritance to his critters, had he?

"You know, I think I remember something about a

scandal in the Jolly or Mopope family years back." Velma's fake eyelashes fluttered against her cheeks as she paused in thought. "Now who told me that little tidbit? Confound it, I can't remember. It was so many years ago."

What? A gap in Velma's encyclopedia of a memory? Middle age must surely have caught up with the woman, despite her attempt to retain youth with hair dye, acrylic nails, and false eyelashes. Of course she swore she didn't use any of those things but Amanda knew better. At close range, she could detect salt and pepper roots under that haystack of red hair that was so stiff from hair spray that even the recent tornado hadn't been able to budge it.

"Oh well, it will come to me eventually," Velma said confidently.

"I'll be curious to hear the story when you remember it," Amanda assured her.

Velma wheeled her hefty body around. "You dry, Millie?"

"Dry as straw," Millie replied. "I think I need a conditioner for my gray hair. Do you have any of that herbal tea and karotene concoction that's supposed to bring dead hair back to life?"

"Sure do. I'll take care of you in a jiffy." Snap, pop. "Let me get Amanda sprayed first."

After Velma had patted and smoothed Amanda's hair into a tall beehive, she circled with aerosol can in hand, gluing every strand in place. Amanda inhaled a deep breath before plunging into the pollution vapor.

"You know, I thought Officer Thorn would have paid you a call by now. The two of you really should get together. You'd make a handsome couple, hon."

So it was true that Amanda's caution and discretion had paid off. No one knew she and Thorn were having a . . . relationship.

"*You* ought to give Nick a call and invite him to dinner sometime. He has to be lonely out there on his farm, keeping the police beat and tending his livestock." Chomp, crack.

Amanda couldn't breathe, much less speak in the suffocating fog of spray. Velma, however, had iron lungs.

"That Randel Thompson has eyes for you, you know." Crackle, snap. "He asked me about you yesterday. He wanted me to fix him up with you. You remember Randel, don't you? The long, lean cowboy who works on Buddy Hampton's horse farm." With fiendish determination, Velma doubled over to mash a fake fingernail against one strand of blonde hair that refused to wrap around the hive. Then she sprayed the contrary tendril into place. "But I think Officer Thorn is more your style." She grinned. "If I were ten years younger, I'd chase Nick around a few blocks myself."

Amanda surged out of the chair, looking for fresh air. "Thanks, Velma. How much do I owe you?"

Snack, crackle, pop. "Nothing, *if* you give Nick Thorn a call." She tried to wink but her false eyelashes stuck together. "Nick needs a classy woman in his life. Invite him to dinner."

Amanda slapped a ten-dollar bill in Velma's hand and smiled as she brushed past Head Cheerleader who was leaning against the wall, coiling her bleached blonde hair around her index finger.

"I'm not kidding about Nick Thorn!" Velma called before Amanda could close the door behind her.

Amanda grumbled under her breath. It wasn't that she

was ashamed to have all of Vamoose know she and Thorn were seeing each other. But the thought of having her love life speculated upon in the fog of hair spray at Beauty Boutique or discussed over coffee at Last Chance Cafe appalled her. But maybe she *should* get their ... relationship ... out in the open, suffer the inevitable wave of gossip, and forget it. Well, perhaps when she was certain that Thorn's feelings for her would last longer than the gossip, she would make it a point to be seen with him in public. But Velma wasn't getting her wagging tongue on any gossip about Amanda until Amanda was damned good and ready, and she wasn't damned good and ready yet. It might be awhile before she disclosed such private information to the local yokels of Vamoose.

The truth was that Amanda wasn't sure how strongly Thorn felt about her. Mother always said that it was illadvised to make a commitment to a man who was only after sex and/or money. How serious could Thorn really be about her if he wouldn't hand over his tax forms to her? She wasn't about to hand her heart over to Thorn or reveal their ... relationship ... to Vamoose until he presented her with his W-2 form. Then, and only then, would Amanda know Thorn trusted and respected her. And while Amanda waited for her knight in shining police car to pledge his devotion, she was going to discover who had bumped Elmer Jolly off. *This* she promised herself as she drove off to tend her errands.

Chapter Five

Amanda and her beehive hairstyle returned home to find Randel Thompson leaning leisurely against his sporty, yellow short-bed pickup, awaiting her arrival. Randel swaggered toward her to swing open the door of her jalopy and assist her to the ground.

"Evenin', 'Manda," he drawled, flashing her a dazzling smile.

Amanda had the feeling she had been catapulted back to the Wild West. She expected Randel to expel a "Why, shucks" or "How-di-do" any second. And he could cut the " 'Manda" crap. Nobody called her "Mandy" or " 'Manda" except her ex. She hated those derivations of her given name. She also hated her ex.

"Can I help you, Randel?"

"I like your hair."

He would, she thought. "Thank you."

Randel struck a provocative pose against the side of the truck, calling attention to his trim-fitting Mo'Betta shirt and clinging Wrangler jeans. Amanda presumed she was supposed to be awestruck by the lanky blond cowboy who was reported to be a whiz at gentling horses and not too bad with women, either. What a shame that, these days, her taste in men leaned more toward the tall, dark, and handsome Tom Selleck—minus the mustache—types.

"I thought I'd come by and tell you that I spoke with your landlady today. Emma Carter was looking for someone to repair your damaged roof. Since the whole town sounds like it's under construction, and all the roofing crews have jobs lined up for weeks ahead, I volunteered to help Emma out. Your shingles will be delivered at noon. I'll start stripping shingles at 8:00 in the morning."

"That's kind of you, Randel." Amanda dropped her keys in her purse and headed for the house.

"Uh . . . 'Manda?" he sauntered along behind her. "I hired Bobby Sherman to help me when he gets out of school."

"Wise choice. I doubt Bobby and his size fourteen shoes will have trouble staying on the roof without a gust of wind blowing him off. The boy's feet are as big as skis."

Randel chuckled huskily as his eyes flooded over Amanda's figure. Curse this Las Vegas showgirl physique of hers. Amanda wanted to be known for her brains, not her body. But the plague of testosterone in males never allowed them to look deeper than a woman's curvy figure.

"See you in the morning, Randel." Amanda pulled out her house key and tried to get away gracefully.

"Uh . . . 'Manda?" Randel clutched her elbow before she could escape. "I thought maybe we could grab a burger or something together."

Amanda opened the door and swallowed a startled

gasp. Her home looked as if a cyclone had blown through it. Someone had ransacked the place! Struggling for composure because she was determined to solve this mystery on her own, Amanda closed the door and spun to face Randel. She could deal with the invasion of privacy far better on a full stomach.

Forcing the semblance of a smile, Amanda addressed the lean blond cowboy. "A burger and fries sound good."

Numbly, Amanda slid into Randel's truck, battling to gather her wits. Who in the hell had been in her house and why? Could it be that someone suspected *she* might have Elmer's will in her possession? Was that why Elmer's bedroom had been torn upside down and then later cleaned? Had the hay loft incident been an attempt on her life rather than a scare tactic? Yikes! She was flirting with disaster.

It had been Amanda's intent to pursue the murderer, not to be pursued. Now what would Magnum P.I. do in a situation like this? Certainly not panic. Amanda Hazard wouldn't, either. She had dealt with harassment when solving her first murder case. She could cope.

" 'Manda?"

Amanda jerked up her head and glanced at Randel. "What?"

"I said . . . is Last Chance Cafe okay with you?"

"Sure. I need a cholesterol fix," she mumbled, distracted.

Randel chuckled. "I love a woman with a sense of humor."

"I'm not all that amusing. We accountants are a dull bunch—what with all those tedious columns of numbers, debits, and credits."

He laughed again, for no reason that Amanda could ascertain. Her remark wasn't that witty. Obviously Randel was easily amused or else he thought the way to a woman's heart was through flattery. Boy, was he in for a surprise. Flattery got a man nowhere fast with Amanda Hazard. If a man was so easy to please, he was also easy to bed and quick to rise. Amanda reminded herself that this ex-rodeo star had probably been in and out of a great many saddles.

"I guess you heard about Elmer Jolly." Amanda decided she may as well gain something from her dinner companion besides dull company and indigestion.

"Yeah, too bad. He was the best of that older Jolly generation."

Amanda blinked like an owl. This was the first kind word spoken about Elmer, other than her own comments, of course.

"One of Elmer's brothers tried to buy a stud from my boss, Buddy Hampton. Melvin Jolly kept the stud for three weeks without paying the quoted price and then hauled the horse home. Melvin claimed the stud was sterile. All that old sidewinder wanted was free breeding for the mares his son is raising. I swear Melvin would steal you blind if you turned your back."

Or murder you when you weren't looking? It made one wonder . . .

Amanda ambled into Last Chance Cafe and missed a step when she saw Thorn ensconced in his favorite corner booth. His dark eyes bounced back and forth between her and Randel who was towering beside her like a stud claiming a mare. Amanda had never been an expert at reading lips, but she was relatively certain that Thorn had expelled several unprintable curses that had her name attached to them. He sat there scowling, refusing to meet her gaze, making a spectacular display of ignoring her. That was not the face of a happy man. And if the rigidity of Thorn's spine was any indication of his present mood, Amanda wouldn't go near him with a lighted match.

"Over here, honey." Randel grabbed her and steered her down the aisle, making a noticeable display of possession.

Amanda gritted her teeth and forced a smile. Here was yet another annoying example of male obtrusiveness. It was the ole look-who-I've-got-on-my-arm-tonight trick. Amanda stifled the urge to kick Randel in the seat of his tight-fitting jeans and scold Thorn for behaving like the lover scorned. Amanda was only here because she hadn't been able to bring herself to walk into her ransacked house quite yet. And she would not report the incident to Thorn on a bet. Thorn had not wanted to get involved in a murder he swore hadn't happened. And so, by damned, he wouldn't be. Amanda could handle this case by herself.

When the patrons at the table beside Amanda broached the topic of Elmer's death, she pricked up her ears. She wished Randel would shut his trap so she could eavesdrop without being distracted. But Randel yammered on with Amanda adding an occasional nod to pacify him.

When Frank Hermann, a crusty old farmer with a pot belly and baggy overalls, leaned over to ask Amanda if she had heard about Elmer, she made a quick strategic decision—a dangerous one. She knew exactly what she was doing—keeping Elmer's killer on tenterhooks.

"Yes, I know, Frank. Elmer made me the administrator of his estate."

All heads turned toward Amanda in synchronized rhythm—all except Thorn's. All she could see of him was his broad, stiff back.

"No kidding?" Glen Chambliss spoke up. "I thought Elmer had turned into a card-carrying woman-hater years ago. No offense, but I'm surprised Elmer put a woman in charge of his accounts and worldly possessions."

"Elmer took a liking to me and I to him," Amanda declared to everyone who cared to listen.

"Then who inherits?" Preston Banks questioned interestedly.

Amanda smiled, but she said firmly, "I am not at liberty to reveal that information until the legal document goes through probate."

There. Now the word would spread lickety-split. News traveled damned fast in this one-horse town.

After Faye Bernard took their order, Amanda eased back in the booth, battling the frustrating vision of her living room in a state of dishevelment. She could imagine what the rest of her house looked like ... and maybe even her office. Good God!

"Will you excuse me a minute, Randel. I need to pick up some files from my office across the street."

Amanda slid from the booth and sailed off like a flying carpet. When she unlocked the office door, she breathed a gusty sigh of relief. The office was just as she had left it. Amanda unlocked the cabinets and located Elmer's file. She would sleep with the damned thing if she had to, but no one was getting their grubby hands on any information that dealt with Elmer's financial accounts!

"New do, Hazard?"

Amanda very nearly jumped out of her skin when the gruff baritone voice boomed at her like a cannon.

"You've been on a fact-finding mission in the local know-it-all's beauty shop, I presume."

If Thorn had been a dog, she would have checked him for rabies, what with all his snapping, snarling, and growling. She glanced back to see if he was frothing at the mouth.

"And by the way, Hazard, I paid a call on the medical examiner. He did a liver test on Jolly at the scene of the *accident*. Elmer died between twelve and one o'clock."

"A lot can happen in the span of an hour, Thorn."

He glared at her. She glared back.

"Ain't that the truth."

"What's that supposed to mean?" Amanda demanded.

"In an hour, you can collect a new boyfriend and make all sorts of discoveries about him." His eyes turned a darker shade of black.

Was Thorn jealous? No, probably just feeling possessive, Amanda decided. It was one of those male things. Territorial rights and all that.

"You need your eyes checked, Thorn. Randel Thompson is no boy."

"No, he isn't, but he does have a loose zipper," Nick muttered.

"A common flaw, characteristic of those of the male persuasion," she shot back with her customary pessimism on the subject of men.

Nick gnashed his teeth. "And where do I fall, Hazard?"

"Into the nearest bed—you, Randel, and the other seventy-five percent of the male population with open flies."

Nick swore under his breath. Damn that Hazard and her sweeping condemnation of the male population. He wanted to pick her up and shake her until he dislodged all those cynical theories.

While Nick was floundering for a suitably nasty rejoinder Amanda fired her question. "Did the coroner find any suspicious wounds on Elmer?"

Nick reined in his temper—to some degree, at least. "No. Elmer had a broken neck and a gash on the side of his head the exact size of the shelving that crashed down on him. He also had two broken fingers and a cut on his forearm from the glass in a broken canning jar. Accidental death, Hazard. You can stop drilling Velma and everybody else full of questions. This is an open and shut case. You can have Elmer's personal possessions—a wallet and ring of keys. I picked them up from the sheriff's office and left them at my house."

He lurched toward the door and then abruptly spun back around. "Oh, by the way, thanks one helluva lot, Hazard."

"For what?"

Nick glowered at her until his black brows formed a single line over his eyes. "You refuse to be seen in Vamoose with me, but you parade through the cafe with Thompson."

"Oh, for heavens sake, Thorn, that was only because—" Amanda slammed her mouth shut like a crocodile. She wasn't going to tell Thorn about her house, especially while he was behaving like an ass. "Because Randel is going to do my roof."

He snorted derisively. "Yeah, right."

"He *is*. Emma Carter hired him."

"I can just hear Randel finagling his way into that. He has the hots for you, Hazard."

"So Velma said."

"What else did Velma say?"

"She suggested I have you over for dinner." Amanda smiled cattily. "I, of course, knew you were too tough to cook."

Nick unclamped his gritted teeth. "I was referring to Velma's comments about Lover Boy Thompson."

"She said he was a whiz with horses."

"You wouldn't enjoy the ride, Hazard."

"Don't start with me, Thorn. Mother has an irritating habit of telling me what I would and wouldn't enjoy. You aren't Mother."

"Well, at least you have me categorized in the correct gender, even if you don't know a helluva lot else about me."

They stood there like duelists at twenty paces before Amanda flung her chin in the air, broke eye contact, and presented her back.

"Jerk."

"Bi—"

The door slammed shut. Amanda decided she was glad she didn't hear Thorn say what she suspected he had said. Ten to one, it wasn't very nice. Mother would not have approved of having her baby girl called a naughty name.

An hour later, after returning to the cafe for her burger with Randel, Amanda was back on her doorstep and

Randel was trying to invite himself in. "Not tonight," Amanda declined. "I have scads of paperwork to catch up on." She also had a house to piece back together.

"Well, I guess I'll see you in the morning, honey."

When Randel leaned close, Amanda doubled over to retrieve Hank the tomcat. Randel kissed air.

"Amusing *and* agile. I like that in a woman," he said as he sauntered away.

Amanda had the feeling Randel Thompson liked *anything* in a woman. The man's testosterone level was exceedingly high.

Prepared to face disaster, Amanda opened the door. To her utter amazement, the living room had been restored to its former state, even though magazines weren't stacked in their usual alphabetical order. Was she dealing with some kind of wacko here? Or were the their two kooks running around loose—one who made messes and who who cleaned them up?

After inspecting the back door, Amanda discovered that a crowbar, or some such tool, had been used to gain entrance. Damn, perhaps whoever had entered her home had still been inside when she had first arrived. If she had gone inside and met with trouble, maybe Randel would have come to her rescue and the culprit would now be in custody. . . .

Amanda glanced out the window to watch Randel drive off. Or was it Randel's accomplice who had wrecked her home while Randel casually awaited her arrival to invite her to dinner? Come to think of it, Randel was the only one in Vamoose who had kind words for the deceased. It could have been a ploy.

It was also interesting to note Randel had appeared at her home the day after Elmer's death. And how convenient that Randel would have a bird's eye view from atop Amanda's house the next few days. Damn, now was not a good time to be at odds with Officer Thorn. Maybe she should inform Thorn of the strange happenings.

In his present mood? Sure, Hazard. The man is just oozing sympathy and concern, isn't he? The glare Thorn had flashed her before slamming out of her office could make a saint believe in hell. He probably wouldn't ever speak to her again. She would have to devise a way to return to Thorn's good graces without groveling like some sniveling female. Amanda didn't snivel or grovel. It was beneath her dignity.

On that thought, Amanda set off to feed her hungry critters. At least somebody around here appreciated her. She was the cat's meow, the twinkle in the pig's eye, and the wag in her three-legged dog's tail. Lucky the duck could take or leave her. As for the chickens, they were in hen heaven in their nests of Cole-Hahn shoe boxes.

The blaring phone brought Nick awake with a start. He automatically grabbed for the pistol he wasn't wearing and then rolled toward the phone. He knocked the receiver from its cradle and it clanked on the floor. After hauling the cord up like the line of an anchor, Nick tried to speak into the wrong end of the phone before flipping it over.

"Who is it at this time of the morning and what do you want?"

"Thorn, my hens aren't laying any eggs."

Nick's head plunked on the pillow. "Damn it, Hazard, it's six o'clock in the morning."

"I know what time it is, but what about my chickens?"

"I don't give a hoot about your hens!"

"Are you still brooding? Hey! Maybe that's what's wrong with the chickens."

"Geezus . . ." Nick rubbed his eyes and sighed. He had never been an early bird, unlike Hazard who usually popped up like bread from a toaster. He was still mad as hell at her. She and Don Juan Thompson were the latest gossip in Vamoose. He'd like to wring both her *and* her chickens' necks!

"So, Thorn. What's the matter with my hens? I fed them, watered them faithfully, and provided accommodations befitting the Holiday Inn. Where are my high-cholesterol-content, farm-fresh eggs?"

Nick did not want to grin. Hazard was not amusing at 6 a.m. He smiled in spite of himself. "Are you doing drugs, Hazard? I may have been off the Narc beat for a few years, but—"

"Quit clucking, Thorn. Just answer the question. Do chickens go on strike or what?"

'Chickens don't strike; they lay."

"Not mine."

"There's your problem. You don't lay regularly, either, Hazard. You're setting a bad example for your chickens."

There was a noticeable pause. "I'll pretend I didn't hear that."

"Don't bother. I'm not going to pretend I didn't say it."

"Just forget I called, Thorn. I'll ask Randel about the hens when he arrives at eight o'clock—"

"Chickens are rather temperamental creatures," Nick muttered in begruding explanation. "Your hens have endured a storm and they were uprooted to a new location. It isn't unusual for hens to miss laying eggs for a few days, but they'll eventually adjust."

"Thanks, Thorn." Another pause. "Could I come by to pick up Elmer's personal possessions later today?"

"I'll bring them to you." It would give Nick a chance to check out Cowboy Casanova who was perched on the roof.

"What time?"

"Five o'clock."

Hesitation. "Would you like to stay for supper, Thorn?"

"Thanks, but no. I plan to sort my socks tonight."

Amanda hung up the phone. So much for a peace-treaty dinner. Thorn was still plenty peeved, but he had softened up a bit. It would be nice if she and Thorn were at least on speaking terms. Before she solved this murder, she might need a good cop, even if he was grumpy at six o'clock in the morning.

The congregation at Vamoose's cemetery was small. Amanda stood apart, studying the individual faces with ponderous concentration. The Jollys were not a jolly lot, though the situation was not conducive to enjoyment. Melvin and Claud's mouths naturally turned down at the corners, giving them a dour expression. Both of the Jolly men reminded Amanda of Elmer with their thin, wiry frames and balding heads. Their wives, the

Mopope twins—Eula Bell and Odie Mae—were as round as the Jolly men were lean. Bertie Ann, widow of the youngest Jolly, and her son Wally were also in attendance. Some of Elmer's nieces and nephews occupied the second row of seats, all of them looking to be between the ages of thirty-five and fifty. Behind them stood a smattering of grand nieces and nephews. There wasn't a teary eye in the lot.

Amanda decided that anyone—from youngest to oldest—could have gotten the best of a frail, brittle, seventy-three-year-old man. In short, Amanda was studying the crowd as if it was a lineup of possible suspects—or maybe none at all. She definitely needed more information. She would have to pay the family a call at a later date.

A sudden burst of wind uplifted Amanda's hair and slapped it across her face. Amanda wondered if Elmer was sending her a message from beyond, urging her to quit dawdling and track down his killer. Elmer never did care for funerals, Amanda mused. He had always said he would rather not even attend his own if he had a choice in the matter.

Amanda's gaze dropped from the bank of clouds that piled on the horizon like knotted fists. Then she turned her attention to the three men who rented Elmer's farm ground. Harry Ogelbee, Abner Hendershot, and Clive Barnstall stood with hats in hand, staring at some distant point. Amanda wondered what was running through their minds. Were they reflecting on Elmer's endearing traits or sighing in silent relief that he was gone?

As for herself, she missed the old rascal. Elmer had been a lively character who had an opinion on everything—much like Amanda. She and Elmer had been kindred spirits in some ways, though Amanda never considered herself quite the social recluse Elmer was. True, the man had his faults. Who didn't? But he was entertaining and fiercely attached to the few people he called "friend." Amanda was proud to have been among that select group. She owed it to Elmer's memory to track his murderer down, even if the citizens of Vamoose seemed content to let his death go uninvestigated.

The strange occurrences at Elmer's farm, and in her own home, suggested that someone had wanted Elmer out of the way, or had disposed of him in a fit of temper. Whatever the case, Bloodhound Hazard was on the trail. And if she didn't find Elmer's will—and quickly— the estate would wind up in probate with a judge determining the outcome.

Amanda reminded herself that the Jolly family didn't even know she had been named executor of the estate. They would have to be told and expenses would have to be paid out of her pocket until she could locate that missing will and the estate was settled according to Elmer's specifications.

Confound it, Elmer, where did you stash that darned will?

When the service came to a close, Amanda pivoted toward her truck and cast a dubious glance toward the darkening sky. What Vamoose didn't need was another thunderstorm following so closely on the heels of the recent tornado. There were leaky roofs all over town.

Inhaling a deep breath, Amanda shifted her jalopy into gear and started toward her office. She would catch up on her paperwork this afternoon and pay the Jolly clan a call the following day. . . . Damn, she had prom-

ised to help Thorn shear his sheep in exchange for per-
tinent information and the loan of his stock racks to collect her critters. And speaking of critters, if those
temperamental chickens didn't shape up and put out, the
feathers were going to fly. She wasn't feeding those
hens just so they could sit there on their Cole-Hahn
shoe boxes like princesses on royal thrones!

A wary frown knitted Amanda's brow when she entered her office. It wasn't that anything looked out of
place, but there seemed to be a lingering scent in the
building—one which her senses couldn't identify.
Someone had been here during her absence.

Amanda checked the back door. Sure enough, the
doorjamb showed evidence of tampering and the lock
was broken. Spinning about, Amanda propelled herself
toward the locked file cabinet. The drawer containing
the files from H to M looked as if a screwdriver had
been wedged inside it. The metal casing was bent. Hell
and damnation! This breaking-in routine was becoming
annoying. Somebody obviously thought she *did* have
possession of that will! What else could he, she, or they
be looking for?

As soon as Thorn delivered Elmer's personal effects,
Amanda was going to take every key on the ring and
open everything that had a lock on Elmer's farm. That
last will and testament had to be somewhere!

Determined to get some work done, Amanda sat
down at her desk and tallied one of her client's expen-
ditures. She worked fervently until noon and returned
home to find the bare-chested Randel tossing the last of
the old shingles into the dump truck he had parked be-

side the house. Randel strutted like a peacock; Amanda ignored him. He invited her to lunch; she declined without offering a believable excuse. With the threat of another storm in the air, Amanda didn't want Randel dillydallying while she had a naked roof overhead.

Amanda made herself a sandwich and began swallowing it down like a python. The phone jingled and Amanda choked down a mouthful of ham sandwich—she was still supporting the hog market—and reached for the receiver.

"Hello?"

"Hi, doll. It's Mother." She cleared her throat, and Amanda took another bite of her sandwich. "I just wanted to tell you that you don't have to bring a covered dish to the reunion tonight."

"Good. I don't have any covered dishes, Mother."

"Mother cleared her throat again. "Do I detect a hint of sarcasm, doll?"

Amanda could visualize Mother standing there with one carefully plucked eyebrow raised in disapproval, looking down her patrician nose at a plump, blonde-haired child in pigtails. Amanda had been the recipient of zillions of those looks. She still remembered that suffocating air of parental authority.

"About the reunion, Mother—"

Mother yowled in interruption. "Don't tell me you aren't coming! I told everybody you would be there. And your brother needs some financial advice. Those kids of his—they'll end up in a juvenile detention center if your brother doesn't get control of them—are bleeding him dry. And that incompetent wife of his!" Mother huffed into the phone. "The word *lazy* was invented to describe her."

Since Mother had strayed from the original topic, ranting about the unpardonable failings of her daughter-in-law, Amanda munched on her sandwich and chased it with a Diet Coke. By the time Mother had circled back to the subject of covered dishes and reunions, Amanda had finished her meal and filed her fingernails. Mother was very long-winded.

"You simply cannot miss this reunion, doll. You missed the last one, you know."

"Does that mean I lost my family membership and I don't have to pay my dues?"

"Your daddy wants to see you. You were always his *little girl.*"

Here came the ole guilt-trip routine, thought Amanda. "Okay, Mother. What time does this damned reunion start?"

A disgusted sniff came down the line. "Ladies do not curse, Amanda."

"The hell you say."

"Mind that tongue of yours, young lady! I raised you better than that!" Mother howled.

Amanda yanked the receiver away before Mother burst the other eardrum.

"Now, I'll cook something good up for you. All you have to do is show up at seven-thirty ... and don't curse! My goodness, living alone has really corrupted you." Mother cleared her throat—for the millionth time. "Are you going to bring your new boyfriend, doll?"

"No. We had a spat."

"Probably because he doesn't approve of your foul language."

Oh yeah? If you could hear Thorn on occasion, you

would wash his dirty mouth out with soap. And you should have heard what he called me the other night!

"Well, tah-tah, doll. We'll see you at seven-thirty."

Amanda dropped the receiver as if she were handling live coals. Damn, she would rather be run down by a speeding car than attend that damned reunion. But it wasn't worth agonizing over. She would immerse herself in work rather than waste time dreading the upcoming evening.

At five o'clock sharp, Nick pulled into the driveway of Amanda's rock-and-timber farm home. The half-naked Randel and Bigfoot Bobby Sherman were hammering shingles into place. Amanda's battered jalopy was parked by the barn. Nick sent Randel and Bobby a quick wave of greeting and headed for the corral. Amanda, with the tomcat, three-legged dog, and waddling duck at her heels, was unloading sacks of pig feed. Her blonde hair was tumbling around her in disarray and the way she filled out her jeans was downright criminal. Damned sexy female. He wished he didn't like Hazard quite so much because there were times when he would be happier if he hated her.

"Grab a sack, Thorn. I'm on a tight schedule here," Amanda threw over her shoulder.

"Big plans for tonight, Hazard?" he questioned sarcastically. "Are you and Lover Boy Thompson painting the town red?"

"No, I've been sentenced to a family reunion, if you recall. Mother sent me on one of her guilt trips. I have to spend the evening listening to her boast about what a successful accountant I turned out to be and dodging free consultation requests from the family." She cast Thorn a disgruntled glance. "I'd rather sort your socks."

I'd rather see you flat on your back beneath me. Nick clamped down on the scintillating thought and stacked the feed sack inside the barn door.

"Did you bring Elmer's personal effects?"

"Certainly. You didn't think I came by just to unload your hog rations for you, do you? I have chores of my own, you know."

"My, we are on a short fuse this evening, aren't we?"

Amanda pivoted to survey the darkly handsome Thorn in uniform. What a hunk. Randel Thompson could strut the whole live-long day and he would never arouse Amanda the way Thorn could in one minute flat. What was this quirk in her constitutional makeup that always caused air bubbles to burst in her bloodstream when she got within five feet of this man? Sometimes Thorn made her so mad she could spit tacks. Sometimes he got her so hot and bothered that her lungs felt as if they were clogged with dust. And yet, she resented the fact that Thorn never took her suspicions seriously. She was irritated with him for demanding that they bring their . . . relationship . . . out in the open, and she could not imagine why he got huffy when he found Randel running around bare-chested on her roof. But despite their conflicts, she felt a natural affinity toward Thorn that wouldn't quit. Sometimes it was damned infuriating to know that she—a highly rational form of intelligent life—was impossibly vulnerable to basic biological attraction.

"Hazard," Nick growled, taking an ominous step toward her. "There are times when I can't decide whether

I want to kiss those sarcastic lips off of you or simply strangle you."

Amanda was not the least bit intimidated. She glanced at her watch. "Well, hurry up and decide, Thorn. I've got places to go and things to do—"

She didn't even have the chance to punctuate the end of her sentence. Nick yanked her to him, slamming her body into his masculine contours. He felt like a rock wall—all that finely tuned muscle and hard—well, he was aroused. So was she. Enough said. He kissed her with forceful possession while his long fingers curled around her throat, just in case the urge to choke her overshadowed the need to suck the breath out of her.

Amanda's blood pressure shot through the roof. She was really going to have to watch her cholesterol count. Greasy hamburgers and fries, supplemented with large doses of this sensual wild man, was a dangerous combination that could contribute to heart trouble.

As quickly as Nick had clutched her to him he set her away. Amanda grabbed the wall for support and panted for breath.

"How's that for second best, Hazard?" he muttered in a bitter tone.

"Are you, by chance, referring to Randel?" Amanda croaked. The volatile chemical reaction Thorn set off had constricted her vocal apparatus. She sounded like a sick frog.

"Is there more competition for your affection besides Randel?" Nick wouldn't have been surprised. He had heard enough coffee shop talk when Hazard strolled in to know that there were several men in Vamoose who entertained fantasies about this gorgeous blonde accountant.

"Oh, for God's sake, Thorn," Amanda said when she could speak without her voice leaping an octave every other word. "Randel has lips like a frog—thin and wet. I pride myself for having better taste. You know I'm not into bed-hopping. I don't believe in casual . . . relationships."

"*Affairs*, Hazard. You started having difficulty with the A-word the minute we became lovers—on a frustratingly irregular basis, I might add. What the hell's wrong with me that you can't admit we have—or at least we *had*—something good going? I'm a cop with sound credentials and I have all my own teeth. What the hell do you want? Mr. Absolutely Perfect, who grovels at your feet and always gives you your way without putting up a fuss?"

"I want to be sure, you idiotic toad!" Amanda burst out and cringed at her vocal outburst. She lowered her voice and continued, "I have one divorce to my credit, thank you very much. I don't want another one. And neither do I want to make the rounds on Vamoosian tongues that wag from both ends. You know I want a relationship that is deeper than a *sheet*. I want a meaningful relationship that will outlast this Nevada showgirl body that I have been cursed with. Don't you think I know what that ex-rodeo star wants from me? Don't you think I'm smart enough to know why he's lurking up on my roof? I know where the man's brains are located—"

" 'Manda honey?"

Amanda clamped her mouth shut when Randel swaggered toward the barn, his chest slick with perspiration. He looked like a well-oiled body builder without his bar bells.

"Me an' Bobby finished the job. We'll be shoving off now."

Nick pivoted to stand behind Hazard and then leaned close to her ear. " 'Manda honey?" he mocked dryly. "Are you sure you and Romeo the rodeo clown don't have something going?'

"Knock it off, Thorn," she muttered out the side of her mouth. To Randel she said sweetly, "Thanks for fixing my roof. I'm glad you completed the job before the next rain sets in."

Randel propped a brawny arm against the doorjamb and graced her with his charming smile, ignoring Nick as if he was just another feed sack on the stack. "I could repair the tin on your barn and sheds in my spare time if you like."

"I would appreciate that. And bring Bobby Sherman with you. I'll pay him, too. I'm sure a graduating senior could use a few extra dollars."

"I'll be back in the morning," Randel informed her with another charismatic smile.

"Thanks for the warning," Nick grumbled.

Amanda gouged Thorn in the ribs with her elbow. "Fine, Randel. And thanks."

When Randel winked and swaggered off, Amanda outstretched her hand toward Thorn. "Give me Elmer's wallet and keys and cut the wisecracks. Romeo the rodeo clown isn't even in your league. I don't hang around men who keep loaded guns. You never can tell when that kind of man will go off." With a saucy smile that made her baby blues twinkle, Amanda pushed up on tiptoe to give Thorn a hasty kiss. "Now hand it over, Thorn."

"What? The loaded gun or the wallet?" His voice

dropped to a familiar husky resonance that reminded Amanda of more intimate times and more private places. Her hormones went wild.

"The wallet and keys, please," she managed to say without panting the words. "I really don't have time to play with loaded pistols right now."

"Let me know when you want to schedule a little target practice, Hazard. I'll bring the firearms and ammunition."

After Nick had dropped the keys and wallet in her hand, he patted her denim-clad fanny and sauntered out the door. "See ya later, 'Manda honey."

"The dreaded reunion should be over by eleven," she called after him.

"I should have my socks sorted by then," he said with a grin.

Amanda opened a feed sack and smiled to herself. Truce at last! She functioned much better when Thorn was his ornery but charming old self. Now why was that?

Chapter Six

Nick parked himself in the booth beside Jerry Jolly who was sipping black coffee and staring at the bulletin board in Last Chance Cafe. "I was sorry to hear about your uncle."

Jerry shrugged a thin-bladed shoulder. "The old buzzard lived to be seventy-three on pure orneriness. It was bound to catch up with him sometime."

Ah, the bereaved nephew, thought Nick. Of course, Jerry had always been too self-engrossed to give a fig about anyone else. He was always looking for an easy way to turn a fast buck. His farming techniques were the joke of Vamoose. His wheat fields looked like sunflower patches and his cattle were skin and bone.

Jerry's one love in life was breeding horses. Nick had once heard that Jerry had stashed several of his brood mares on one of Elmer's pastures to fatten them up. Elmer had run the horses through the fences with the blast of his shotgun. One of the mares had suffered a broken leg and had to be put down. The horse, of course, was proclaimed to be the most expensive animal Jerry owned. Melvin had gone to bat for his son, much to everyone's surprise, and had gone a few rounds with Elmer over the incident. Damned near started a family feud, according to rumor. Nick hesitated in handing Hazard that tidbit of information. Sure as hell, she would make something of it.

"I'd like to know who inherited Elmer's property," Jerry said between sips of coffee. "I hear that lady accountant was named executor of the estate. It was news to the family. I never could figure out why Elmer got so attached to that city-born woman."

"Maybe he was just a sucker for a pretty face," Nick offered jokingly.

"Elmer?" Jerry expelled a snort. "He was a woman-hater after—" He took another sip of coffee.

"After what?" Nick prodded, thoroughly appalled at himself. Suddenly he was sniffing for clues like Bloodhound Hazard, and he was certain Elmer's death had been an accident.

"Nothing. It doesn't matter now. Elmer is gone."

Nick let the matter drop. "How are your folks taking the death? Your dad spent a lot of years with Elmer. Melvin and Elmer were only four years apart in age, weren't they?"

"Dad is the second oldest. He and Elmer had their share of trouble because Elmer was at the top of the family pecking order and Dad resented being told what to do. But Mother always felt sorry for Elmer."

"Any reason why?"

"She's kind-hearted. But that's enough on that subject."

In other words, you aren't prying any more information out of me, Nick thought to himself.

"Well, my condolences to your family, Jerry." Nick

grabbed his steak sandwich-to-go and headed home. He had cattle and sheep to feed and several strips of tin to batten down on the barn before another rain storm set in, and given a sixty percent chance of precipitation that was likely. Nick wanted to repair the leaks above his stack of alfalfa hay before the bales got wet and moldy. His flock of sheep didn't need to founder on rotten hay. Some of the ewes were already hobbling around after being struck by flying debris.

Amanda drove home from the dreaded family reunion in Oklahoma City in a steady downpour. Very soon, she would be able to determine if Randel Thompson was as good at roofing as he was reported to be with horses. Her new shingles were undergoing their first waterproof test and she was anxious to see the results.

The family reunion had been everything Amanda had anticipated. She had been forced to give a few freebies in financial consultation. Mother had blathered about her daughter's smashing success, and Amanda had artfully dodged comments and questions suggesting she should tie the matrimonial knot again instead of fumbling around by herself in that piddling little town west of the metropolis. Exasperating!

Amanda was eternally grateful that she had not subjected Thorn to the family circus. She had some relatives who were in a galaxy all their own. Talk about a colony of kooks! Amanda wondered how she had come to have such a strange clan. She sometimes wondered if she and Daddy were the only sane ones in the bunch. And she wasn't always too sure about Daddy!

Arriving home, Amanda remained in the car a moment and shined her headlights on the front door, hoping no unexpected visitors were awaiting her. The fact that a person—or persons—unknown were prowling around her private domain was giving her the creeps. She never knew what to expect when she entered her home or office. Perhaps she should dig a moat around her home and stock it with alligators. Tossing in a few piranhas would be a nice touch.

Checking her watch, Amanda decided she had enough time to drive out to the Jolly farm to poke around before Thorn arrived at 11:00. Amanda backed out of the driveway and headed northwest, cursing the sloppy roads that had more gravel in their ditches than on the beaten path. She dodged a variety of wildlife along the way—turtles, frogs, snakes, an occasional armadillo. Only the rabbits had enough sense to stay out of the rain. She could imagine what the rabbits were doing for entertainment.

Once she finally made it to the farm, Amanda reached into her purse for Elmer's key ring and dashed for the porch. A flick of the light switch illuminated Elmer's living room. Amanda glanced at her watch and then set to work. She had an hour and ten minutes to search the house. She tried out the keys on every lock. Inside a tool chest that was stuffed under the sofa she found junk mail envelopes with research notes on wheat breeding that were dated in the '50s. She also found an instruction manual for a grain thrasher that had been obsolete for decades.

On the top shelf of the kitchen cabinets she found another locked box containing two diamond rings. Amanda slipped them on her finger and frowned, puzzled. Had the wedding set belonged to Elmer's mother?

The rings obviously had not belonged to Elmer's wife since he never had one.

Amanda replaced the rings and plucked up the aged, yellow letter that lay at the bottom of the box. She blinked in surprise when she unfolded the note to read its contents. It was a Dear John letter—a Dear Elmer letter in this case—penned in a sweeping scrawl. It was undated and unsigned, but the author begged for Elmer's understanding and forgiveness. She claimed to have fallen for someone else. It had just happened, a quirk of fate, a twist of destiny, and so on and so forth.

Was this mysterious woman the reason Elmer had never married? Had he been head over heels in love and then betrayed? Had the experience ruined him for life?

After folding the letter, Amanda returned it to the container and searched the other rooms of the house. She even checked the basin of the antique, wringer-style washing machine that sat in the utility room, hoping Elmer had stuffed a valuable clue inside for safe keeping. No such luck. But Amanda had acquired a broader perspective of the man who had puttered around his house for years on end.

Amanda cast another hasty glance at her watch and pivoted toward the door. Switching off the lights, she hurried toward her truck. The rain was coming down in sheets and Amanda was drenched by the time she dived into her jalopy. She was a mile down the road when she felt a jarring thud. Her vehicle swerved in the mud when it was rammed from behind by a truck that was driving without headlights. Amanda clamped a deathgrip on the wheel and tried to keep her jalopy on the road. Another thump on her rear bumper sent her skidding sideways toward the ditch. Her headlights spotlighted the bridge over Deep Creek. Amanda swallowed air.

When the unidentified vehicle slammed into her the third time, with enough momentum to send her plunging toward the swift-moving water, Amanda gritted her teeth, sent up a prayer for divine deliverance, and spun the wheel. She barely missed the flimsy guard railing. The jalopy went into a free-gliding skid on the muddy road and nose-dived into the ditch, missing Deep Creek by a span of only ten feet.

Amanda had plowed through enough snow drifts with Thorn at the wheel last winter to know it was better to accelerate in a situation like this rather than apply the brakes. If she stopped, she might never gain enough momentum to get going again. She floorboarded the jalopy and skidded through the ditch, fishtailing forward, afraid to stop for fear of sinking to the axle. She was not going to give the driver who had tried to force her into the creek the chance to get close to her again!

In the rearview mirror, Amanda saw the incongruous shadow of the other vehicle backing up the hill and out of sight. She concentrated on the task ahead of her. When she located a spot where the grade of the ditch wasn't quite so steep, she made a run for the road. No matter what, she was not going to climb out of this truck and risk being run down.

Damn! Another close call like this and her hair would turn prematurely gray. She really should reveal her near brushes with calamity to Thorn. Of course, he would dream up plausible explanations, ones which he swore were unrelated to a murder he was certain didn't happen. Amanda made a mental note to jot down all the frightening occurrences she survived and leave them for

Thorn in her safety deposit box at the bank—just in case . . .

A safety deposit box! She should have thought of that earlier. Maybe Elmer had stashed his will, or at least another copy, along with his grain research data, at the bank as a precautionary measure. She would check on that the first chance she had.

Although the headlights were covered with mud, impairing visibility, Amanda's jalopy plowed up the incline of the ditch, gurgling and spluttering. Amanda cursed in a manner that would have singed Mother's ears. Her head smacked against the side window when the jalopy bounced over the clumps of mud and weeds that lined the road. With hammer down, Amanda cleared the obstacle and swerved into the middle of the road. Safe at last. Praise the Lord, safe at last!

Hyperventilating, Amanda drove home. She was still shaking when Thorn knocked on the door five minutes later. Amanda flung open the door and sailed into Thorn's arms to kiss the stuffing out of him. God, wasn't it great to be alive? There was nothing like a close encounter with catastrophe to put one's senses on full alert and get the old ticker pumping full steam ahead.

Nick reared back his head and looked down at those sultry pink lips and tangle of wet blond hair. He had never received such an enthusiastic greeting from Hazard. It piqued his curiosity.

"You should attend more family reunions. At least I assume that's what caused this overflow of emotion."

"Did you come here to fool around or play twenty questions, Thorn?"

Nick frowned at Hazard's mood. She was behaving

more strangely than usual. She was also shaking like a tuning fork. "What's going on, Hazard?"

"Nothing's going on, thanks to you," she said as she wrapped her arms around his neck and savored the warmth and contentment that holding him provided.

Nick eyed her for a long pensive moment before he said, "You're *too* anxious to jump my bones, Hazard. And I'll have you know that I don't rent out my body for fast flings. I have more respect for myself than that. There is more to me than just muscle and hormones, you know. I may be easy but I am not cheap."

Amanda laughed at his attempt at wounded dignity. The release valve on her emotions popped off and she couldn't stop giggling.

For years now, when the pressure built inside her and the stress—which she was always reluctant to admit she was experiencing—built up, she was seized by hysterical laughter. When she was in one of these moods, it took very little to set her off. She was in one of these moods . . .

"I'm,"—guffaw, snort—"sorry, Thorn." Amanda valiantly tried to sober up, but when she looked up at Thorn's bewildered frown, she burst out laughing again—only worse. Tears blurred her eyes and her ribs ached.

"Damn it to hell, Hazard. What has turned you into a giggle box?"

The jangling phone did nothing to jolt Amanda back to her senses. She was still struggling for control and failing miserably.

"Get a grip, Hazard," Nick muttered as he propped her against the wall and strode toward the phone. "Hazard's house."

"A . . . a . . . who is this?" came an unfortunately familiar voice.

"It's Officer Thorn of the Vamoose PD. Hello, Mother." He cast Amanda a stern glance that ordered her to get herself together—pronto. "Sorry I missed the reunion. I had to work late. Just got off duty, in fact. Amanda tells me I missed a super supper and interesting conversation." Hazard had told Nick nothing of the kind. He was ad-libbing while Hazard got herself under control.

Mother cleared her throat and presented Nick with a long-winded commentary of the reunion, listing names and explaining family connections. Nick wondered if he was supposed to be taking notes.

"I've been trying to call Amanda for an hour and no one answered. I thought she would have been home long before now. With all this rain, I wanted to make sure she arrived safe and sound. Is Amanda all right?"

Safe? Yes. Sound? Hazard was a basketcase. "She's fine," Nick lied.

Just where had Hazard been the past hour? Something told Nick that there was more going on than Hazard wanted him to know. He remembered seeing her muddy truck in the driveway and he was pretty certain something had upset her—hence her odd behavior.

"Well, I won't bother you, but you really must come visit us soon. We are all anxious to meet you." It sounded like an order rather than a request.

Nick smiled wryly. "Thank you for the invitation."

That sobered Amanda up damned quick. "God, whatever it is, don't accept, Thorn. You'll regret it."

"Sorry, Mother, I've got to go. It's been a long, trying

day. I just wanted to ensure Amanda returned home safely."

Nick hung up the phone and stared into those misty blue eyes that were fringed with wet lashes. "I want to know what happened, Hazard."

Her chin went airborne. "Nothing happened."

So she was going to be stubborn, was she? That was nothing new. "Fine then. I think I'll leave."

"Leave? Why? I thought you wanted—"

"I did. I do, but not tonight. You're acting weird and you won't explain why."

Nick ambled past the stunned Hazard. Maybe he needed to turn *her* down more often. It was good therapy for her overinflated feminine ego. And if she didn't think enough of him to confide in him, then she wasn't getting any satisfaction, even if it meant denying his own raging hormones.

"Be at my place at ten o'clock in the morning. We have sheep to shear, cattle to separate, and calves to inoculate. 'Night, Hazard."

Amanda watched in frustrated disbelief as Thorn strode out her door. The man was turning down sex? Was he sick? He had been grumbling about the infrequency of their intimacy for months. And here she was, ready to deliver and relieve her bottled anxiety, and wham! The man walked out on her. She had obviously repelled him with that outburst of unladylike snorts, hiccups, and guffaws. But if Thorn really cared about her, he would have overlooked her hysterics.

Get over it, Hazard. Thorn is gone and that's that. What you need is plenty of rest. You have been running on adrenaline and raw nerves for days. You nearly nose-dived into Deep Creek. Go to bed and thank the powers that be that you're still alive and kicking.

Amanda took that good advice and shut off the lights. She was sound asleep in seconds.

Nick had purposely requested that Amanda arrive at his ranch at ten o'clock, giving himself time to drive out to Elmer Jolly's farm. He had also taken time the previous night to inspect her muddy pickup. Nick would have recognized that red mud anywhere. The area where the Jollys resided was notorious for sticky, clay soil. In fact, the land was better suited for making bricks rather than cultivating crops. If not for soil testing and plenty of fertilizer, that part of the country would only raise sunflowers.

The missing hour for which Hazard refused to account, the caked mud on her jalopy, and her frazzled emotions caused Nick grave concern. True, he had declared he was not going to get involved in Hazard's investigation of an imaginary murder, but something was going on and Hazard wouldn't confide in him. It was time Nick had a look around.

Bringing the four-wheel drive truck to a halt, Nick surveyed the tire tracks that led into a ditch east of Elmer's farm. Nick was willing to stake his reputation on the fact that Hazard had gone off the road. Climbing down from his truck, Nick examined the area, finding another set of tracks that suggested a second vehicle had stopped and backed up the hill. Frowning at the implications, Nick piled into his truck and drove to Elmer's farm. To his bafflement, he saw Elmer's pickup perched on the hill, caked with the same red mud that covered

Hazard's jalopy. There were also scrapes on the front bumper of Elmer's old truck.

If Nick were making an educated guess, he would suspect someone had tried to force Hazard off the road. Elmer's truck had definitely been driven sometime during the past twenty-four hours. Nick clearly recalled that the truck did not have a speck of mud on it when Hazard had dragged him out here after the storm to see the body that was no longer laying on the floor of the cellar.

Nick opened Elmer's pickup door, noting that the key always left in the ignition was in its usual place, granting easy access to the vehicle. But then, who would have ever tried to steal Elmer's truck when the old man met unwanted visitors with a loaded shotgun? Besides, what was the point? The battery was as old as Methuselah. If the truck ever stopped, it would require jumper cables to get it going again. But as a precautionary measure, Nick retrieved the keys.

Mulling over the possibility of Hazard being run off the road by a dead man's truck, Nick ambled to the farmhouse. A thorough search turned up nothing unusual. A tour through the barn, however, had him frowning. Hay bales had been knocked down from the loft. Nick also noticed dried mud on the ladder that led to the loft. Grimly, he climbed up the ladder toward the five-feet-wide opening which held loads of hay. When he glanced down, he saw the broken bale on the ground below.

Damn! Was this the scene of another incident which Hazard failed to mention to him? What in the sweet loving hell was going on around here? Was Hazard actually correct in suspecting foul play in Elmer's death? She had been right a few months earlier when another local farmer was found floating in his cattle's water tank. Hell's bells, it was going to kill him to have to admit Hazard might be right—again. She would gloat herself sick.

After a thorough search of the grounds, Nick noticed several sets of galoshes tracks that circled the house and outbuildings. He had the uneasy feeling someone was looking around Elmer's homestead. And it would also appear that Hazard had become a target. The unnerving thought caused fiercely protective feelings to hurtle through Nick's bloodstream. It was one thing for Nick to threaten to shake Hazard until her teeth rattled, but it was quite another for somebody else to lay a hand on that woman. If her life was in jeopardy, she should have told him, damn her!

Nick whirled on his heels and headed home. He was going to get to the bottom of this mystery, even if he had to pry the truth out of Hazard with a crowbar!

After Amanda had presented Randel Thompson and Bobby Sherman with a list of needed repairs, she drove into town, hoping to glean information at Last Chance Cafe. Amanda veered into the service station to fuel up her gas-guzzling truck. The owner, Thaddeus Thatcher, waddled out to greet her.

"Did you get stuck, girl?" Thaddeus surveyed the muddy vehicle as he stuffed the gas nozzle into the empty tank. "I got stuck clean up to my bumpers in my fuel truck while I was making a delivery to Abner Hendershot's farm yesterday. Those dadblamed country roads are hell ... er ... heck on vehicles. If you get that dried mud stuck in your starter, you can burn the damned ... er ... darned thing plumb out. And mud gets so packed up inside the tire wells that your vehicle will vibrate like crazy. You ought to get your truck washed real soon."

"I'll do that, Thaddeus." Amanda gestured toward the windshield. "Could you clean that off for me."

"Sure, sure." Thaddeus lumbered over to grab a squeegee and sponge that dripped with industrial-strength cleaner. "I hear you're the administrator of Elmer's estate. Everybody's anxious to know what the old buzzard did with his money."

"I'm sure they are, but that information is still confidential." Amanda watched in dismay as Thaddeus smeared mud in her line of vision. But after about five minutes, Thaddeus managed to restore the windshield to a reasonable state of cleanliness.

"Yep, it was a crying shame that Elmer never spent his money on himself. He just hoarded it all his life. He could have helped out his nieces and nephews when they got into scrapes. But not Elmer. He wasn't very generous."

"Did you know Elmer well?

"As well as anybody did." Thaddeus pulled the hose from the gas tank and wiped his hands. "Elmer used to come by the station every two weeks to fill up and borrow my newspaper to catch up on local news. He was too cheap to buy his own subscription. And he wasn't too friendly, either. He barely spoke to his own family, much less the rest of us Vamoosians. After he had that row with Melvin and Claud five year's back, he really cut himself off from his family and society."

Amanda handed Thaddeus the cash for her fuel. "What was the disagreement about?"

"The three brothers used to farm together. They would pull all their tractors and machinery into the same field to disc or plow. But Melvin had been hitting the sauce pretty heavy and he dozed off. His tractor veered toward Elmer's and ran into the plow Elmer was pulling. The plow broke in two and had to be welded back together. Melvin's tractor tires were slashed to ribbons. I ordered him new tires and he raved because they cost a fortune."

Thaddeus propped himself against the side of the truck and leaned toward the window to convey the next bit of information. "I heard Elmer took a hammer to Melvin and Claud had to come between them. Those three old coots nearly beat each other to pieces. I guess the old gripes started pouring out after that. The Jolly brothers decided to do their own field work. No more brother helping brother. That was when Elmer decided to rent out his ground. He was getting too old to keep up the grinding pace of wheat planting, harvest, and haying."

"What old gripes?" Amanda quizzed curiously.

Thaddeus took off his baseball cap and raked a grimy hand through his gray-blond hair. "Now that's the funny thing about the Jollys and Mopopes. They kept their lips zipped. The only reason I know about the royal battle was because Frank Hermann saw it happen and told me about it."

Damn, another deadend. Amanda slumped behind the wheel. Several people held grudges against Elmer, but Amanda would never be able to find out who had done away with him.

Amanda drove off before Thaddeus became engrossed in some tidbit of trivia he had read. The man was a walking encyclopedia of little-known facts. Amanda had gotten off lucky this morning by firing questions about Elmer Jolly. During previous visits to Thatcher's Gas and Oil, Amanda had listened to long spiels about the manufacturing of rubber for tires, the process of cleaning petroleum, to name only two.

Amanda parked outside the Last Chance Cafe, anxious to treat herself to a few cups of coffee before driving to Thorn's farm. After she had doctored her coffee with enough cream and sugar to make it taste like hot chocolate, Clive Barnstall, Harry Ogelbee, and Abner Hendershot eased down into the booth beside her.

Harry smiled and the sun reflected the silver caps on his front teeth. "I don't suppose you're going to tell us who inherited Elmer's farm ground. Me and Ab and Clive are interested to know who is going to be our new landlord."

Amanda sipped her steaming brew. "Sorry, fellas, but no information until after probate." And besides that, she didn't have a clue who had inherited. She couldn't get her hands on that damned will!

Knowing how cantankerous Elmer could be, he probably left his fortune to that pack of critters." Clive chuckled. "Gawd, I'll probably be renting wheat ground from that three-legged dog."

"It would serve you right," Harry piped up. "You were the one who ran over Pete while he was following you around the field."

"You ran over Pete?" Amanda questioned in disbelief.

"Well, not on purpose, of course." Clive levered his bulky body back on the seat and stretched his tree-stump legs out in front of him. "Pete liked to follow tractors and hunt rabbits. One evening, a jackrabbit darted out of the weeds in the fence row. Pete gave chase and ran smack dab into my disc. Chopped his leg smooth off. I carried Pete to the house and Elmer had a conniption fit. He also raised my rent that year."

Amanda waited until Faye Bernard had filled the coffee cups before trying a new tactic to gain information. "Would any of you be disappointed to have one or both of Elmer's brothers as your new landlords?"

"Are they getting the property?" Abner inquired.

Amanda shrugged and smiled evasively.

"I could deal with Melvin or Claud if I had to," Clive declared. "Better them than their offspring. The younger ones would raise the rent in one minute flat. Melvin and Claud aren't too free with their money, but those kids of theirs always felt they were deprived. If you've ever seen Claud's and Melvin's homes, you'd know what I mean. The Jolly men spent a fortune on tractors, implements, cattle, hogs, and sheep, but their houses were practically bare. Those kids grew up without a single luxury. Now they like to spend money and Melvin and Claud have trouble keeping the clamp on them."

"What about Elmer's youngest brother Leroy?" Amanda asked.

"Leroy never did take to farming," Harry explained. "He worked for the family farm because he had no choice. But when he was old enough, he joined the army and served in the war."

Abner took up where Harry left off. "After Leroy married Bertie Ann Mopope and moved to Oklahoma

City years ago, they didn't come around Vamoose much. Leroy was completely out of the farming picture. I guess he must have sold his land to his brothers. I can't say for sure, though. Nobody knows much about their business and it was a long time ago."

Curse it, this subtle investigation was proceeding at a snail's pace. Amanda could be retirement age before she solved this perplexing case!

Amanda glanced up to see all three older men ogling the woman who was sauntering down the aisle with two platters of eggs and bacon in her hands. The new waitress looked to be in her mid-thirties, perhaps one or two years older than Amanda. After setting the plates on the table, the brunette struck a Cleopatra pose and graced her customers with a blinding smile. That was one way to ensure a big tip, Amanda decided.

"I didn't know Jenny Long was back in town," Harry commented, still all eyes.

"She just got back this week." Clive was still assessing the curvaceous waitress, too.

Clive must not have eaten breakfast yet, Amanda surmised. He was licking his chops. However, Amanda doubted the middle-aged man was salivating over the toast, bacon, and eggs. Typical man. The males of this world would have to be in their graves before they stopped ogling a well-sculptured feminine body.

"Faye has decided to work part time so she can take night classes in college," Abner reported. "Jenny is in training until the summer school session begins."

"I hear Jenny divorced that no-account deadbeat she married. She's living with her parents and they're baby-sitting her little boy."

"You think Nick Thorn knows Jenny is back in town?" Harry questioned.

Amanda felt as if someone had stuck a fist in her stomach.

"That's right!" Clive piped up. "They had a thing going while they were in high school, didn't they?"

"Pretty hot and heavy for awhile, as I recollect. Those two were inseparable," Harry put in.

Amanda wished he hadn't. She did not want to hear this.

"We all thought they would tie the knot, but Jenny started running around with that hippie from the city when Nick went into basic training with the marines."

Amanda decided it was time to make her exit. She had seen enough of Thorn's old flame, thank you very much. The woman was receiving plenty of attention. Amanda recognized obvious flaunting when she saw it. Jenny had "available" stamped all over her—what with that scoop-necked, skin-tight cotton tank top that displayed the hills and valleys of her bosom to their best advantage, and jeans that looked as if they had been painted on. Jenny was definitely eye-catching in her clinging clothes, her dark shiny hair, and vivid green eyes. Contacts, Amanda decided. Nobody had eyes *that* green.

So Thorn's old flame was back, Amanda mused as the plunked into her pickup. Was that why Thorn had made a hasty departure the previous night? Had he and Jenny tripped the light fantastic for old time's sake? And *he* accused *her* of fooling around with Romeo the rodeo clown! He had his nerve!

Amanda was not in the best frame of mind when she reached Thorn's farm. She was ready to take a pair of sheep shears to that two-timing rascal. And Thorn had better not turn Amanda loose with a branding iron if he knew what was good for him. And if he was foolish enough to put the surgical instrument that changed bull calves into steers in her hands, he was really asking for trouble!

Chapter Seven

Nick glanced up when he heard the jalopy splattering through the mud. The minute Hazard climbed down from her truck, up went her chin. Nick had learned to recognize that mannerism for what it was—stubbornness and simmering temper. Hazard had a bee in her bonnet and it was buzzing.

"Good morning, Hazard," he greeted.

"Is it? What brought you to that conclusion?" she smarted off.

Nick ignored the snide question and handed her a whip, gesturing for her to follow him to the corral where he had penned the Salers cows, calves, and bull. He fully intended to keep Hazard occupied all day. She wouldn't have time to go snooping around and getting herself into more trouble. Nick had not quite decided how to broach the subject of her investigation of Elmer's death. Considering the mood she was presently in, he decided to let her work off her frustration first.

"We have to cut out the bull before we separate the calves," he announced. "You work the gate and I'll single out the bull. Just be careful not to let the calves out when the bull heads for the pasture. I don't want to waste time rounding up the calves again."

Amanda said nothing. She was still trying to cope with the thought of Thorn screwing around with his high school sweetheart while Amanda had been suffering through the dreaded family reunion and avoiding a drowning in Deep Creek.

"Hey! Wake up over there!"

Amanda jerked up her head, jarred from her wandering thoughts by the fifteen-hundred-pound Salers bull that romped toward her. She was supposed to be manning the gate between the corral and pasture, waiting to swing the gate shut after the bull trotted out. Instead, she was dawdling in thought, ill-prepared for the snorting creature that charged at her with fire in his eyes and steam rolling from his ears. Amanda didn't have time to swing open the gate, only time to scale the fence before she was churned into butter. The bull lowered his head and crashed into the gate. If Amanda had not clamped her body on the metal tubing she would have catapulted to the ground in front of the irate creature.

"Damn it, Hazard, watch what you're doing!" Nick railed at her.

With the snap of his whip, he sent the bull circling the corral again, hoping to bring the gargantuan animal along the fence so Amanda could let him out in the pasture. Unfortunately, the bull preferred to remain with his harem of cows and refused to be separated from them again.

"One of the cows is in heat." Nick circled the corral, giving the contrary bull all the space he wanted—and then some. "I'm going to bring the cow and the bull around together. Let both of them out."

Amanda swallowed down her heart which had lodged in her throat and hopped to the ground. Working cattle was going to require her undivided attention. One more mental lapse and she would be a doormat—one that the irascible bull walked over—literally.

"Swing open the gate just wide enough to give the bull a clear view of the pasture," Nick ordered before he snapped the whip over the reluctant livestock.

Amanda obeyed. This definitely wasn't her field of expertise. She knew nothing about cattle and had to depend on Thorn for guidance, unappealing as that was to her.

When the bull and his favorite mate-of-the-moment trotted toward her, Amanda backed off. The cow balked; the bull pawed the mud. Nick popped the whip and cursed the air purple. If Nick had not been so fleet of foot and daring, the cow would have cut sideways and fled back to the rest of the herd that was huddled in the opposite corner. Nick cracked the whip on the cow's nose, forcing her to switch direction. The bull charged. Amanda yelled and Nick expelled several more oaths. Mud splattered in Amanda's face as the cow slid sideways and collided with the edge of the gate before scampering into the pasture.

Amanda froze to the spot when the bull suddenly stopped and focused those smoldering black eyes on her. It looked as if the bull was trying to decide if this was to be the day Amanda died. With the careless ease of one who knows he is king of the corral, the bull stared at her and then at the cow that had scrambled out the gate to the pasture. Having made his decision to let Amanda live a little longer, the bull moseyed through the gate, switching his tail and sniffing the air. Amanda swore the bull tossed her a consider-yourself-lucky stare before he joined his mate.

"Why do you keep that damned animal around?" Amanda muttered. "Wouldn't it be safer to artificially inseminate your herd?"

"Safer, yes," Nick agreed. "But far more time consuming and not as effective. I have enough trouble juggling my chores with shifts on patrol. And why should I deprive my bull of his fun?"

Amanda wished Thorn had kept his trap shut. That remark stoked the fires of her temper. "Why indeed? That's all the male of any species lives for."

Nick refused to be baited. This definitely was not the time for the argument Hazard seemed to be spoiling for. "Lock the pasture gate and open the one that leads to the west pen. I'm going to cut out a few calves at a time and bring them along the fence. When you have them shut in the lot, run them down to the south end so they don't try to double back while you aren't looking."

Amanda slogged over to the assigned gate and held it open while Nick cut out four calves and sent them trotting in her direction. The calves scattered like quail and returned to their bawling mothers, forcing Nick to repeat the process amid a raft of muttered curses.

"It must be my red shirt that scares them off," Amanda speculated.

"Cows only see black and white," Nick informed her. "That business about waving a red cape is a myth. Cattle naturally become skittish in confined places. Besides that, they're just plain stupid creatures."

"You can say that again," Amanda seconded. "They stare at an open gate as if it were a door to hell. Then they turn tail and run."

Amanda was pretty sure that her brilliant observation was wasted on Thorn. The cattle were bawling to beat the band and even shouting couldn't drown them out.

After thirty minutes of scrambling to open and shut the gate when Nick commanded, thirty calves were penned in the west lot, much to their mother's dismay. Nick swung the pasture gate open wide and gestured for Amanda to help him run the herd of cows out with the bull.

"Come help me gather the medicine and supplies we'll need to innoculate the calves," he requested, heading for the barn.

Amanda found herself laden down with bottles of Vitamin K, ear tags, and penicillin. She and Nick traipsed back to the pen and set their supplies on the makeshift table that consisted of wooden planks.

"I'll run the calves down the lane to the squeeze chute." He indicated the large metal implement that was secured to the end of a narrow aisle. Then he pointed toward the far end of the squeeze chute. "Open the head gate. When the calf sees the opening and tries to dart through, use that lever on top to lock the calf's head in place."

Amanda was new at this business. There weren't all that many head gates and squeeze chutes in the city neighborhood where she grew up under the ever-watchful eyes of Mother. But Amanda was willing to learn. Poised and ready, she waited for the calf to scrabble through the chute and thrust its head through the narrow opening. The instant the calf made a leap for freedom, Amanda yanked down on the lever. The calf's head was trapped. The frightened creature went berserk for a minute before it realized it couldn't escape.

"Nice catch, Hazard," Nick complimented as he dropped the metal gate in place behind the squirming calf. He shoved the lever on the side of the squeeze chute upward, sandwiching the calf so it couldn't move while Nick injected the medication.

"What is all this stuff, Thorn?" Amanda questioned curiously.

"The Vitamin K controls bleeding for surgery. The inoculations are combinations of medicine which prevent infection, such as Black Leg, Foot Rot, and Lump Jaw, and act as vaccinations against common diseases," Nick patiently explained. "The ear tags release chemicals into the bloodstream to protect against flies and ticks."

"Ear-tag earrings. What a novel idea." Amanda smiled for the first time all day. "I can wear a pair to the Hazard family reunion on the Fourth of July. Do the tags repel unwanted relatives as well as flies?"

"Don't try to be a comedienne," Nick said as he held up the bottle and filled the syringe. "We have work to do. You're in charge of the ear tags. I'll give the innoculations."

Clamping the yellow tags in place was no easy task, Amanda soon found out. The calf objected to being touched, as well as having his ear pierced. He bawled his head off and his eyes rounded until Amanda swore they would pop out.

When Nick dropped the side gate of the squeeze chute to brand the calf, the smell of burned hide filled the air and smoke rolled.

Amanda stared at the circle T brand with distaste. "That seems rather barbaric, Thorn."

"Until modern technology invents a better way to identify livestock, branding will have to suffice," he said matter-of-factly. "Now hand me the pliers and the scalpel."

Amanda obliged. With fascination, she watched Thorn reach between the bars to make an incision. He worked quickly and effectively, performing surgery on the bull calf. The calf, of course, didn't seem to care how effective Thorn was; it bawled at the top of its lungs.

"Hand me the wound protector. No, not that. Give me the spray bottle of purple medication. And then go open the head gate to release the calf."

Amanda strode around to unfasten the gate. The calf leaped free but it walked very gingerly toward the fence to lie down. The bull-calf-turned-steer was not having a good day, either, Amanda decided.

"Feeling better, Hazard? I was sure that watching the males of the world be castrated would lift your sagging spirits."

"Only if you're next in line, Thorn. Do I get to perform the surgery?"

Nick pivoted on his haunches to meet Hazard's disgruntled glare. "What the hell did I do, besides commit the unpardonable sin of being born a man?"

"As if you don't know," she said through curled lips.

"You're peeved because *I* turned *you* down last night, aren't you? Did it put a dent in your ego?"

"It's *why* you turned me down that peeves me, Thorn."

"You don't like to be used and neither do I, Hazard." Nick flung a leg over the fence and hopped down to chase another calf into the squeeze chute. "Do you want to tell me why you were in such an emotional frenzy last night that you threw yourself at me to forget what had upset you?"

The man's perception was a little too good for her taste. "You don't want to know, Thorn."

"As it turns out, I do want to know why you were an hour late returning from the reunion and why your pickup was covered with red mud and gravel." Through the fence that separated them, he pinned her with a probing gaze. "Level with me, Hazard. What happened?"

"Nothing." Amanda presented her back to shield herself from that penetrating stare. Up went the chin. "I just hit a slick spot on a wet road and spent a little time in the ditch, that's all."

"Hazard . . ." The tone of his voice indicted he wasn't buying her explanation.

The chin went up another notch. "That's my story and I'm sticking with it."

Nick ran another calf down the lane and Amanda locked the animal's head in place. Nick flung her another pointed glance. "I want to know what is going on in your voluntary investigation of Elmer's death. Somebody tried to run you off the road by Elmer's farm last night. I examined the tracks this morning."

"I thought you said you weren't involving yourself in another of my imaginary murder cases and ridiculous investigations," she shot back.

"I changed my mind." Nick hopped over the fence and squeezed the calf in the chute. "I also want to know what happened in Elmer's barn. I saw the strewn hay bales. Did that incident involve you, too, Hazard?"

Thorn was willing to admit that Elmer might have been murdered and someone did not appreciate her nosing around? Bless the man . . . and curse him for lollygagging with his former sweetheart! Amanda sighed. These conflicting emotions were frustrating her to death.

"We'll be working cattle for another hour. And while we're working, you can tell me everything," Nick ordered as he tended his next four-legged patient.

Amanda was relieved that Thorn was finally willing to listen, really listen. She definitely needed to release the pent-up anxiety of two near disasters. Inhaling a deep breath, Amanda organized her thoughts and proceeded in chronological order. Nick interrupted with several curses while she related the unnerving incidents in Elmer's home, in the barn, and in the bumper-car collision. He paused to stare incredulously at her when she mentioned that someone had searched her house and office.

"Damn it, Hazard, you should've reported that to me immediately!" he insisted, brandishing the scalpel in her face.

"I reported every incident immediately after it occurred when I was investigating my *first* case. You thought I was inventing the whole story to gain your assistance. I had no intention of letting you refer to me as a lunatic again, Thorn."

Nick was silent for a moment while he focused his attention on the surgery he was performing. "And what do you intend to do if you can't locate Elmer's missing will? Obviously, whoever has been dogging your steps thinks you have the will in your possession. What the hell are you trying to do? Set yourself up as a target, hoping your unidentified suspect will try to trap you so you can try to trap him first?"

"What a brilliant idea, Thorn. I should have thought of it myself!"

"Absolutely not, Hazard!" Nick blared. "I was only being sarcastic. I was *not*, repeat *not*, serious. I think it's time I conducted an informal investigation while you tend to your own accounting business."

"Elmer Jolly *is* my business." Amanda's chin tilted a notch higher. "I am the administrator of his estate. And beside that, I don't know why you should care if I get my butt in a few tight cracks while dealing with this case."

Nick did a double take. The calf in the squeeze chute bawled for its mother. "What the hell kind of thing is that to say? You know I care about you. I wouldn't have been snorting and growling about Romeo the rodeo clown sniffing at your heels and escorting you to dinner in town if I didn't care."

"Then what is this fling with your former sweetheart all about?" It was a wonder she had withheld the question as long as she had. Curiosity was about to kill her.

When Amanda slapped the scalpel in his hand and wheeled to grab the bottle of wound protector, Nick smiled wryly, studying her rounded derriere and the rigid set of her back. "You must be referring to Jenny Long."

"Yeah, that's the one—Ms. Bosom in painted-in clothes. And don't think for one minute that I don't know exactly why you turned me down last night, Thorn." Amanda shoved the bottle of wound protector at him and flashed him a scatching glare. "I went through this during my divorce. I will not do it again!"

"Are you questioning my faithfulness in an affair that you absolutely refuse to make public?" Nick twisted on his haunches to tend the calf in the squeeze chute. "You seem more concerned about your sterling reputation being tarnished than my personal feelings in the matter. You won't make any commitment and yet you expect me to bow and scrape over you. Rather a one-sided loyalty, don't you think? Now that Randel Thompson is panting and drooling over you, Vamoosians think the two of you are an item. Now just where does that leave me?"

Amanda stared at the seat of his pants, wishing she could kick him to Vamoose and back. "So, is that what this fling with Ms. Bosom is all about? A way of getting even with me?"

"Jenny is somebody I used to know."

Amanda really was going to kick him if he didn't answer her question. Thorn was purposely annoying her, refusing to deny or to admit to her accusations. "Did you or did you not fool around with Ms. Bosom last ni—?"

The calf bellowed at the top of its lungs and leaped straight in the air. Nick cursed foully and flung himself out of the way after a flying hoof connected with his arm. The calf panicked in tight confinement, trying to jerk its head loose and kick at everything within range. Nick scrambled to his feet, shaking his forearm, waiting for the calf to realize there was no way out.

"Are you all right, Thorn?"

"No, my arm hurts like hell. You'll have to castrate the next calf. I'm sure you'll derive spiteful pleasure from that."

"I've never performed surgery in my life, well, except for doing a hysterectomy on a laboratory rat in my college physiology class," Amanda amended.

"I'll teach you the procedure step by step. You'll do fine. We only have one bull calf left."

When the last calf was secured in the head gate and the squeeze chute was pressed firmly against its ribs, Amanda squatted down with pliers in one hand and a scalpel in the other. Nick crouched behind her and Amanda followed his instructions to the letter. She was not as swift and efficient as Nick, but she completed the surgical procedure without the calf keeling over in a dead heap.

"Nice work, Hazard." Nick opened the head gate to release the calf. "We'll let the calves recover from surgery for the rest of the day. Then I'll load them up and haul them to the pasture three miles east."

"Why don't you just lock them in the pasture across the road?" Amanda inquired.

"Because these calves are ready to ween. If there are no more than two fences between the cows and calves, they'll tear down the wires to be reunited. I have enough repairs to make after the storm without replacing a half mile of fence posts and barb wire." Nick picked up the left-over ear tags and strode off. "Let's take a lunch break before we shear the sheep. My arm could use the rest."

"Thorn?" Amanda replaced the supplies on the shelves in the barn and turned to find Thorn standing directly behind her.

"Yeah, Hazard, what is it?" He reached around her to set the medication in its customary place, purposely brushing against her shoulder.

His close proximity had the same effect on Amanda that it always did. All laws of physics and chemistry were suspended and time screeched to a halt.

"*I* don't like being second best, *either,* Thorn," she managed to get out.

"Nobody said you were, Hazard."

His voice rustled, assuring Amanda that she had some degree of effect on him, too—biologically speaking at least.

"Nobody said *you* were second best, *either,* Thorn."

"Then why haven't the citizens of Vamoose seen you walk through the door of Last Chance Cafe on my arm instead of Romeo Thompson's?"

"I've got a sudden craving for a greasy burger and fries," Amanda assured him.

He propped his hands on either side of her, trapping her between his brawny body and the wall. "Hamburger isn't the only thing I'm craving."

"Right now? I smell like a cow." She looked up at lips that were only a hairbreadth away. Thorn, she had long ago decided, had the most sensual lips ever carved on a male face.

"I have a shower with hot and cold running water. And you know how I love spontaneity." He waggled his eyebrows suggestively.

"I thought you wanted to make an appearance at Last Chance Cafe. Something about needing a little respect and consideration that has to do with masculine pride, and all that."

"Yeah, I need that, too."

He was so tantalizing close. Her nostrils flared with the scent of his cologne, even if the aroma mingled with the smell of cow hide. Thorn was still a picnic to her senses—all five of them. Her lips involuntarily parted in an invitation which he quickly accepted. His slow, penetrating kiss soothed those feelings of inadequacy and betrayal that had assaulted her since the moment she learned Thorn's old flame was back in Vamoose.

When Nick finally came up for air, Amanda fanned herself and inhaled several deep breaths. The man definitely knew how to kiss. And he had better not have been practicing on Ms. Bosom—again.

The thought put a question on her tongue and it leaped off before she could think to bite it back. "Aren't you afraid Ms. Bosom will be envious when we show up at Last Chance together? Eternal triangles can be really messy."

Nick didn't respond to the comment; he grabbed Amanda's arm and propelled her out of the barn. "Let's go eat, Hazard. Nibbling on you whetted my appetite."

"You aren't going to tell me, are you, Thorn?"

"About Ms. Bosom—I mean, Jenny Long? Nope. I know how you like to dabble in detective work. I'll let you figure it out for yourself."

When he graced her with a mischievous grin, Amanda felt her fist knotting involuntarily. If Mother did not have such a high regard for pearly white teeth, Amanda would have considered knocking a few of Thorn's out.

Last Chance was packed. Amanda felt as if she had just walked on stage before a captive audience. Every pair of eyes in the restaurant zeroed in on her and Thorn. Amanda saw Jenny Long's face fall and her hand stall in midair over an empty coffee cup. Jenny's all-too-green eyes bounced back and forth between Nick and Amanda. Jenny whirled around to occupy herself with her task while Nick and Amanda ambled down the aisle.

Randel Thompson and Bobby Sherman were lounging in a nearby booth, and Amanda noted that Randel didn't look all too pleased to see her with Thorn. The rest of the patrons began talking among themselves. *Gossiping,* Amanda corrected as Thorn escorted her to the two vacant seats at the counter.

From out of nowhere Ms. Bosom appeared, all cheery smiles and seductive poses. She leaned over the counter, granting Thorn a tantalizing view of cleavage. Being a man, of course, he stared pointedly at the proffered display. Amanda gnashed her teeth.

"Hi, Nicky? What can I get for you?"

Amanda swore she felt a draft when Ms. Bosom batted her lashes.

"I'll have the chicken basket with tater tots."

"Breasts or thighs?" Ms. Bosom's coo was followed by another flapping of eyelashes and sugary smiles.

Amanda reached for the Rolaids in her purse, anticipating a bad case of indigestion, if this nauseating scene was anything to go by.

"I'll take a combination of both, Jenny," Nick replied, doing a damned miserable job of hiding his grin—in Amanda's opinion.

"And what can I get for you, Miss Hazard?" Jenny inquired without taking her hungry eyes off Thorn.

A big stick, thought Amanda. "I'll have the High Cholesterol Special and coffee with plenty of cream."

That got Ms. Bosom's attention. "Come again?"

"I want the bacon cheeseburger and fries," Amanda translated.

Ms. Bosom absently poured coffee into the cup she

retrieved from beneath the counter. Her aim was bad, what with her vivid green eyes soaking up every contour of Thorn's body like a sponge. Amanda grabbed a napkin from the dispenser and blotted the spill. Ms. Bosom was too absorbed in her visual fantasy to notice the mess she had made.

"What are you drinking, Nicky?"

Nicky? Thorn did not look like a Nicky, thought Amanda. He was six-feet-two-inches and two-hundred pounds of solid muscle. Not the cuddly Teddy bear type. And if Ms. Bosom didn't stop drooling all over Thorn, Amanda was going to get the poor woman a bib. Watching Ms. Bosom in action made Amanda's stomach roll over like a trick poodle. She popped her last Rolaid tablet in her mouth. Slobber and greasy French fries were not going to set well on her stomach.

"Ms. Bo— . . . um . . . Jenny, would you hand me another pack of Rolaids please?"

Amanda saw Thorn's shoulders shaking in silent laughter when Jenny wiggled her jean-clad fanny over to retrieve the tablets. Amanda wanted to pound him flat as a flounder.

After Jenny dropped the Rolaids in Amanda's hand, she reluctantly moved away to place the dinner order. Amanda was about to make her irritation known when Randel swaggered over to lean on the counter, purposely brushing his shoulder against Amanda's.

"I thought you'd want to know that me and Bobby are about finished with your repairs."

"Good." Amanda smiled more gratefully than necessary. "Thanks, Randel."

"Oh, by the way, your phone was ringing off its hook all morning. I saw an old truck drive by a couple of times, but I couldn't tell who was in it because me and Bobby were working on the hog shed. I got the idea somebody was looking for you."

Nick's dark head was bent over his coffee cup, but he was listening intently.

Amanda felt herself tense. "An old pickup? What color?"

"Green, I think. It was covered with mud."

Damn. Her stalker had been casing her home again. Amanda was definitely going to have to bait a trap to catch that rat. If she announced a date to reveal the contents of the last will and testament, perhaps it would force her antagonist to make a last-ditch effort to confront her. At least then she would know with whom she was dealing! This not knowing was making her crazy.

"Uh, 'Manda honey, how about taking in a movie and dinner with me tonight?" Randel asked, leaning a bit closer. "We could go to the city. There's a new western out that I've been wanting to see."

"Sorry, Randel, she already has plans for the evening," Nick said in Hazard's behalf.

When Ms. Bosom jiggled past, Amanda added—for Thorn's benefit—"Maybe some other time, Randel."

Randel winked and smiled. "Don't worry about paying the labor for the repairs. It was on the house, honey. I'll give Bobby a little something for his help."

When he pushed away from the counter and sauntered off, Nick shot Hazard a dour glance. "I wonder how Romeo plans to exact his wages for services rendered?"

"Probably the same way Ms. Bosom intends to be repaid for the preferential treatment you're receiving—"

The fire whistle resounded around the cafe and ten

men—Thorn included—bounded to their feet. The Vamoose volunteer fire department was off and running.

"Hazard, bring my pickup over to the fire station and follow us. I'll catch a ride with one of the other men.

Amanda threw down the money for the meal she didn't have time to eat and scrambled out the door. No great loss on the meal, Amanda assured herself. She didn't need highly saturated fat setting on her churning stomach. If she got hungry later she could always chew on her fingernails.

When Amanda stepped outside, she glanced in every direction at once, searching for rolling smoke that indicated a fire. She half expected to see a black cloud just outside of town—in the exact location of her rented farm house. Instead, there was a curl of smoke to the northwest. Damn it to hell! Although it was difficult to judge puffs of smoke at a distance, Amanda had the unshakable feeling she knew where the fire was. And she could guess why a fire might "accidentally" break out in that vicinity.

Amanda hopped into Nick's four-wheel drive black Ford with its hayfork protruding from the rear bumper and took off like a speeding bullet. The byways of Vamoose were suddenly a flurry of activity. Amanda very nearly rear-ended a compact car that pulled out in front of her while the absent-minded driver was craning her neck to locate the fire.

"Crazy women drivers—" Amanda blinked and shook her head in dismay. "Good Lord, what am I saying?"

Vamoose's shiny red fire engine—with lights flashing and siren blaring—pulled out of the station while bodies clambered into position. Amanda saw Deputy Benny

Sykes buzz past in his patrol car, following behind the fire truck. Amanda shifted gears and joined the cavalcade. All the while, she kept asking herself questions that only had speculations for answers. As Thorn constantly reminded her, it was best not to go jumping off cliffs to ill-founded conclusions. She would wait to see if the fire was where she suspected it was before she began analyzing how, why, and who had set it . . .

Chapter Eight

Amanda sat in the driveway of Elmer Jolly's farm, watching flames engulf the old house, thinking of all the antiques that were lost and grieving the fact that an old man's life had been obliterated. It was as devastating as the losses caused by tornadoes, hurricanes, earthquakes, and floods. In this case, it was worse because intuition told Amanda this fire had been deliberately set. Had Amanda's would-be assailant come to the conclusion that she had *not* really located the will as she wanted everyone to believe? Had the house been destroyed to erase all evidence? And if so, what evidence had she overlooked that could have led her to the criminal?

"Well, whoever was to inherit Elmer's house won't have much left," Preston Banks observed while he stood beside Amanda. "Our volunteer fire department does the best it can, but it looks as if all they can save is the foundation."

"The Lord sure works in mysterious ways, doesn't He?" Harry Ogelbee mused. "First Elmer gets killed trying to hide from a tornado and now his house burns down."

"I don't think the Lord had anything to do with either incident," Amanda declared.

The crowd of bystandards closed in around her.

"What are you suggesting?" Abner Hendershot demanded.

Amanda stared at the farmers who clustered around her.

"Do you think Elmer was murdered?" Clive Barnstall questioned.

If Amanda answered the question honestly, word would be all over Vamoose by sunset. Thorn would be fit to be roped and tied. He would hate it if she divulged information that could put her life in jeopardy and interfere with the investigation he had finally taken seriously. But the truth, Amanda reasoned, was not only a threat but also her protection. Her mysterious stalker might think twice if he tried to dispose of her after she announced her suspicions aloud. On the other hand, she might force the murderer to panic, provoking him to act without careful forethought. Recklessness could lead to his exposure. It was a risk Amanda felt obliged to take.

"I believe Elmer's death was anything but an accident."

Several in the crowd gasped.

"Any probable suspects?" Harry wanted to know. "I'm not on the list, am I? You don't think I bumped Elmer off because he raised my rent after I ran over his precious dog and he came after me with a two-by-four! Sure, I was mad as hell at Elmer, but I didn't push him down the steps of the cellar!"

Amanda's blue eyes narrowed on Harry. "Who said anybody pushed Elmer down the steps?"

Harry raised both arms, as if he were being held at

gunpoint. "Hey, that was only speculation. I just heard the rumor that Elmer was found in the storm shelter under a pile of shelves."

"Were you the one who notified the ambulance?"

"It wasn't me," Harry insisted, eyes wide as silver dollars. "Maybe it was Abner. He said he might pay Elmer a call that morning."

"Now hold on, Harry, don't go dragging me into this!" Abner's pudgy face turned the color of raw liver and he puffed up like a toad. "I was mad as hell, too, when Elmer ran over one of my cows that broke through that sorry fence around his pasture. I had to destroy the cow and I lost the calf she was carrying. And true, Elmer raised my rent after that, but I didn't try to kill him!"

"Why did you go by to see Elmer the morning of his death?" Amanda prodded.

Abner looked in every direction except at Amanda.

"You may as well tell her," Clive Barnstall insisted, thrusting his hands deep in the pockets of his OshKosh overalls, as if he were hiding something.

"You stay out of this, Clive." Ab's jowls puckered to match his lips. "You've got a few skeletons in your closet, too." He turned toward Amanda and continued talking. "He might point an accusing finger at me, but I can damned sure point back. I know Clive went to see Elmer that day, too, because I saw his truck in the driveway. And don't forget that Clive is married to one of Elmer's relatives. His wife Patricia is one of Claud's kids, you know. Clive was always asking special favors because he claimed to be family. He was more than a little irritated when Elmer accused him of swiping some hybrid wheat grain to plant in his fields."

"I just wanted to see if that miracle seed was as good as Elmer claimed it was," Clive defended himself without thinking. When he realized his mistake, he slammed him mouth shut.

"So you admit you swiped seed wheat from the granary," Amanda said.

"Okay, yeah, I did," Clive begrudgingly admitted. "It was only a few bushels. It wasn't as if I was trying to steal his formula for cross-breeding to make a killing in the certified grain market. The old buzzard was as crazy as all get-out and paranoid to boot. And if I did decide to give him a shove down the cellar steps, it wouldn't have been unjustified. That old goat tried to part my hair with a shotgun last week. I should have filed a complaint."

"Should have?" Harry piped up. "You threatened Elmer, didn't you? We all know you were behind the move to get Elmer declared incompetent and put him in a home. You had the inside angle, what with your wife being a Jolly. And you think you've got clout around here just because your dad used to be mayor. You're always trying to throw your weight around because Cyrus was once the grand pooh-bah of Vamoose."

It was amazing how quickly accusations started flying when individuals with a motive for murder felt threatened. Neighbors and acquaintances started flashing suspicious glances and flinging speculations in an effort to cast shadows of guilt on others. Amanda was beginning to think if Elmer's resentful renters had banned together to put Elmer out of their misery. And she was damned sure going to put a double lock on the granary before she left here, just in case somebody decided to help himself to Elmer's hybrid wheat seed—again. The secret formula of cross-bred wheat grain would remain confidential until Amanda found that blasted will and discovered who had inherited Elmer's research data and the grain bin of super-duper wheat!

"Now, see here, Harry, you were as much in favor of having Elmer put away as anybody. He was a menace to anyone who came near him." Clive glowered at Abner. "What did you do, Ab? Trot over to tell Elmer we were going to start the paperwork to have him placed in a retirement home if he didn't lower the rent and hand out his miracle grain to the three of us?"

Suddenly all three men were standing toe-to-toe and eye-to-eye, ready to tear out each other's throats. Amanda felt herself being yanked back by her shirt collar and hauled away from the shouting match which could have revealed even more interesting facts.

"Damn it, Hazard. Can't I leave you alone for fifteen minutes without you inciting a riot? I can't even fight a fire without you setting off a few sparks of your own."

Shaking herself loose from Thorn's grasp, Amanda pivoted to stare into his smudged and scowling face. "All I did was field the questions tossed at me and pose a few of my own. Those three monkeys—See No Evil, Hear No Evil, and Speak No Evil—suddenly broke their vows of silence and commenced chewing each other up one side and down the other."

"In other words," Nick seethed. "You're the match that sets dry kindling ablaze."

Up went the customary chin. "Apparently not. I was unable to light your fire last night. But I'm sure you'd already burned the end off your wick before you arrived at my house."

Nick stuck his face into hers—eyes narrowed to hard slits, lips curled, prepared to bite off her head.

"Damn it, Hazard, don't try to sidetrack me. You're brewing trouble again. Didn't you learn your lesson after you fumbled through your first murder case? You constantly flirted with disaster. Sometimes I wonder why I bothered to fish you out of the ice water in Whatsit River that cold January night—"

"You want to know why? I'll tell you why, Thorn. You rescued me because you hadn't maneuvered your way into my bed yet. You couldn't stand the thought of a challenge lost!"

Nick recoiled as if he had been slapped. "Hazard, that is the stupidest thing that has ever popped out of your mouth."

"Oh yeah?" Wow, Hazard, there's a clever comeback. You really knocked him dead with that one! Got any more of those zingers tucked under your tongue?

"Yeah. And believe me, you have made some pretty idiotic statements in your time!"

When the volunteer fire chief—Thaddeus Thatcher—ambled over to confer with Thorn, Amanda stood back to listen to Harry, Abner, and Clive fling another round of accusations at each other. It was entirely possible that all three ranchers could profit from Elmer's death. Clive might very well be in line for part of the inheritance, since his wife was a Jolly. Harry and Abner would be well rid of a cantankerous, unpredictable landlord who raised their rent and threatened to pull the farm land and pastures out from under them every other week. Desperation and anger could have sent one or all three farmers over the edge. Amanda also knew that these men did not always operate in the black. They borrowed astronomical amounts of money to purchase cattle, tractors, and implements. She was their accountant, after all.

One could not rule out Randel Thompson, either. He had certainly been paying Amanda a great deal of attention since Elmer's death. Was that just a coincidence?

Amanda frowned when she saw Randel in deep conversation with Jerry Jolly. She couldn't overlook the possibility that Randel had concocted the story of a mud-caked pickup cruising past her house and a phone ringing off its hook. It could have been Jerry Jolly who had back-ended her with Elmer's truck and then driven past her house. Randel might have been the accomplice who was trying to sweet-talk her into confiding in him. The old enemy-trying-to-be-your-friend trick was a popular gimmick in the world of criminology. One always had to be on the lookout for wolves in sheep wool where murder was concerned.

"Let's go, Hazard," Nick ordered, jostling Amanda from her suspicious deliberations. "We have sheep to shear."

Amanda followed Thorn to his truck, but not without casting one last glance at the smoldering remains of Elmer's home. "Did the fire chief determine what caused the blaze?"

Nick slid beneath the steering wheel. "Thaddeus thinks the fire might have been deliberately set, even if it was made to look like faulty electrical wiring. The insulation on the circuits was outdated, but Thaddeus has decided to call the fire marshal—"

"At your request," she surmised.

"At my request," Nick confirmed.

Amanda smiled triumphantly. "So you *are* ready to admit that my conclusions are correct."

Nick gnashed his teeth. He always hated it when Hazard proved herself right. She tended to rub it in his face. "Yes, I have," he said begrudgingly.

"I told you something was amiss when I found Elmer in the cellar, still wearing his store-bought teeth."

Nick rolled his eyes skyward. Only Hazard could come up with such an outrageous clue to launch her into a mission for truth. The woman was a born crusader and a stickler for noting details. Nothing got past those eagle blue eyes and pert bloodhound nose.

"I don't think I've got the hang of this sheepshearing business," Amanda grumbled as she levered the wriggling ewe against her hip and went back to work on the sheep.

Nick swallowed a chuckle when he glanced over to see Hazard wrestling with the ewe that was propped on its rump, legs outthrust and head flung back. The ewe struggled to maintain its balance against the novice sheepshearer. Nick was getting even with Hazard for gloating about the Jolly case. It did his heart good to know she was having a devil of a time learning the knack of shearing.

The aforementioned ewe had patches of wool dangling from her body and nicks on her skin. No doubt, the ewe would hang her head in shame for weeks—she and all the other ewes Hazard had scalped. A worse set of haircuts Nick had never seen.

In addition to the humiliated ewes, Hazard looked as if she had been through the wringer. The lanolin from the wool put a sheen on her hands and arms. She kept blowing errant strands of blonde hair from her oily face, and the fragrance she now wore was one only a sheep would appreciate. Hazard was exercising muscles that were rarely used as she twisted and contorted herself around the squirming ewe. Hitherto, only Hazard's jaw muscles and tongue received regular workouts. Nick predicted Hazard would be stiff and sore, come morning. Now wouldn't that be a shame?

Nick was three times as fast with shears as Hazard was. And if Nick hadn't been aggravated with Hazard for instigating arguments at Jolly Farm, he might have relented and dismissed her from the exhausting chore. But Nick wasn't feeling that charitable. Hazard was getting what she deserved, even if the ewes weren't.

Finally Amanda clipped the last of the wool from the ewe. Working the kinks from her spine, Amanda struggled to stand erect. "How many more, Thorn?" she asked with a groan.

"Only Atilla the ram is left."

"Oh no, I'm not handling that cantankerous son of a buck," Amanda objected. "I haven't forgiven Atilla for butting me off my feet last winter. I could barely walk for a week."

"And if Atilla isn't sheared, he'll die of heat stroke this summer."

"He should have considered that when he selected my derriere as his target. He can sweat to death for all I care."

"You won't have to prop Atilla up on his rump to shear him. He's too heavy. Rams are sheared standing up."

"And you think he'll stand still for it?" She looked skeptical.

Nick glanced up from shearing the ewe's hind quarters and grinned broadly. "I didn't say that."

"Forget it, Thorn. The only way I'll ever go near Atilla again is if he's laying on a plate and I have a knife and fork in hand."

"Spiteful little thing, aren't you?"

"He knocked me flat!" Amanda said in offended dignity.

"Okay, Hazard, don't work yourself into a tizzy. I'll shear Atilla if you'll bring him out of the pen while I finish this ewe."

"And how am I supposed to do that?" she wanted to know.

Nick smiled scampishly. "Just bend over in front of him like a target and he'll follow you anywhere."

Amanda refused to be amused. Turning on her heels, she walked over to fetch the Hot Shot that Nick had used to prod the contrary sheep down the lane to the corral. Atilla was as cooperative as his counterpart—the bull. Wasn't it interesting, thought Amanda, that the male of every species shared the same annoying characteristics. They were all stubborn, arrogant, and insufferable.

Encouraging Atilla to go where he did not wish to go was frustrating and time consuming. Amanda utilized every curse in her vocabulary before she convinced the ram that he must walk through the lane to be sheared—or else. The oversized ram sent Amanda scrambling up the fence twice before she finally managed to get him in the corral. To her amazement, Atilla stood reasonably still while Nick sheared him. Kindred spirits, thought Amanda. Thorn and Atilla could both be buttheads when they felt like it.

"If you can spare me for a few minutes, Thorn, I'll go fix us a cold drink," she volunteered.

"Sounds good. There's beer in the fridge and Coke in the cabinets. I'll take a beer."

Amanda ambled toward the house. Her nose wrinkled distastefully when the breeze stirred the scent of sheep that clung to her clothes and mingled with the smell of sweat and cattle. God, what she wouldn't give for a bath! She could offend a skunk with her odoriferous aroma.

The thought of quenching her thirst with beer had no appeal whatsoever. Frozen strawberry daiquiries were more her style. Instead, Amanda settled for a Diet Coke. Problem was, it took five minutes of searching Thorn's disorganized cabinets to locate the Coke. He definitely needed to adopt the alphabetical system Amanda utilized. The man had no logical sense of order.

Before Amanda could pour the drinks, the phone rang.

"Hello. Thorn's zoo. Who are you?"

Amanda's unexpected greeting gave the caller pause.

"A . . . a . . . is Nicky there?"

Amanda made an awful face at the receiver. It was Ms. Bosom.

"Mr. Thorn is shearing sheep at the moment. May I take a message?"

"Yes, tell him to call Jenny when he comes in."

"Got it." Amanda hung up the phone and cursed colorfully. The man was obviously on a twenty-four hour sex schedule these days. Ms. Bosom must be calling to verify their next appointment.

With drinks in hand. Amanda stalked back to the corral, spitefully hoping Atilla had butted Thorn around a few times, incapacitating him for the evening. When Nick released the ram and hopped over the fence before

Atilla turned on him, Amanda thrust a beer into his hand.

"Ms. Bosom called," she told him. "She wants you to get in *touch* with her ASAP."

Nick leaned against the corral fence, wiped the perspiration from his forehead, and savored his brew.

"Well?"

"Well *what?* Thank you for the beer?" he questioned in mock innocence.

Amanda glowered daggers. "Forget the damned drink. What about Ms. Bosom?"

"What about her? Was she thirsty, too?"

Amanda resisted the urge to pour Diet Coke on Thorn's shiny raven head. "If you are finished with me," she said through clenched teeth. "I'm going home to shower."

"We're finished." Nick took another sip of beer. "Thanks for the help, Hazard."

Amanda guzzled her Diet Coke and handed him the glass. Thorn didn't know how gracious she was being. She really wanted to stuff the ice cubes down the front of his jeans.

"Later, Thorn."

"*Adios,* Hazard."

Amanda hoped he would ask her to spend the evening with him. He didn't. He simply smiled in amusement.

"You *are* going to investigate the Jolly murder and arson tonight, right, Thorn?"

"Wrong. It's my day off."

"Fine. I'll proceed as usual with my investigation."

"Just back off before you get into trouble—again," Nick advised.

"A lot *you* care," Amanda muttered on her way to her pickup.

"What was that, Hazard?"

"Go to hell, Thorn, and take Ms. Bosom with you!'

His teasing laughter followed her to the truck. Amanda gunned the jalopy and took off with mud flying. It was a spectacular exit, even if she did say so herself.

After the livestock had been fed, and Hank the tomcat was sprawled in his favorite chair, Amanda headed for the shower. It took forever to remove the smell of cattle and sheep from her hair and skin. The cool water did nothing to diminish her aggravation. Visions of Thorn and Ms. Bosom together kept hounding her. Amanda was sad to report that she was jealous.

She would sic the IRS on Thorn. That would show him.

We are being rather childish, aren't we, Hazard? You're the one who refused to allow a public acknowledgment of this ... relationship ... with Thorn. Only after you were seen with Randel Thompson did you permit Thorn to escort you to Last Chance Cafe. And that incredibly clever tactic only proved that you were not keeping company with any one man in particular.

"Oh, shut up," Amanda snapped irritably.

Why should I? I'm not the one in a rotten mood because it's Saturday night and all you have to look forward to is uninterrupted peace and quiet. You could have invited Thorn over for the evening before he accepted a rendezvous with Ms. Bosom.

"It was Thorn's place to do the asking," Amanda

pointed out as she scrubbed another layer of skin off her body in her fit of temper. "Thorn suggested as much at Last Chance Cafe this afternoon. Obviously that was just Thorn's way of staking his claim for Randel's benefit. If Thorn wanted to be with me instead of Ms. Bosom tonight, he could have said so."

After having that conversation with herself, Amanda stepped out of the shower and grabbed a towel. When she veered around the corner toward her bedroom, she gasped, startled. Her bare feet automatically retreated two steps at the sight of the intruder.

"What are you doing here?" she demanded in a strangled voice.

Randel Thompson's gaze raked over her barely concealed body in wolfish appreciation before he finally got around to meeting her suspicious gaze.

Amanda clutched the towel protectively around her and backed away. This was it. Randel had come to finish her off, or to torture her into revealing the location of Elmer's will. She could scream from here to Tripoli, but it would do no good. She would still be just as dead.

This was Thorn's fault. If he hadn't been lollygagging with Ms. Bosom, Amanda would have been with him at this very moment, protected from the "trouble" Thorn had mentioned earlier.

"Hey, 'Manda honey, don't freak out on me," Randel cooed when she looked at him like a homicide victim. "I knocked on your door and nobody answered. Since your truck was parked in the driveway, I just wanted to make sure everything was all right."

Amanda did not let her guard down for even one second. Her eyes darted hither and yon, contemplating her best avenue of escape. "What do you want?"

"What's under that towel would be good for starters," he said with a rakish leer.

"This isn't the Old West, Randel, and I don't swoon at sexual innuendoes from bowlegged cowboys."

Randel propped himself against the wall in the hall and wiped the silly grin off his face. "I want to know what you were doing at Last Chance Cafe with Nick this afternoon."

And I want to know what you were discussing so seriously with Jerry Jolly after the fire, thought Amanda. Unfortunately, this vulnerable situation, and the lack of clothing, were not conducive to such pointed questions. She could be strangled by her own towel, electrocuted in her bathtub, drowned in her farm pond. The possibilities were endless.

"I was eating lunch with Thorn," Amanda replied belatedly.

"I could see that for myself. But what exactly does it mean?"

"It means that I'm starved to death because I didn't get to eat my meal before the fire whistle went off. All I swallowed at noon was smoke."

"That's not what I meant, 'Manda."

"Then perhaps you should have been more specific . . ."

Amanda's voice disintegrated when the screen door creaked. To her relief and/or dismay—she wasn't sure which—Nick Thorn walked in as if he, too, owned the damned place.

Thorn glanced in Randel's general direction, but his obsidian eyes bored into Amanda. When confronted with such freezing disapproval, Amanda, who was rarely at a loss for words, could not pry her tongue loose from the roof of her mouth.

"Excuse me, I didn't know I was interrupting. I thought Hazard and I had plans for the evening. Obviously I was mistaken," Nick said, and not very nicely, either.

Randel grinned victoriously when Nick wheeled around and stalked out without a backward glance.

Amanda scowled. "Take a hike, Randel. I would like to get dressed without an audience."

"But—"

Amanda showed him the door, as if he were too dense to know where it was. "Vamoose. I am not accepting visitors this evening."

"But—"

Amanda whirled around and stomped to her bedroom, slamming the door behind her. Well, at least Thorn's unexpected arrival saved her from being molested and/or murdered, if that was Randel's true intent. Thorn would know Amanda was last seen with Randel. Even that cowboy had enough sense to know he would become a prime suspect if Amanda turned up dead. As for Amanda's . . . relationship . . . with Thorn, it was on the rocks. She could no longer trust Thorn when she was convinced he had hopped in the sack with Ms. Bosom the minute Amanda turned her back. And Thorn certainly wouldn't trust her after the scene he thought he had witnessed. Thing's were sure getting interesting.

Chapter Nine

The next morning, Amanda marched out of her house, prepared to face the work-a-day world. Her first stop was the accounting office across from Last Chance Cafe. The sight of Thorn's patrol car at the restaurant turned her mood pitch black. It took the jingling phone to jolt Amanda from her bitter thoughts.

"Hazard Accounting."

"Mandy?" the feminine voice drawled.

Amanda cringed. She hated being referred to as "Mandy."

"This is Billie Jane Baxter."

Amanda recognized the human gong's voice without being prompted. "Yes, Billie, how can I help you?"

"I'm flying in from Nashville Saturday to see how well my new house withstood the storm, and to visit my mother. I wanted to come by and check on the accounts I opened at Vamoose Bank."

Then why are you calling me? Amanda wondered irritably. She soon found out.

"You know what a ninny I am about checkbooks. Never can remember to keep a record of my withdrawls."

Billie Jane laughed it off. She laughed alone. "I wondered if you could run over to the bank and pick up my statements and balance my checkbook for me before I get to town. I'm so busy with concert tours I just don't have time for financial details."

Why anyone would pay good money to listen to this country singer whine and wail was beyond Amanda. Obviously, there was no accounting for some people's tastes.

"I was hoping I could come in Saturday afternoon and pick up the statements after you have the accounts balanced."

"Sure, that will be fine, Billie Jane."

"Thanks, Mandy. You're a peach."

Amanda Hazard was nobody's peach. At the moment, she felt like the world's biggest crab apple.

"Well, see ya Saturday, Mandy."

"Fine, Billie Jane." It sounded like the appropriate thing to say.

Amanda wasn't sure Billie Jane would have any cash left in her account, considering the monstrosity of a country mansion she was building in her hometown. Billie Jane could accommodate her entire musical band and all her relatives in that house. The woman had spared no expense in construction. Amanda rather thought Billie Jane was rubbing Vamoosian noses in her stardom, but who was she to criticize the country star's startling success, or the methods used to display it?

Grabbing her purse, Amanda stuffed the file she had been updating in the cabinet and headed toward the door. Thorn emerged from the cafe just as Amanda stepped outside. They glared across the street at each other like two enemies from opposing war camps.

Flinging her nose in the air, Amanda climbed into her jalopy and aimed herself toward the bank to fetch Billie Jane's financial statement and see if Elmer Jolly had stashed a copy of his will in a safety deposit box.

Of course the will wasn't there. Amanda should have realized that she'd have to earn every penny of the fee she might charge as administrator of the Jolly estate.

Casting a wary glance toward the gloomy sky, she drove to Melvin Jolly's farm. The spring weather patterns had become downright depressing. Storms and gray skies were broken only by an occasional day of sunshine. Amanda wondered if she would have to grow fins and gills to survive until summer.

After slopping down the country roads, and cursing Commissioner Brown a half dozen times, Amanda arrived at Melvin Jolly's home. The driveway resembled a used car lot. Amanda supposed she should have done the polite thing and reversed direction since Melvin looked to be entertaining company, but this was an excellent opportunity to meet the Jolly clan. She wanted a complete list of possible suspects at her disposal before beginning her analytical deductions.

Once Melvin opened the door, Amanda practically invited herself inside the modestly furnished home, as if she had no notion she might be intruding. "I wanted to tell all of you how sorry I am about Elmer," she said for openers. "I know you prefer to have the matter of Elmer's estate settled as soon as possible. I have been working on the legal end of the matter."

Like hell you have, Hazard. You're fumbling around in hopes of tripping over a few clues and stumbling over the missing will.

Melvin Jolly's expression never altered. He looked as if he were chewing on a lemon.

"Won't you sit down, Ms. Hazard," Odie Mae said in a neutral tone.

Amanda sat. With a pleasant smile plastered on her face, she surveyed the tribe that had gathered for some sort of powwow. Jerry and Wally Jolly were lounging on the sofa beside their cousin Patricia who was bookended by her husband Clive Barnstall. Clive nodded a greeting that was as cold as the Klondike. Apparently he had not forgiven Amanda for instigating the argument at Elmer's charred home. Eula Bell and Claud Jolly—looking like cigar store Indians—occupied the threadbare loveseat. The children—if one could call middle-age adults children—were scattered around the small living area that had not been redecorated for a half century.

"So, who is inheriting Elmer's estate?" Claud questioned without preamble.

Amanda smiled; she was the only one who appeared to know how. "I'm afraid I have to keep you in suspense awhile longer. I have to contact the county courthouse to set a date for probate first."

"Why don't you just come right out and tell us that you managed to get yourself included in my brother's will," Melvin sneered.

Amanda would have liked to pound Melvin's bald head, but she almost never relied upon physical violence when senior citizens were concerned.

"Melvin! You shouldn't say such things." Odie Mae's face turned the color of paste.

"Well, it's true," Melvin snorted in disgust. "Elmer

took a shine to this Jezebel and she made the most of it. She buttered him up for his money and—"

"Is that why you disposed of your brother and then drove off like a house afire the day of the storm?"

Amanda came to the quick conclusion that she may as well fling a few accusations. She wouldn't acquire any information if she did nothing more than defend herself against this biased jury of Jollys. "I am well aware that the whole lot of you were barely on speaking terms with Elmer after the tractor incident five years ago. And just because Elmer had his own way of discouraging unwanted visitors at his home, you decided to have him declared incompetent and become the guardians of his affairs. How very convenient."

"My brother was becoming dangerous," Claud put in huffily. "He could have injured someone with his hostile actions. Elmer was paranoid—"

"Apparently he had legitimate reasons to be, wouldn't you say?" Amanda interrupted. "If not, we wouldn't be here discussing Elmer in the *past* tense."

"If you are implying that some of us had reason to do away with Elmer when we all know he suffered an unforeseeable accident, then you are out of your mind, Ms. Hazard," Jerry Jolly spoke up.

"No," she contradicted. "I have several reasons for drawing that conclusion."

"Would you mind naming a few of them," Wally Jolly requested.

"I was the last one to speak with Elmer the day he died—with the exception of his murderer, of course. I know for a fact that Elmer was feeling threatened because—"

"Hi, everybody! So what's new with Elmer's—?"

Bertie Ann Jolly burst through the door and screeched to a halt. Her gaze landed on the intruder and then darted questioningly to her sisters.

Every pair of eyes leaped from Bertie Ann to Amanda, who felt as if she had just stepped into a searchlight. And then, just as suddenly, the Jolly clan clammed up and looked everywhere except at Amanda.

"I want you to leave my house, Ms. Hazard," Melvin demanded, eyes blazing.

Amanda got up and left. You could have heard a feather drop in that room before she closed the door behind her. Amanda wondered how many invisible daggers were stuck in her back by the time she walked off the porch. She knew how Julius Caesar must have felt.

Ah, Amanda would have given most anything if she could have sneaked back into that house to eavesdrop on the conversation that proceeded her visit. Amanda had infuriated plenty of people the past few days. It was rather like stirring up a nest of hornets and waiting to see which one was going to deliver the sting. Baiting traps was such unpopular business.

Raindrops splattered on the windshield as Amanda navigated down the soupy road. Her destination was the courthouse. She was not setting a court date; instead she was going to check the records of property and titles. She might turn up some intriguing facts while she waited for the murderer to get restless and come after her again.

Amanda had come to the conclusion that this was one case that wasn't ever going to proceed in the customary manner—there would be no picking up clues that led like footsteps to the killer. She had no other alternative but to lure the murderer to her. She only hoped she was prepared when that happened.

Thank goodness Thorn had finally come around to her way of thinking. If anything went awry, Thorn could follow-up the investigation. That was a reassuring and yet unsettling thought. She was still mad as hell at Thorn for screwing around with Ms. Bosom, but if Amanda wound up dead, Thorn would take the case. He would feel sufficiently guilty, too. That, Amanda imagined, would be her only consolation when she joined Elmer at the pearly gates.

Amanda had a field day at the county courthouse, rifling through the records of property transactions. It was fascinating to discover how the Jolly land had been claimed during the Land Run in 1889, and how it had been handed down through generations. Ancestors had deeded the land over to their survivors, decade after decade. Some generations had been buyers who acquired more property to be divided among their kinfolk. Other Jollys had simply maintained what they had inherited without expanding.

When Amanda came across the name of Therrel Thompson in the records, a frown knitted her brow. According to the deeds, Therrel Thompson had sold a quarter section of land to Elmer. Could Therrel Thompson have been Randel's grandfather? Were the Jollys and Thompsons related in some way or another? Or had Therrel simply sold the land to the highest bidder? It certainly bore checking out.

Another intriguing tidbit of information leaped out at Amanda while she was studying the land transactions and property owners on the maps. Agnes and Vernon Jolly had deeded their land to their sons—Elmer, Claud, and Melvin. Amanda wondered if the youngest Jolly sibling—Leroy—had settled for cash or mineral rights when his parents' estate was finalized. That would explain why Leroy had packed up and moved to the city after he returned from war. Leroy, it was said, had no interest in farming traditions. He had married Bertie Ann Mopope and taken to city life like a duck to water.

Amanda also came across another land transaction that piqued her curiosity. The Hendershots had also sold eighty acres of land to Elmer Jolly. Was Abner Hendershot renting land that had once belonged to his family? Was he distantly related to the family, too? Amanda's mind reeled. There were too many connections between families in small-town America. They boggled the brain. A person couldn't turn around without bumping into somebody's relative. There were double cousins, kissing cousins, cousins by marriage. . . . Lord, where did it all end?

If Agnes Jolly had been a Hendershot or Thompson, or a niece or cousin to them before her marriage, the connections could be complicated. Amanda would never figure out which old grudges and which new resentments were responsible for Elmer's death. One thing was certain. Elmer could not have offended anyone without stepping on some kind of relative's toes! Why, Elmer appeared to have had family ties to everybody north and west of the Vamoose railroad tracks!

By the time Amanda had poured over the records for several hours, she was nurturing a queen-size headache. She still had accounts to update in her office before she could call it a day.

Heaving a weary sigh, Amanda stepped outside the courthouse to face the drizzling rain. It seemed the monsoon season had settled on Oklahoma. The meteorologist who interrupted the music on her favorite country station predicted another round of showers. Goodie, goodie, thought Amanda. Her pigs would have mud holes galore. Lucky duck could take a swim without waddling down to the pond. But Amanda would have to purchase Pete the three-legged dog one and a half pair of fins and floaties. He wasn't much of a swimmer these days.

Maybe what Amanda needed was a vacation from downpours and frustrating murder cases. The desert sounded inviting this time of year. And it wasn't as if anyone would miss her if she vamoosed from Vamoose. The Jollys thought she was a gold-digging floozie, and Thorn had a grand distraction in the form of the top-heavy Ms. Bosom.

That's it, Hazard. Feel sorry for yourself, why don't you?

She did, all the way back to Vamoose.

On impulse, Amanda took the long way back to town, detouring to the charred remains of Elmer's home. The farm looked more remote and forsaken than ever with a backdrop of gray clouds against the blackened ruins of a home that boasted no more than rubble and a sooty foundation.

Amanda carefully stepped up to where the kitchen had been, to pilfer through the debris, searching for the metal box that had contained a love letter and wedding rings. The fireproof container had survived the blaze, much to Amanda's relief. At least she had salvaged some memorabilia that had once meant something special to Elmer.

A curious frown puckered Amanda's brow as she stepped over the rubble to stand in what had been Elmer's bedroom. Amanda hunkered down to survey what looked like a trap door in the buckled floor. Was this Elmer's cache? Were his valuables and his will hidden beneath the floor?

Excitedly, Amanda scampered back to her jalopy. Hang the bookwork at the office, she decided. She was going home to change into grubby clothes and hotfoot it back to Elmer's with a shovel and high hopes of discovery!

Amanda had just veered out of the driveway when the patrol car stopped in the middle of the road. Thorn unfolded his sinewy frame from beneath the steering wheel and ambled toward her.

"Any new clues for the Hazard Amateur Detective Agency?"

"Sarcasm doesn't become you, Thorn. Do you want something important or did you simply decide to put a little sparkle in this dreary day by harassing me?"

"I just thought I would tell you I checked with the county sheriff's office this morning and ran a M.O. on some of the Jolly clan."

"And?" Amanda prompted.

"Clean. None of the Jollys ever pressed charges against each other after their squabbles. However, your boyfriend was charged for larceny in Texas. The charges were later dropped."

"Be more specific, Thorn. Since I don't have a boyfriend, I haven't the faintest idea who you are referring to," Amanda replied with cool aplomb.

"Romeo the rodeo clown, of course," Nick snapped. "I don't have the details."

"Thank you, Thorn." Her voice did not sound the least bit appreciative.

Neither did Thorn's. "You're welcome, Hazard."

They glared at each other for a full minute before Amanda shifted gears and drove off, spitefully splattering Thorn with mud. It was the only enjoyment she'd had all day.

An hour later Amanda was appropriately dressed and shoveling debris out of her way to investigate the trap door. When she had the area cleared, she grabbed her flashlight and sank down into the musty hole. She found herself surrounded by cardboard boxes and wooden crates that had been gnawed by mice.

Amanda had to crawl beneath the floor joists to inspect the old man's hidden treasures. She found a set of china and crystal that looked as if they had never been used, and an eight piece setting of tarnished silverware. Why had Elmer kept the goods stashed from sight? Had they once belonged to his long-departed mother? And if so, why had he been keeping them? To Amanda's further bafflement, she found a box containing sheets and a comforter that the mice had chewed to pieces to make their nests.

Using her elbows to propel her, Amanda slithered toward a wooden crate that looked as if it was filled with canning jars. She had just begun to pry the nails loose from the lid when she heard a "crunch" somewhere above her. Damn, it was probably Thorn. He must have decided to shadow her so he could catch her doing something stupid and needle her about it . . .

The trap door slammed shut above her and Amanda cursed soundly. She had the inescapable feeling it wasn't Thorn standing over her. She could hear the scraping noises of objects being dragged over the scorched flooring. Amanda bolted toward the trap door and konked her head in her haste to prevent being locked in the foundation. By the time she reached the hatch, it had been sealed shut by pounds of debris. Amanda couldn't budge the door.

Quickly, she shined her flashlight around, searching for an alternative escape route. But before she could crawl toward the sliding wooden door that granted access to the plumbing and sewer line beneath the bathroom, she heard thumping noises coming from that direction. Damnation! Who the devil had confined her to this foundation-of-a-tomb?

Amanda pricked up her ears when she heard the cranking of an engine. She had the sinking feeling that her jalopy was going for a drive without her. Not that she would be needing it anytime within the next century, of course. She had been buried alive and left to starve. Where was Thorn when she really needed him?

Get a grip, Hazard, Amanda ordered herself. It was up to her to escape from her most recent scrape. Now what would Magnum P.I. do in a situation like this . . . ?

Amanda's thoughts scattered when she spied the snake that was sharing her prison. She opened her mouth and screamed bloody murder. The snake—one that Amanda swore was at least twenty feet long with fangs the size of soda straws—recoiled at the sound of her voice. Amanda hated snakes as much as she hated mice. For that matter, she didn't care for spiders and scorpions, either. No doubt, she was trapped with all sorts of disgusting varmints that were waiting to make a feast of her.

The sight of the snake spurred Amanda into action. She slithered toward the sliding door beneath the bathroom, spun about, and hammered her boot heels against the wood with every ounce of strength she could muster. Meanwhile, she screamed at the top of her lungs, praying the snake would keep its distance.

Two eternities later, the casing around the door gave way. Whatever objects had been barricaded against it shifted. Amanda kicked like a mule a few more times for good measure and then shoved the blockade sideways to emit light into her sepulcher. Several minutes elapsed before Amanda had cleared a path wide enough for her to emerge. She inhaled a fortifying breath, stood up, and dusted herself off. Damn it, this was getting monotonous, not to mention scary!

When she was sure her spaghetti legs would support her, she wobbled toward Elmer's old truck that sat upon the hill. Her jalopy was long gone, just as she predicted. At least she had the keys that Thorn had given her to Elmer's vehicle for transportation. Once she had rolled Elmer's green truck down the hill and popped the clutch, the engine purred like a sick kitten.

Amanda left the truck idling while she returned to the trap door to gather the wooden crates containing canning jars. Although Amanda had been distracted before she could inspect the crate, she had caught glimpses of the contents—junk mail envelopes. Amanda was now reasonably certain she knew where Elmer had stashed his research notes from the last two decades. He had sealed his notes in the jars and hidden them under his house to protect them from nibbling rodents and nosy neighbors.

Amanda gathered her treasures and left the boxes of dishes and silverware behind. She hadn't driven two miles before she discovered what had become of her gas-guzzling jalopy. The top of the truck was barely visible in the swift-flowing waters of Deep Creek. Her stalker must have wanted all of Vamoose to assume she had drowned. Of course, the creek would have been dredged to locate her body, but no one would ever have guessed that she had been buried alive inside the foundation of Elmer's charred house.

It was fortunate that Amanda had as many lives as a cat. Otherwise she would have died more than once during this exasperating investigation. Someone had been staying up nights to devise ingenious ways to scare her to death—all because she had befriended a cantankerous old recluse by the name of Elmer Jolly.

Exhausted and happy to finally reach her home, Amanda trudged toward her house, but not before she cast cautious glances in every direction. She cursed the air blue when she realized all her keys had gone down with her jalopy. She had to break into her own house!

Carrying the box of jars with her into the bathroom for safekeeping, Amanda stripped and showered. Although her pride was still smarting, Amanda could think of only one safe place to stash Elmer's research notes— Thorn's farm. She was going to put the research papers in police custody, and she was going to do it pronto.

She and Thorn may have been at odds, but she was dignified and mature enough to set aside her personal problems with that miserable two-timing lout in the interest of this investigation.

Clean and revived, Amanda strode over to retrieve her crate of jars. The phone rang. She snatched up the receiver and offered the caller and impatient greeting.

"Hi, doll. It's Mother. You've certainly been busy lately. I usually get your answering machine instead of you. I just hate talking to that thing. . . . What have you been doing, working yourself to death?"

It wasn't the work that was coming close to *killing* Amanda but she let Mother think so. At the moment Amanda could use a dose of sympathy, even Mother's. "I've been extremely busy as a matter of fact."

"Well, it seems to me that since you are pushing so hard you should take more vitamins. You know they have those stress vitamins on the market these days."

While Mother grabbed the bit between her teeth and dashed off on a colloquy concerning the benefits of supplemental vitamins, Amanda gathered and alphabetized the magazines that Hank had knocked off the coffee table.

Mother finally cleared her throat and broached another subject. "Your Uncle Dean and Aunt Lydia invited us over for dinner Saturday. Your brother and his family are coming and your cousins will be there, too.

Dear God, spare me another family gathering in the same month!

"I thought this would be the perfect chance for us to meet this Thorn fellow."

"Sorry, Mother. I can't make it. I'm planning on being ill that night."

"Amanda, you are being sarcastic again." Mother clucked her tongue. "You know your father and I are curious to meet your man friend. It seems to me that you have gone to great lengths to avoid introducing him to the family."

"Mother—"

"Now I will hear no more of your excuses and that is that. You have this Thorn fellow at Uncle Dean's on Saturday night at seven-thirty. We want to know if he is good enough for—" Mother cleared her throat when she realized her blunder. "That is to say, we want to get to know him."

"I can't—"

"You can and you will, doll. Seven-thirty Saturday. Be there."

Amanda blinked when the line went dead with a resounding clank. Mother had hung up on her. Now there was a switch.

Muttering at Mother's persistence, Amanda grabbed the canning jars and headed toward the green truck that she had parked on the slope of her lawn. With a pop of the clutch, she was off and running. Thorn probably wouldn't be any happier to see her than she was to see him, but that was tough.

And Mother could forget about putting Thorn on the firing line Saturday night. She and Thorn barely had a civil word to say to each other these days. Maybe she should send Thorn and Ms. Bosom to Uncle Dean's house. Amanda smiled devilishly. Now that would be an interesting scene. Thorn and Ms. Bosom would receive a full helping of exactly what they deserved at the Hazard family barbecue.

Chapter Ten

The patrol car and black four-wheel-drive pickup were parked in front of Thorn's small brick home. Amanda grabbed her treasure of canning jars and marched to the door. She knocked repeatedly before Thorn appeared. Amanda took one look at his damp hair and gaping shirt and concluded that Thorn had just stepped out of the shower. The scent of soap and cologne filled her nostrils. He smelled better than any man had a right to.

"Hot date tonight, Thorn?" she inquired, striving for an aloof tone that suggested she couldn't care less. Feminine pride was spurring her like a merciless jockey. She would be damned if she let this big ox know how it hurt to see him and Ms. Bosom running fast and loose in Vamoose.

"What do you want, Hazard?" Nick growled unpleasantly.

"A haven for my treasure." She buzzed past him without invitation. "I finally located Elmer's research data. Since my home and office have already been searched by person or persons unknown, I hesitate to stash the notes in either place. And since another attempt was made on my life, I decided not to waste any time."

That got Thorn's attention in a hurry. *"What?"*

"I had heard that too much sex impaired a man's hearing. I guess it must be true," she said flippantly.

"Damn it, Hazard—"

"Stop blustering and pay attention. I'm sure you are pressed for time and I wouldn't think of detaining you from your rendezvous—"

Nick's arm shot out, indicating the chair he wanted her to park herself in. "Sit, Hazard."

Amanda plopped down dutifully.

"Now what's this about another attempt on your life," he demanded in a no-nonsense tone.

Amanda proceeded to tell him about locating the stash of dishes and canning jars under the trap door and being barricaded inside the foundation while her jalopy drove off without her.

"My truck, along with the keys to my house, office, and chastity belt, are at the bottom of Deep Creek."

Nick's dark brows formed a V over his slitted eyes. "Let's try to keep our personal differences out of this, shall we, Hazard? When I am conducting a professional investigation—informal or otherwise—I can do without your smart-ass remarks."

"And I can do without your condescending and very obtrusive attitude of superiority, thank you very much!" Amanda snapped back. "I am not a criminal suspect under investigation. *I* am the victim!"

His fingers itched to clamp around her lovely but irritating neck. Hazard didn't know how narrowly she escaped becoming the victim of another murder attempt.

There were times when he felt like killing her. This was one of those times.

"Picking and replacing your locks will be no problem, Hazard," he managed to say without biting her head off. "Tell me what leads you have found in the case."

Amanda's pent-up frustration poured out in a long-suffering sigh. "I'm afraid I know a little of everything and a lot of nothing. I have a mile-long list of suspects with comparable motive. No single suspect seems more likely to have benefitted from Elmer's demise than the others. Motives differ but not to noticeable degrees, unless one considers adding bursts of volatile temper. In that event, anyone could have gone over the edge while dealing with the spirited but irascible Elmer Jolly."

Nick sank down beside Amanda on the sofa and stared at the far wall. "And which of your suspects seems clever enough, and physically able, to perform the deeds that had you scrambling for your life? Bucking hay bales and scooting heavy objects over escape routes suggests a certain amount of strength."

"A male suspect," Amanda murmured pensively. "But I can't rule out the possibility of an accomplice. And there are scads of men over the age of sixty around Vamoose who can still buck bales without gasping for breath."

Nick was silent for a moment. "I think you need round-the-clock protection."

Amanda cast Thorn a skeptical glance. "And who do you know who wants to bother trailing me twenty-four hours a day? You know perfectly well that posting guard detail around me wouldn't bring the culprit out of hiding." She shook her blonde head. "No, it would be better to bait a trap to catch Elmer's killer—"

"No daring heroics, Hazard. You suffer too many grandiose delusions when it comes to cracking murder cases. I hate to burst your bubble, but you are not the Lone Ranger and Superwoman all rolled into one."

An energetic knock at the door interrupted Nick's objections.

Amanda bounded to her feet and scurried toward the kitchen to hide her canning jars, only to hear Thorn grumbling behind her.

"Damn it, Hazard. Are you so afraid that somebody might think we actually care about each other?"

She pivoted to face his scowl. "Do we, Thorn?"

"Once upon a time I thought we did. But then I have never claimed to understand the workings of the fickle female mind."

"Me? Fickle? You're the one who—"

Another insistent rap sent Amanda around the corner to the kitchen and prodded Thorn toward the door.

"Coming!"

Nick swung open the door and Jenny Long stepped inside to curl one arm around his neck while she balanced a baking dish in the other.

"Hi, Nicky!" Jenny greeted him with a kiss hot enough to reheat her casserole. "I thought I'd surprise you with dinner. I'll just pop it in the oven."

Jenny sashayed toward the kitchen, her denim-clad hips swaying like a porch swing. She pulled up short when she spied Amanda sitting on the counter, rearranging the insides of Nick's cabinets into alphabetical order.

"Oh . . ." Jenny stared bewilderedly at Amanda. "I didn't know Nicky had company."

"He doesn't." Amanda grabbed a box of rice and strode toward the living room, smiling nonchalantly. "No big deal, Ms. Bo—Jenny. I just stopped by to borrow some rice." She gestured toward the box in her hand and grinned spitefully at Thorn who stood a few feet behind Jenny. "It's the *minute* variety. Somehow it doesn't surprise me that you cook the *quick* stuff, too."

Nick gnashed his teeth at the sarcastic dig. Of course, since Jenny's largest commodity wasn't brains, the comment flew over her head.

"Thanks, Thorn, I'll pay you back," Amanda promised as she sailed toward the front door.

"Ditto, Hazard," he called after her.

The instant Amanda stepped outside her pretentious smile slid off her lips. She was losing Thorn to one of those domestic types whom men seem to favor. Jenny had probably been Future Homemaker of the Year while in high school. No doubt she loved to wash windows, dust furniture, and set a fine table. Jenny treated Thorn as if he were God's gift to womankind. Amanda didn't know how to cook anything that didn't come from a can, box, or didn't have microwave directions. She despised housework, but she hated clutter and disorganization more. She had never kissed up to a man in her life and she was not about to start now.

Amanda drove home through the drizzling rain to dine on tuna in a can and stale crackers—one of her traditional, no-fuss meals. She left the living room when the tomcat began switching channels on the TV. Hank had become quite amused by his new talent of standing on the remote control and watching the lights flash.

Amanda shut herself in the bedroom and called it a night. She was exhausted—physically and emotionally. She hoped she would sleep like a rock and not let the unnerving incident of the day evolve into a nightmare.

And curse Nick Thorn, Amanda mused as she flounced onto her side. Knowing that Ms. Bosom had plans of satisfying Thorn's sweet tooth with her special recipe for dessert gave Amanda indigestion. She hoped Thorn's pearly teeth decayed and his legs grew together!

Geez, give the man a break, Hazard, her noble conscience fussed at her.

"Okay, I hope he *breaks* his arm." There. That should shut up her nagging conscience.

It did.

Nick stretched his long legs out on his scarred coffee table and flipped through the television stations to catch the late evening news and weather report. The radar indicated another band of showers marching across the state. Damn, just what Vamoose needed. More heavy rain. Wheat fields that were still standing, after being hammered by hail, were now flooded. Harvest was only a few weeks away and agricultural experts predicted a reduction in crops. That should force the wheat prices up, and the wheat market could definitely use a boost.

Muttering about the farm economy, the excessive rain, and the woman he couldn't get off his mind, Nick absently pressed the remote control in hopes of finding a program to distract him. Jenny Long's unexpected arrival—on the heels of Hazard's appearance—had frustrated Nick. When a man wanted a woman around, there usually wasn't one in a hundred miles. Then suddenly he had two females on his doorstep. One had an over-stocked supply of sass and supersensitive pride; the other had no shame. Damn it all, there were times when Nick wondered if Elmer Jolly hadn't had the right idea. There was something to be said for the life a hermit led . . .

Thoughts of Elmer sent Nick's mind circling back to Hazard. He couldn't figure out who was antagonizing the administrator of his estate and why? Maybe whoever wanted Hazard out of the way *thought* she knew something she wasn't supposed to know—like what was in the missing will. Of course, Hazard was stubborn to the core and she refused to let it be known that she didn't have a clue as to what was in the document. Where was that damned will anyway?

The jingling phone derailed Nick from his train of thought. He picked up the receiver and mumbled a greeting.

"Nick Thorn? Is that you?"

"Mother—I mean . . . Mrs. Hazard, is that *you?*"

"You recognize my voice? I'm impressed." Mother cleared her throat. "I know it's late, but I just wanted to call and confirm that you and Amanda are coming to the city Saturday night."

The comment took Nick by surprise. The only invitation Nick had received from Hazard lately was: Go to hell and don't come back.

"Saturday night?" he repeated.

Mother sighed melodramatically. She reminded Nick of a heavy breather from an obscene phone call.

"I knew Amanda would neglect to tell you that you are invited to dinner at Uncle Dean's."

"Well, I—"

"This is nothing formal, you understand. It's just a casual get-together and barbecue. We were all so disappointed that you couldn't come to the family reunion. We're all so anxious to meet you." Mother cleared her throat again. "Well, I won't keep you any longer since it's so late. We'll see you Saturday. Bye—"

The line went dead and Nick stared at the receiver. Hazard was right. It was difficult to get a word in edgewise when Mother was yammering ninety miles a minute.

Nick barely had time to hang up the phone before it blared at him again. He wondered what Mother had neglected to say.

"Hello?"

"Nick? Deputy Sykes here. I know you're on a 10–10, but I've got a 502 doing a 505. I could use a Code 3."

Nick rolled his eyes ceilingward. Deputy Sykes belonged on a metropolitan police force. Benny was a precision-honed, "by the book" sort of guy who thrived on jargon. It would have been much simpler for Benny to say that he knew Nick was off duty but he requested assistance with a drunk driver whose reckless driving on bad road conditions landed him in a ditch.

"Where are you, Benny?" Nick questioned.

"Three miles south and two miles west of Vamoose. I can't rouse Cecil Watt and his tow truck. Could you bring your four-wheeler to pull the 502 out. He's got mud and water up to his hood grill."

"I'll be there in five minutes," Nick confirmed.

"Five minutes. Right. 10–4."

Nick stuffed his stocking feet in his galoshes, grabbed a rain coat, and headed for the door. In five minutes flat he was at the scene of the accident. Sure enough, Clive Barnstall had been sipping the sauce and slid off the muddy road into a ditch that resembled a canal. Deputy Sykes had Clive propped against the squad car, reading him the riot act.

"I don't have to tell you what Patricia is going to say when she sees you in this condition," Benny said, wagging a bony finger in Clive's face. "You're going to catch hell for a week, maybe two!"

"I had cattle on the road," Clive slurred. "I had to get the damned things back in before somebody hit 'em."

"Well, hell, Clive, you didn't have to celebrate the success of your mission with a whiskey bottle."

While Benny chewed on Clive's ears, Nick hooked up the chain and waded into the ditch to fasten the tow to Clive's bumper. "Benny, will you man the steering wheel while I pull the vehicle out."

"Man the wheel. Right," Benny repeated as he scampered into the ditch.

Leaving Clive draped over the hood of the black-and-white, Benny signaled he was ready by blinking the headlights. Engines groaned and the smell of rubber and waterlogged motors permeated the air. By the time Nick had the vehicle in the middle of the road, Clive was snoring on the hood of the police car.

"You want to haul Clive to the county sheriff's office?" Benny questioned.

"No, just write him up and take him home. The county sheriff's department probably has plenty of serious accidents on hazardous roads to keep them busy tonight." Nick smiled wryly. "Besides, Patricia Barnstall will work Clive over for the stupid stunt in ways no cop's lecture could touch."

"Couldn't touch. Right."

Nick shook his head in amusement as Benny nudged Clive awake and stuffed him in the squad car. One of these days, when Benny didn't take his duties so ridiculously seriously, Nick was going to resign the force and farm full time. But young Benny Sykes still had a few things to learn before Nick, in good conscience, turned him loose on Vamoose.

When Benny drove off, Nick parked Clive's truck in front of the pasture gate. With the situation in hand, Nick aimed himself toward home, cursing the steady rain that was turning Vamoose into a swamp.

Amanda awakened to the sound of pigs squealing, chickens squawking, and a duck making enough racket to raise the dead *and* the exhausted. Even Pete the three-legged dog was barking his head off. Pete had not assumed his duties as watch dog since he changed his address, but he was definitely putting up a fuss tonight. Amanda swung her legs over the edge of the bed and stumbled off to investigate. She switched on the kitchen light and crammed her feet into her galoshes. With broom in hand, she stormed out the back door. Her first thought was that coyotes had wandered near the chicken coop, alarming the occupants—ones that would probably refuse to lay eggs for another week.

It was still raining steadily when Amanda stepped off the porch in her flimsy nightshirt. Her critters were still squawking and squealing. Pete, however was now silent, and where he was was anybody's guess. The dog didn't hobble up to greet her the way he usually did.

Amanda shivered as the rain soaked through her

clothes and clung to her skin, but she was on an unswerving crusade to save her critters from coyote attack. Nobody messed with her chickens and that was all there was to it. She had too much invested in those feathered freaks that had been on strike since she toted them home. If hungry coyotes or packs of stray dogs . . .

Pete! Amanda cursed the thought of Pete turning on the hens. Maybe she had an egg-sucking dog on her hands. Maybe that was the reason there were never any eggs in those Cole-Hahn shoe box nests.

Amanda poked her head into the henhouse, but there were no unwanted intruders. The hens were still clucking in their nests, all present and counted for. It came as a relief that Pete was not the guilty party.

Since the henhouse wasn't under siege, Amanda slogged toward the hog pen to see the shadowed, grunting forms huddled in the corner of their shed. Whatever had alarmed the animals must have trotted off.

"Pete!" Amanda called and then whistled. Nothing. The dog was not to be found.

Just as she rounded the corner of the barn, an unidentified object collided with her skull. Reflexively, Amanda swung her broom at her attacker, but pain escalated until it exploded in her mind. Amanda folded at the knees, dropped her broom, and pitched forward in the grass. The sound of dripping rain vanished into complete and utter silence . . .

Nick took an impulsive turn into Hazard's driveway on his way back from pulling Clive out of the ditch. Although it was after eleven o'clock, he wanted to know what the call from Mother was all about. A curious frown plowed his brow when his headlights swept across the barn. Nick swore he could see a shadow dart-ing around the corner into inky darkness. He cast a worried glance toward the house and drove up to the barn. When he noticed the prone form on the ground, he slammed on the brakes.

"Damn it to hell!" Nick bounded out of his truck and rushed forward to find Hazard—in her wet nightie—sprawled beside her broom. It was obvious the little witch must have met with trouble during her midnight ride.

Grabbing Hazard by the shoulders, he turned her limp body into the crook of his arms to examine her for wounds. There was no blood—thank God—only the outline of a very voluptuous chest that was easily discernible in the clinging nightshirt.

Nick scooped Hazard up and carried her to his truck. Once he had propped her inside, he headed for the house. Several curses later, Nick toted Hazard through the back door and stretched her out on the kitchen floor. Within seconds he had located the knot on her head. The flesh was bruised by the blow she had sustained, but the wound wasn't severe enough to require stitches. Whoever had whacked Hazard upside the head must not have known he was dealing with a rock-hard skull. This was one witch whose head was a pretty tough nut to crack.

Nick bounded up to fetch a towel and dry clothes. He considered calling Deputy Sykes to track down the mysterious shadow that flitted away, but Nick doubted Benny had yet returned from delivering Clive Barnstall home.

Nick's foremost concern was Hazard's condition. He wanted her dry and conscious. Kneeling back down, Nick peeled away the wet shirt.

Within a few minutes Nick had dried Hazard's skin

and maneuvered her into a T-shirt and sweatpants. He had just tugged the hem of her shirt into place when her head rolled sideways and she groaned aloud.

"Hazard?"

Amanda heard her name echoing through a fuzzy tunnel. Her head was pounding in rhythm with her pulse. She trembled involuntarily and brought up a shaky hand to examine the bump on her head. When she pried open one eye, she saw a blurry face looming over her. Amanda instinctively recoiled.

"Hey, Hazard. It's only me. Are you okay?"

"Is that you, Thorn?" she mumbled in question.

"Hell, yes. Who were you expecting? Your fairy godmother?"

The familiar baritone voice finally registered in her groggy senses. Amanda collapsed back to the floor. "What are you doing here?"

"Never mind about me. Why were you out riding on your broom at this time of night?" Nick demanded.

"Cute, Thorn," Amanda muttered, casting him the evil eye. "I was chasing coyotes, or so I thought. I think I stumbled onto the two-legged variety. . . . Where's Pete?"

"More than likely he's recovering from a similar headache or a dose of Mace," Nick speculated as he watched Hazard prop herself up on a wobbly elbow. "If I hadn't come along when I did, you may have suffered more than a headache, Hazard."

Gradually, Amanda became oriented to her surroundings. When she realized she was not wearing her wet nightclothes, she frowned accusingly at Thorn. "How many women do you have to undress in the course of one night before you're satisfied, you pervert!"

Nick had expected that kind of reaction. "This was all in the line of duty," he told her calmly. "I was also checking you for wounds. It was nothing personal."

Nothing personal? Ouch, that hurt! Damn the man. To hear Thorn talk, he could have been dressing a turkey. His nonchalance was worse than his perversion. It was glaringly apparent that Thorn had taken up with Ms. Bosom and that his . . . relationship . . . with Amanda was ancient history. That knowledge pained her more than her headache. She still harbored tender feelings toward Tom Selleck's look alike, though she denied those emotions in saner moments.

"I'm placing you under protective custody, Hazard," Nick said in no uncertain terms. "You're coming home with me."

"Over my dead body, Thorn!"

Nick glared at her. "Your dead body is exactly what I'm concerned about. And this subject is not open for discussion. As Vamoose's symbol of law and order, I am *telling* you what you are going to do. If you fail to comply, I will dream up some charges and have you hauled off to jail for a few days." His obsidian eyes glittered dangerously when Hazard opened her mouth to protest. "Don't argue with me, Hazard. I am the man who can ensure threats become promises and you damned well know it. If you get yourself killed, I'll have another case to investigate."

"You haven't busted your butt in search of clues about *this* case," she said snidely. "Of course, I know how pressed for time you must be with Ms. Bosom chasing you around with her casseroles. Her delicious dishes are undoubtedly laced with aphrodisiacs and you—"

"Knock it off, Hazard. There are more important things going on around here besides Ms. Bosom—I mean Jenny's culinary pursuits. Otherwise, why would I have been hanging around with you? You can't cook."

Amanda found herself hoisted to her feet. The twenty-year-old faded yellow linoleum spun furiously beneath her feet and she latched onto Thorn for support.

"Not now, Hazard. Save your amorous advances until we get to my house," he teased her.

"Only in your dreams, Thorn," she hissed.

"You've certainly got that right," Nick said under his breath as he half carried Hazard out the back door.

Much to Nick's dismay, Amanda refused to be up-rooted from her home until she knew the physical condition and whereabouts of her beloved dog. Swearing colorfully, Nick stashed Amanda in his truck, grabbed a flashlight, and tromped toward the barn. Just as Nick suspected, Pete was wandering around between the barn and pigsty, dazed and disoriented—the victim of a dose of Mace.

"Is he still alive?" Amanda demanded the second Thorn slid into the truck.

"Pete will be fine when the Mace wears off," Nick diagnosed.

In silence, they drove to Thorn's farm. Amanda wrestled with the exasperating realization that she had allowed Elmer's killer to escape her again. She had the intuitive feeling that if she could ever get her hands on the will and publicize it, her stalker's plans would be foiled and he, she, and/or they would finally leave her alone.

"I wish I could locate that cursed will," Amanda grumbled two miles later. "I'm sure it holds a valuable clue. Where could Elmer have stashed that confounded document?"

"Obviously Elmer hid it some place that no one else would think to look." Nick veered around the corner and shifted to four-wheel drive to maintain traction on the slippery road. "Remember where he stashed his research notes? How many people would have gone snooping under the foundation?"

Despite her headache, Amanda brightened. "Maybe the will is stuffed in the jars with the research data. I didn't examine them closely."

"Maybe, but don't even think of starting that project tonight. It's midnight and I have to be on patrol at eight in the morning."

"I didn't ask for your help, Thorn."

He tossed her a quick glance and turned in the driveway. "No, you didn't and you haven't since I doubted your suspicions in your first murder case. If you would quit being so muleheaded, and so gung-ho, maybe you wouldn't find yourself the victim of disaster every few days."

Amanda climbed out of the truck and hurried out of the rain. She headed directly toward the kitchen to retrieve her crate and carted it to the spare bedroom that Nick had converted into a den. Amanda plunked down on the carpet, amid shelves of stereo equipment and video tapes. Without ado, she began unscrewing jar lids.

Nick propped his shoulder against the doorjamb and watched Hazard sort through the junk mail envelopes. "If you do decide to come to bed tonight, will you be sleeping with me or using the hideaway in the living room?"

As if he didn't know. Since Nick had been suffering

a drought of affection, he didn't really expect a flood of emotion from Hazard just because it was raining outside. Her amorous moods had never been affected by weather conditions.

Okay, Hazard, here's your chance to get back into Thorn's good graces, and he into yours, Amanda mused as she thumbed through Elmer's notes. She could use a sturdy shoulder to lean on after her most recent bout with disaster. . . .

"Well? Make up your mind. I'm tired."

"I'm sure you are." Amanda gritted her teeth when the vision of Thorn and Ms. Bosom exploded in her aching head. No way was Amanda going to climb into a bed where Thorn and his old flame had been stoking new fires!

"I'll take the hideaway bed. I'm sure your bed has seen enough action to qualify for the Purple Heart."

Nick erupted like a geyser. "Damn it, Hazard, all we did was share a goddamn casserole! You're letting your hang-ups from the divorce wars warp your thinking. I'm getting sick and tired of being judged by the standards your ex-husband established. I AM NOT HIM!"

"God, Thorn, you don't have to yell." Amanda groaned and grabbed her sensitive skull. "I already have a splitting headache."

"Ah yes, the standard excuse."

Nick pushed away from the door and stamped down the hall. In no time flat, he had unfolded the bed and collected sheets. This was the end of the line, Nick decided. It was over, finished. No more, Mr. Nice Guy. No more pampering Hazard and her screwy hang-ups. If she had no faith in him then to hell with her!

Without a sideways glance, Nick retraced his steps

down the hall and veered into his bedroom. He had wasted enough time on a woman who didn't have enough respect to be seen in public with him as an "item." He was fed up with Hazard's cautious reserve in their affair. Yes, damn it, an *affair!* She couldn't even say the word! She was using his body for her own purposes on those rare occasions when she finally admitted she wanted a man. Well, by damn, no more! Ms. Bosom had practically run him down to get his attention. Maybe it was time Nick did a few of the things Hazard *accused* him of doing!

Nick flounced in bed and cursed into his pillow. He really hated Hazard. She drove him nuts. . . .

"Thorn?"

Nick rolled onto his back and stared at the shadowed silhouette beside the door. "Now what in the hell do you want?"

"Do you mind if I raid your icebox? I'm hungry."

So was Nick, but there was nothing in the refrigerator that could appease his appetite.

"No, go ahead and take whatever you want." For spite, he added, "Jenny's chicken casserole was delicious. Try it—Argh!"

Nick wasn't sure what hit him. He rather suspected it was Hazard's boot. Lucky for him that she wasn't carrying an ax.

Chapter Eleven

Amanda moaned when something nudged her—none too gently.

"Get up, Hazard. The price for sleeping on my hide-away bed is your help."

"My help with what?"

"It's been raining all night and the creek is probably flooded. I've got to check my cattle and count the calves. If I meet with trouble, I want an extra hand on board. Hurry up, Hazard. I have to be on patrol at eight."

"What time is it?"

"Six o'clock."

Amanda groaned tiredly and pushed into an upright position. She had stayed up until three o'clock, opening canning jars and rifling through Elmer's notes—and all for nothing. She had learned more than she wanted to know about cross-pollinating wheat seeds. Ordinarily, she was a morning person who bounded up and readily accepted the challenges of the day. However, she could have done with a little more sleep today. Thorn was punishing her for choosing the hide-a-bed over him. She should have expected as much.

When Nick tried to play tug-of-war with her sheet, Amanda twisted it around her like a toga and stood up. The world shifted on its axis and Amanda sat down more quickly than she had intended.

"You aren't calling in sick, Hazard," Nick insisted. "I'll get you a cup of coffee, but I want you up and dressed when I come back. You got that?"

Amanda aimed and fired her imaginary howitzer in Thorn's back when he lurched around and stomped toward the kitchen. The man didn't have a sympathetic bone in his magnificent body. She was still nursing a tender knot on her head, but did he care? Hell no.

Nick pulled up short when he returned to the living room to see Hazard wearing nothing more than bikini panties and T-shirt that barely descended past her hips. The coffee cups shook in his hands while he restrained himself from throwing her down on the bed and forgetting the cattle and the 8 a.m. check-in. Damn, that was one exceptionally fine set of legs. Too bad there was such a sassy mouth attached to them.

This woman was hard on a man's blood pressure. She was also hard on his . . . well, Hazard wasn't the only one with a headache. The pressure in his lower extremities was sure to cause a blood vessel to burst in his brain—or somewhere else.

"Here, Hazard." Nick tore his gaze away from visual temptation and extended his arm. When Amanda retrieved her cup, Nick pivoted to sip his coffee and examine the cobwebs in the corner. "You want some aspirin?"

Amanda set her cup aside to wriggle into her jeans.

"You know perfectly well that aspirin makes me nauseous, Thorn."

"Do you want some Alka-Seltzer?" he asked gruffly. "It will only take me a second to find it. Somebody arranged my cabinets in alphabetical order when I wasn't looking."

"Well, it wasn't Ms. Bosom. She never learned the alphabet."

Amanda picked up her cup, noting that Thorn had doctored her coffee just the way she liked it—heavy on the cream and sugar. After two welcomed sips, Amanda glanced up to see Thorn holding a packet of Alka-Seltzer tablets and a glass of water.

"Thanks, Thorn."

"You're welcome, Hazard."

Nick polished off his coffee and propelled himself toward the front door. Amanda followed after him, studying his lithe stride and his broad shoulders. She wished Ms. Bosom hadn't entered the picture to bombard her with self-doubt and old torments. Thorn was right. He wasn't her ex-husband and she shouldn't judge every other man by Jason's contemptible standards.

"You drive, Hazard. I'll get the gates," Nick volunteered as he slopped toward the corral.

Amanda put the truck in four-wheel drive and eased off the clutch. Mud flew up beside her as she plowed through the corral. By the time Thorn opened and shut the gate that led from the corral to the pasture, he looked as if he had contracted brown measles. She knew Thorn thought she had intentionally splattered him when she fishtailed through the gate because he flashed her one of his glares.

"Thanks, Hazard. I suppose you thought I deserved that," Nick grumbled as he sprawled on the seat.

"It was an accident."

"Yeah, right."

"It was!"

"Then you drive like you conduct an unofficial murder investigation—hap*hazard*ly. And while we're on the subject, did you locate Elmer's will last night?"

"No, but if there is anything you want to know about cross-germinating wheat to breed out susceptibility to disease, just ask."

"Elmer may not have gotten along with his family and neighbors, but he was a whiz in agronomy," Nick said. "It was his hobby and his obsession for over fifty years."

"I wonder who inherits the data from his lengthy research?"

"We may never know." Nick gestured west. "Cut across the pasture to the creek. Let's get these cattle counted so I can get some work done today."

Three minutes later, Amanda applied the brakes and listened to Thorn curse the air blue. One of the young calves had become stranded on a knoll of land that was now surrounded by water. The mother cow was standing on the opposite shore, bawling her head off. The calf bawled back, refusing to swim through the swift current.

Amanda assessed the situation carefully. It was obvious that the cow couldn't ford the swollen creek, lift the frightened calf onto her back, and swim to safer ground. It was also apparent that the red calf could not pole-vault the creek. The thought gave Amanda an inspiration. She put the truck in reverse and whipped around.

Nick stared incredulously at her. "What in the hell are you doing?"

"I'm going to gather lumber to build a bridge. I saw your stack of wooden fence posts. I also noticed some long planks lying beside them."

Nick muttered at Hazard's infuriating habit of taking command of every situation she encountered. "This is *my* farm and *my* rescue mission."

Amanda stopped beside the stack of posts and stared at him. "Do you have a better idea, Thorn? We can't jump the creek. And even if we did, we couldn't carry the calf through floodwater without the risk of drowning."

Nick jerked open the door. "We'll get the damned planks and do it your way."

Amanda smiled to herself while Thorn sulked. He hated it when she devised a brilliant solution before he could think of one himself. Fragile male ego and masculine chauvanism at their worst. Even after all these years of emphasis on equality of the sexes, men still had the ridiculous notion that women could not entertain ideas in their female brains unless men had dreamed them up first.

Amanda picked up her end of the sixteen-foot plank and maneuvered it into the bed of the truck. When the second and third planks had been loaded, Nick climbed into the driver's seat. Amanda presumed the gesture to be a subtle statement—one of those male ego things again.

After the planks were positioned above the gurgling creek, Nick tested the improvised bridge. Although the planks were barely long enough to span the frothy water, they were sturdy enough not to be swept downstream. Nick grabbed his lariat from behind the pickup seat and paced across the bridge with Amanda trotting on his heels. Of course, the wide-eyed calf was not the least bit enthused about sharing his island with humans. The calf darted hither and yon while Nick swung the loop and waited for the opportunity to strike.

Amanda felt that funny little tingle of awe trickle through her when Thorn roped the calf on the first attempt and then dashed forward to wrestle the squirming animal to the ground. Thorn rammed his knee into the calf's ribs, holding the struggling animal in place.

The calf bawled and squalled as if it had been skinned alive when Thorn dallied the rope around its legs. The mother cow trotted back and forth along the far edge of the creek, bellowing in protest and making such a commotion that the entire herd came romping over to investigate.

"You carry the head end, Hazard," Nick commanded. "And take it slow and easy across the planks. They're slippery as hell. If we fall off, the calf will drown for sure."

Amanda grabbed her designated end of the calf. On the count of three, they lifted the wriggling animal and carried it toward the makeshift bridge. Amanda yelped in alarm when the calf writhed and bucked when they were halfway across the creek. Her foot slipped and Nick cursed mightily. In the nick of time, Amanda recovered her balance and backed toward solid ground. The mother cow, followed by the rest of the herd, trotted forward.

If Amanda had expected appreciation and gratitude from the twelve-hundred-pound cow, she was doomed to disappointment. The cow wanted her calf back *now,* and she wanted Nick and Amanda as far away from her precious baby as they could get—*immediately!*

Amanda was knocked sideways, dropping the calf much sooner than she had planned. If Thorn had not stepped in front of her like a shield, Amanda swore she would have had four hooves stuffed down her throat. Mother would have been beside herself if Amanda had her teeth knocked out after the fortune she had spent on orthodontic braces for her daughter.

While Nick was flapping his arms and yelling obscenities at the mother cow, Amanda scrambled over to pull the loop off the calf's neck and untangle its legs. The calf bounded up and raced to its mother to compensate for the meal it had missed the previous night and early that morning.

Amanda stood back to watch Thorn wander among the herd of Salers cows and calves. One minute he was cursing them to beat the band and the next second he was smiling in satisfaction. It reminded Amanda of their stormy . . . relationship. There were times when Amanda wanted to knock the stuffing out of Thorn. And there were times when she wanted to squeeze the stuffing out of him. Now was one of those times when she wanted to squeeze that sinewy hunk of man and kiss his lips clean off him.

Watching him interact in his chosen environment always got to her. Each time she accompanied him on his farming chores, she felt as if she had been transported back to the Old West, seeing life as it had been in another time. She could easily envision Thorn, with holsters strapped to his lean hips and a Stetson setting on his raven head at a jaunty angle, swaggering through some dusty cowtown at the end of a trail drive. . . .

"Hazard? Are you all right?"

Amanda made a quick leap through time and ambled over to fling her arms around Thorn's broad shoulders. He was still staring warily at her when she pushed up on tiptoe and planted a steamy kiss to those deliciously sensual lips. And as usual, chemical and biological reactions sizzled through Amanda like firecrackers. Damn, the man could really get to her when she let her guard down.

Thorn clutched Amanda against him and feasted on her lips like a starving man. Apparently, he was feeling the effects of biological attraction himself, if the bulge in his jeans was any indication.

"Hazard, I swear you are the most exasperating woman ever to draw breath!" Nick wheezed when he finally surfaced for air. "Where were you last night while I was flat on my back, afraid to turn over for fear of breaking something off?"

Mother would have yowled if she could have heard *that* remark!

Amanda pivoted around and sashayed over to retrieve the lariat, emulating Ms. Bosoms drumroll walk.

"You're really asking for it, Hazard." Nick's eyes followed every seductive movement. When Hazard bent over to pluck up the lariat, he groaned aloud. The woman had a fabulous fanny and she knew it. Nick had made the mistake of telling her so on a few occasions.

"I thought you had to be at work at eight o'clock."

"I'm thinking of calling in ... horny." His black brows waggled and he grinned in cavalier devilment.

Amanda grinned back. "You are absolutely impossible, Thorn."

"No, I'm easy," he contradicted. "Or at least I could be with a little cooperation from a certain accountant who fancies herself a detective. My problem is keeping you alive long enough to get any satisfaction."

"There's always Ms. Bosom," Amanda flung back before she climbed into the truck.

Nick hopped in beside her. "And you have Romeo the rodeo clown at your beck and call."

"He does lay . . . a good roof."

"And Ms. Bosom can appease a starving man . . . with chicken casserole." Nick tossed her a discreet glance as he drove toward the corral. "So where do we go from here, Hazard? Back to pistols at twenty paces?"

"No, back to the house for another cup of coffee."

"I'm serious, Hazard."

"About *what*, Thorn?"

Nick recalled the vow he had made the previous night. He had been ready to throw in the towel and call it quits. That was last night. It seemed he and the ducks woke up in a new world every day.

There was a long pause before Nick said, "About *you*. Hazard. About you . . ."

Amanda felt an odd satisfaction ripple through her. Now don't blow it, Hazard. Tell the man you're still crazy about him, even if he does aggravate the hell out of you sometimes.

Amanda inhaled a deep breath and released it out slowly. "I'm serious about you, too, Thorn."

"Serious enough to work up the nerve to invite me to dinner at Uncle Dean's so Mother and the rest of the Hazard tribe can get a look at me and decide if I'm good enough for you?"

Amanda gaped at him. "How did you know about that?"

"Mother called last night to confirm my reservation at the barbecue."

"She had no right. And believe me, Thorn, you don't want to go. You'll wind up as the main course."

"I'll wear my bulletproof vest."

"You'll need a full coat of armor," Amanda warned.

"I'll take my chances, Hazard." Nick gestured toward the corral. "It's your turn to get the gates."

"That's what I like about you, Thorn. You believe in equality." Amanda opened the door and climbed down. She knew she was about to be splattered with mud.

Sure enough, she was.

While Nick took a quick shower and dressed in his uniform, Amanda sipped coffee and thumbed through Elmer's junk mail envelopes. She was still puzzled about the location of Elmer's last will and testament, but she was sure that her stalker did not have the document in his possession. Amanda could think of no other reason why she would become the target of attack, if not because of that will. No other explanation made any sense . . . unless . . .

"Are you ready to go?" Nick strode from the kitchen with coffee cup in hand.

The inspiration that Amanda felt was about to gel in her mind skipped away like a breeze when Nick interrupted her thought process. "Let me put these notes away. Will you drop me at my house to change clothes?"

"Only if I get to watch."

"You're on duty, Thorn."

"I'm also on a slow burn."

"You just had a cold shower."

"It didn't help."

Amanda glanced below his belt buckle and smiled impishly. He was right. It didn't help.

His gaze followed hers. "Told you so, Hazard."

"I think you need to see a doctor."

"I already know how to cure what ails me." Nick escorted her toward the door. "You name the time and the place and I'll be miraculously healed. But I guarantee it will take longer than one minute, despite your snide remarks to the contrary."

"Get over it, Thorn. I was only kidding around. We both know you're good for a full two minutes."

"Just for that, I'm going to keep you in bed for a full twenty-four hours, the first chance I get."

Amanda tossed him a provocative smile. "I was hoping you would say something like that."

Nick pulled up short. "That's it, Hazard. I'm not going to work."

Amanda tugged him out of the way and shut the door behind him. "Save it for tonight, provided you're still in the mood after you meet my family."

Nick drove Amanda home in the squad car, envisioning a romantic evening of sensual delights and long-awaited fantasies come true. He checked her house for signs of intrusion before he deemed the place safe. While Amanda showered, Nick volunteered to feed her critters. Pete the three-legged dog had recovered from his bout with Mace, but the chickens still hadn't produced any eggs. When Nick returned to the house, the tomcat was switching channels on the remote control.

"You have a strange cat on your hands, Hazard," Nick declared.

"He's all male. And when I let him out of the house, he goes tomcatting around the countryside. He exhibits all those peculiar tendencies common among males." Amanda tucked the hem of her blouse in her skirt and stuffed her feet in her navy blue pumps. "Will you drop me by the beauty shop. I need to see Velma."

Nick groaned. "Is this another fact-finding mission?"

Amanda graced him with her most innocent smile. "Of course not, silly man. I just wanted to have my hair styled in case you invite me to lunch." She batted her eyelashes at him for good measure.

"Cut the crap, Hazard. You aren't fooling me for a minute," Nick grumbled.

"So you won't take me to lunch?"

"Of course I'm taking you to lunch. You're under protective custody, remember? You aren't going anywhere alone until this case is solved. And if you *accidentally* dig up any information at Velma's boutique, I intend to be there when you follow it up. Understood?"

Amanda saluted him like any self-respecting private greeting a general. "Whatever you say, sir."

Nick grabbed her arm and propelled her out the door. "Don't be so agreeable. It makes me suspicious."

Five minutes later, Nick dropped Amanda at the Beauty Boutique and drove off to monitor the teenage drivers who had a habit of showing off a tad bit before they arrived at school. Amanda entered the shop to find Velma sweeping a pile of hair into the dustpan. Damn, it looked as if someone had been scalped!

"Hi, hon." Chomp, crack. "I don't remember your calling for an appointment."

"I didn't. I just came by on the chance you could squeeze me in."

Velma indicated The Chair. "You're in luck. I had a perm cancellation this morning so I can give you one."

"I just wanted—"

"Sit yourself down, hon, and I'll fix you right up."

"But I—"

It was too late. The Amazon beautician had decided Amanda needed a perm and a perm she would have. While Velma washed and rolled her hair, Amanda glanced around the shop. It looked as if Velma had decided to remodel after the water damage left by the storm. She had selected the southwest decor and had placed artificial cacti at strategic points around the shop. Paintings of rugged mountains, howling coyotes, and half-naked Indians cluttered the walls. Velma's interior decorating talents left a lot to be desired.

"I hear you had lunch with Randel Thompson and then with Nick Thorn last week." Snap, pop. "Playing the field, are you?"

Amanda grimaced when Velma wrapped her hair so tightly around the rollers that it raised her eyebrows two inches. "They invited me to lunch and I accepted."

"If you ask me, Nick ought to be your pick." Velma grabbed another roller and twisted several more strands of blonde hair. "Randel isn't as dependable as Nick." She blew a bubble, sucked it back into her mouth, and grabbed another clump of hair in her fist. "Randel used to be as wild as a March hare. He even got hauled to jail in Texas during a rodeo. So the story goes, Randel and some of his friends were celebrating their winnings and ended up in a bar fight with the local yokels who weren't too happy when Randel started hitting on their girlfriends." Snap, crack, pop. "One of the drunken cowboys stole a portrait of John Wayne off the wall after the fight was over. The proprietor brought charges against the whole bunch of them."

"Does Randel have any other crimes to his credit?" Amanda questioned.

Crack, chomp. "Not that I know of. He'd been straight since he came back from Texas."

"Did Randel once live in Vamoose?"

"A long time ago." Velma plucked up the setting lotion and dribbled it over the rollers until it was running down the sides of Amanda's face. "His family left when Randel was just a baby. The Thompsons sold their property to the Jollys and moved to Texas."

So Randel did indeed have old ties to Vamoose. He was not here by coincidence, Amanda mused.

Velma dabbed at the drips on Amanda's chin and wrapped the plastic cap around her head like a turban. "And speaking of the Jollys." Snap, crackle, pop. "I finally remembered that tidbit of gossip that escaped me the last time you were here. Do you know Bertie Ann Jolly?"

"I've met her."

"Well, talk about wild! In her day, Bertie Ann was a holy terror. She was a lot younger than Eula Bell and Odie Mae and she was a handful and a half! Bertie Ann made Randel Thompson look as tame as the tooth fairy."

"Bertie Anne?" Amanda blinked, bewildered. "Are we talking about the same Bertie Anne with hair like steel wool, wire-rimmed glasses, and no waistline?"

"One and the same." Crack, snap. "I hear she was really a looker in her prime. Her family was serious-minded, but Bertie Ann was a rebel deluxe." Velma finished cleaning the shop while Amanda waited for the perming lotion to set. "The Mopopes had it all arranged for her to marry Elmer, even though she was twelve years younger than he was. At first she balked at being told what to do. Then she thumbed her nose at propriety and just moved in with Elmer. It was her way of getting back at her family, and her parents nearly had heart attacks over it. Of course, Elmer didn't complain since he had been single for so many years. You know how men are. They don't usually turn down that sort of thing."

Amanda nodded in understanding. *That sort of thing* always got the best of most men.

"Of course, the older generation of Jollys threw a royal stink, too." Chomp, chomp. "Elmer decided to do the right thing and marry her to make it respectablelike."

Visions of boxes crammed with silverware and crates of China popped into Amanda's mind. She had the feeling she knew why those boxes had been stored under Elmer's house, and why the wedding rings were stashed with the "Dear Elmer" letter.

"The wedding was supposed to take place in the summer," Velma continued as she swept the floor. "But Leroy returned the war hero and wham. Bertie Ann and Leroy were rumored to be fooling around together. The two families tried to keep it hush-hush, and before the rest of Vamoose knew what was going on, Leroy and Bertie Ann got hitched and moved to the city. They didn't come around much after that. Melvin, Elmer, and Claud never mentioned their younger brother and neither did their parents. Odie Mae and Eula Bell tried to get Elmer and Bertie Ann back together years later when Leroy passed on. But Elmer wouldn't have a thing to do with her."

Amanda could imagine how well that suggestion

went over with Elmer. No wonder he had turned bitter and resentful. Bertie Ann had walked out on him to marry his youngest brother. Elmer had already bought all the proper paraphernalia to give the bride he couldn't keep so he stuffed them, and the bitter memories, under his house. Bertie Ann's conscience must have gotten the better of her if she felt obliged to write to Elmer to tell him she had fallen for another man. But Lord, did it have to be Elmer's brother?

Velma shepherded Amanda toward the sink to rinse out the setting lotion. Only when Amanda's neck was stretched out like a giraffe's was Velma ready to hose her down. After scrubbing Amanda's scalp off, Velma propped her up and dribbled the neutralizer all over her head.

"You're really going to catch the men's eyes with this new perm," Velma said with perfect assurance.

Amanda said nothing. Neutralizing lotion was dripping on the corners of her mouth.

"How do you like my new decor?" Crackle, snap.

Amanda had sincerely hoped Velma wouldn't ask. "I always did like an occasional change," she said after wiping the lotion from her mouth.

"I thought I would give the shop a new facial after the storm hammered the roof and water leaked down the walls. A fresh coat of paint and some cacti do wonders, don't they?" Pop, crack.

Did they ever!

"After all the rain we've had, pictures of a drier climate are a welcome relief—"

The last word flew off Amanda's lips when Velma grabbed her head and plunged it back into the sink. A few minutes later, the solution had been rinsed away and Velma was fluffing the new perm in satisfaction.

"This is really *you*, hon. You're going to love this." Velma spun The Chair toward the mirror.

Amanda didn't faint, but she would have liked to. With a phoney smile and empty words of appreciation, Amanda climbed out of The Chair to pay Velma for the "damages."

When Amanda staggered outside, very nearly overcome by the shock of seeing what had happened to her hair, Thorn was waiting in the squad car. Velma poked her bouffant head between the edges of the curtains, grinned, and gave Amanda two thumbs up.

Nick stared at her in disbelief. "Good Lord, Hazard! You look like Medusa with snakes coiling out of your head!"

"That is one way of describing it," she said sickly. "Velma swore I would catch your eye with this new do."

"The perm definitely does that." Nick's lips twitched as he backed around the water puddles in the driveway. "I only hope that the information you acquired was worth the price you paid. So, Curly, do you want to pick up the other two stooges, or what?"

Amanda flashed him a glance that indicated that she didn't find the comment the least bit amusing. "Just take me out to see Opal Mae and Eula Bell Jolly."

"They're on your list of suspects?" Nick crowed. "Get real, Hazard. Those two little old ladies are perfectly harmless."

"You might be surprised what a couple of senior citizens can do. On one of the episodes of *Magnum P.I.*—"

Nick groaned in interruption. "Spare me the details. I don't want to know."

"Okay, Thorn, but don't come whining to me when I crack this case wide open and you're still compiling your list of probable suspects."

"You crack this case and I'm yours for the entire weekend," he said, onyx eyes glittering and pearly white teeth sparkling.

"Can you get Ms. Bosom to cater all our meals for the weekend?"

"If you can get Romeo the rodeo clown to feed the livestock."

"*If* he isn't locked in jail."

Nick sobered instantly. "Do you think Randel could be the culprit?"

"I'm not prepared to rule out anybody just yet. I think the past is closely tied to the present in Elmer's case."

"Well, you can scratch Clive Barnstall off your list. I found him drunk in a ditch last night while you were being terrorized and hammered over the head."

"Or it could be that Clive was a decoy to keep you occupied while I was being konked on the head and dragged off to become the victim of another convenient accident," she postulated.

Nick considered the possibility. "We'll see what leads develop after we talk to Eula Bell and Odie Mae."

"And then you can take me to lunch. I'll buy," she generously offered.

"Call me old-fashioned, but I still believe in picking up the ticket when I take a lady to dinner."

"Okay, Old-Fashioned, but I'm not a lady. Just ask Mother."

Nick grinned. "That's one of the things I like about you, Hazard."

"What? The fact that I'm not a lady?"

"No, I like the fact that you have finally come to think enough of me to let me meet Mother."

"I promise you, Thorn, I am not doing you any favors. You think the Spanish Inquisition was a nightmare? Just wait until Mother gets ahold of you."

"Forget Mother. I'm anxious for *you* to get hold of *me*."

Amanda couldn't wait to get her hands on Thorn, either. Unfortunately, with this perplexing case hanging over her curly head, Amanda already had her hands full, just trying to stay one step ahead of her mysterious stalker!

Chapter Twelve

Amanda sensed immediate hostility when Melvin Jolly opened his front door. If Thorn had not been with her, Amanda wondered if she would have been tarred, feathered, and chased off the farm.

"I'm not impressed with the company you're keeping these days, Officer Thorn," Melvin muttered. "I suppose *that woman* has sweet-talked you into siding with her."

Nick mustered a polite smile for the grouchy Jolly. "May we come in, Melvin? I have a few questions I'd like to ask you and Odie Mae."

"Is *that woman* coming in, too?" Melvin's gray brows formed a single line of his wrinkled forehead when he glared at Amanda.

"I'll have you know—"

Nick cut Hazard off before she antagonized Melvin even more. "I am conducting an investigation concerning Elmer's death and I request your cooperation, Melvin. Since Ms. Hazard is the administrator of the estate, she has a few questions to pose, too."

It was with visible restraint that Melvin stepped aside to admit the unwelcomed guests. Odie Mae wrung her hands nervously while Amanda and Nick sank down on the faded couch. Her gaze darted from Amanda to the doorway that opened into the dining room. Amanda had the feeling someone was just around the corner and she guessed it was Odie Mae's twin sister.

"Eula Bell, you may as well come in here. It will save us all some time," Amanda stated.

Eula Bell stepped tentatively around the corner and scuttled over to her sister. They both stood there wringing their hands in synchronized rhythm.

"I don't know why you see the need to investigate," Melvin grumped. He cast Amanda another mutinous glower. "*That woman* is taking all the money and property Elmer amassed. What else does she want? What Claud and I have left, too?"

Amanda gritted her teeth. She had very little regard for this old buzzard—the same regard, she imagined, that he had for her.

"Ms. Hazard's character is not in question here, Melvin," Nick said. "The near accidents she has survived are the cause of concern."

Amanda noticed that no one in the room seemed surprised and/or concerned that she had been stumbling over pitfalls lately. Very interesting, she thought.

"I have come upon some intriguing pieces of information," Amanda began. "One of them pertains to a land sale that transferred the deed from Therrel Thompson to the Jollys. The price of the property seemed unusually high, considering the year of purchase."

Odie Mae and Eula Bell sank into two chairs and glanced at each other. It was as if the twins were staring into mirrors. Their expressions were exactly the same—worried.

"From what I gather, the Thompsons moved to Texas immediately after selling their property."

"So?" Melvin's defiant gaze zeroed in on Amanda—again. "And what is that supposed to prove?"

Amanda made a stab in the dark, based on the tidbits of gossip she had gleaned from Velma and facts from the courthouse. "I think the sale of that land was a result of blackmail. I also think Bertie Ann was fooling around with Therrel Thompson, and the Jollys and Mopopes decided to force Thompson into selling out and leaving town. You promised to keep the affair quiet if Therrel and his wife packed up and left. Therrel was married to the daughter of an influential citizen in the community—Mayor Cyrus Barnstall. No one wanted to face the scandal. The Mopopes certainly didn't want their youngest daughter involved. They were having enough trouble controlling her without her affair with a thirty-eight-year-old married man, who had just become a grandfather, hitting the headlines."

Eula Bell and Odie Mae simultaneously sank a little deep in their chairs. Their faces turned the color of baby powder.

Bull's eye, thought Amanda. She had scored a direct hit and she knew it.

"What has that ridiculous rumor got to do with anything?" Melvin challenged belligerently.

Amanda smiled. Melvin didn't fool her for a minute. *He* knew that *she* knew the supposed rumor was fact. "Old grudges, Mr. Jolly," she contended. "If I am not mistaken, and I do not think for one minute that I am, it was Elmer who purchased that particular piece of property from Therrel. Elmer had been hopelessly fascinated with Bertie Ann because she possessed the spark and spirit that he never felt he was permitted to display, being the eldest son of a serious-minded family. He wanted to protect her. And she was, after all, supposed to become his wife, by decree of the ruling patriarchs of both the Jolly and Mopope families."

Eula Bell and Odie Mae turned even more pale.

Bingo. Another assumption proved to be fact, thought Amanda.

Melvin surged forward in his chair like a guard dog, baring his false teeth. "What are you trying to do, woman?" he growled. "Blackmail the family into dropping our lawsuit against you after you publicize the fact that you—the local Jezebel—have inherited Elmer's fortune? That's why you've been stalling, isn't it? You wanted time to dig up some dirt so we wouldn't oppose you?"

Nick glanced curiously from Melvin to Hazard. How did Melvin know that Elmer had willed his fortune to Hazard? Or was that wild speculation? Nick decided to make his own stab in the dark.

"Did you and Elmer argue about his decision to leave his inheritance to Ms. Hazard?"

Melvin shut his mouth like a drawer and his pointed chin elevated to a stubborn angle.

Dead end, thought Amanda. Melvin wasn't going to incriminate himself. Amanda decided to turn her arsenal of weapons on Eula Bell and Odie Mae before they wrung their fingers off their hands.

"The two of you have always protected your younger sister to the best of your ability, haven't you? I'm sure you and your family were dismayed over her affair, or should I say *affairs?* Bertie Ann was very much the free spirit. She defied the family's strict traditions and she delighted in playing by her own rules. It must have been a shock to the Mopopes and Jollys when Bertie Ann, in another act of rebellion, set up housekeeping with Elmer after you forced one of her previous lovers out of town. But Elmer was prepared to forgive Bertie Ann almost anything. He had been bewitched and he wanted your spirited little sister any way he could get her. Love does that to a man sometimes, doesn't it?"

Another direct hit. Eula Bell and Odie Mae nearly swallowed their dentures. Melvin was chewing on his false teeth like a cow on its cud.

"And I'm sure you all suffered another devastating blow when the flighty and very fickle Bertie Ann took up with Leroy when he returned a war hero. Leroy was closer to Bertie Ann's age. And I imagine that after enduring war, Leroy was ready to live every moment of life to the fullest. He and Bertie Ann must have made a perfect match—wild, reckless, pleasure-seeking.

"It was bad enough that Bertie Ann took up with married men, but it was totally unforgiveable for her to carry on with the *brother* of the man both families had decided she should marry."

Good Lord, thought Nick. Where did Hazard dig up all this stuff? As if he didn't know. Velma Hertzog was a walking encyclopedia of hush-hush information. Hazard had shoveled up facts dating back to the turn of the century! Nick wouldn't have been surprised if Velma knew of every great-great grandmother who had fooled around with somebody's great-great grandfather. The fact that most families of Vamoose were related somehow or another left scads of skeletons dangling in every closet. Nick wondered what Hazard could dig up about *his* family if she put her mind to it. Lord, he didn't think he wanted to know all the sordid details!

Melvin's bony arm shot toward the door. "Get out," he snarled. "I will not have you tearing my family apart at the foundations!"

Funny that he should mention *foundations*, thought Amanda.

"You have no proof of any of your accusations," Melvin raged.

"Ah, but I do have proof, Mr. Jolly," Amanda contradicted. "I found a full set of china and silverware under Elmer's house. I also located the wedding rings Elmer intended to give Bertie Ann. The "Dear Elmer" letter that broke his heart and turned him into a bitter recluse was among the memoriabilia that survived the fire—a blaze intentionally ignited to dispose of all evidence."

A fleeting thought sailed through Amanda's brain, but she didn't have time to grab hold of it before Melvin's blaring voice demanded her attention.

"Lady, you don't know what the hell you are talking about!"

"Oh, yes I do," Amanda said with great certainty. "Elmer had done everything possible to protect the reputation of the woman he loved. Despite her faults, Bertie Ann intrigued him. Maybe he was even a bit envious of her daring, her fanatic zest for life. Elmer thought the marriage was going to take place, just as the older generation of Mopopes and Jollys originally planned. But Bertie Ann wasn't through rebelling quite yet. It was that next act of betrayal that broke Elmer's heart. He turned his anger inward and pushed all of society away. He was trying to protect himself by never allowing anyone close enough to hurt him again."

Amanda frowned when another thought leapfrogged through her brain. "I wonder if the youngest daughter in a family with twin girls always feels the need to create her own special attention? Bertie Anne must have felt as if she were standing in double shadows. It would seem that she devised a pattern of unacceptable behavior to gain her unique kind of attention. Bertie Ann did succeed in calling attention to herself with her antics, didn't she? Her name was on every tongue—"

"I said . . . GET OUT!" Melvin roared.

Amanda decided to make her exit before Melvin worked himself into a seizure and the twins fainted dead away.

Once outside Nick walked alongside Hazard, smiling in amusement. "You were really on a roll, weren't you? You dropped a few grenades in the senior citizens' laps and watched them explode."

"At least I know the gossip is true and that the land transactions I noted at the courthouse were not just a simple sale from one family to another. I also have the feeling that the Thompson affair was not the only one Bertie Ann had in her wilder days. Melvin and Claud both purchased land from neighbors—"

"Such as?" Nick prompted curiously.

"Such as a liaison with Abner Hendershot's father," Amanda replied. "I'm beginning to wonder if that land transaction might also have been made over the barrel of a shotgun."

Nick folded himself into the squad car and revved the engine. "Melvin's reaction to the accusations that he and Elmer argued about the will leaves me to wonder if the shouting match might have become a pushing match. Two cantankerous old men gouging at each other could have resulted in a fall—down the cellar steps. Perhaps Melvin's son Jerry started targeting you to protect his father. With you out of the way, the will might not be located. Elmer's property will then revert to Melvin and Claud."

"That's an interesting theory," Amanda agreed. "It would also explain the possible connection between Jerry Jolly and Randel Thompson. Randel could be playing up to me while he and Jerry are covering tracks and protecting the real culprit. Maybe Jerry bribed Randel with the land that once belonged to his family before the scandal."

"That is a definite possibility," Nick affirmed. "I know Randel has grown restless working for Buddy Hampton and is anxious to start his own horse ranch. Randel's built a name and reputation for himself in training cutting horses. Jerry Jolly is obsessed with raising horses. They could have all sorts of connections and might have struck a bargain. Maybe we should talk to Jerry."

Amanda glanced at her watch. "I have an appointment with Billie Jane Baxter after lunch."

"Then I'll question Jerry and Clive Barnstall while you're meeting with Billie Jane. You should be reasonably safe with the country music star in your office."

"I think you are taking this protective custody business too seriously, Thorn," Amanda insisted. "I can take care of myself."

"Oh really? Then how do you explain the fact that you came exceedingly close to being knocked out of a barn loft, imprisoned in the foundation of a burned-down house, forced off the road, and konked on the head? Have I left out any of your close encounters, Hazard?"

"I'm still alive, aren't I?" Let him argue with that!

He did. "Only by sheer luck, if you ask me. Next time you might not be so fortunate. The longer you keep stalling about Elmer's missing will, the more danger you attract. Whether your near accidents were scare tactics or death wishes, you would be well advised to announce that you can't find the will and turn the matter over to the courts."

"No," Amanda said adamantly. "That is not what Elmer wanted. I promised him that I would see his wishes carried out. I intend to keep that vow, no matter what!"

"God, Hazard, you can't be serious! Your life may be the risk you take to grant Elmer his dying wishes! You have not been properly groomed and trained to deal with this kind of thing. And if you get yourself killed, my only opportunity to meet Mother will be at your funeral."

"Geez, Thorn, you don't have to be morbid."

"I am making a vital point, Hazard. Magnum P.I., you are not! And you aren't Perry Mason, either."

"Thank you so much for your vote of confidence." She flung up her nose and looked down at him. "Despite what you think, I believe I have found my true calling in life."

"As a detective?" Nick scoffed. "Nobody I know gathers information at beauty boutiques and coffee shops and then plows ahead like a bulldozer, making one stab in the dark after another. You *stumble* onto evidence, Hazard. Or rather, it *stumbles* onto you. Your methods are totally unorthodox. The OKCPD would laugh themselves silly if they saw you in action. And this had better be your *last* case!"

Amanda raised a perfectly arched brow over piercing blue eyes. "Is that an ultimatum?"

"Yes, it is difficult to carry on an affair with a dead woman," he said bluntly.

"We are not having an—" Her voice evaporated.

"Affair, Hazard. A—F—F—A—I—R. And if you weren't so damned worried about your public image, we could be *going together* or *dating*. That would be respectable. Affairs suggest secretive activities and illicit behavior like Bertie Ann Jolly's. Do you want to be lumped in the same category with her?"

Amanda grimaced. "Certainly not."

"Then I think the time has come to establish some rules."

"But you once said—"

"Never mind what I said!"

"Good Lord, next you'll be telling me that somebody is going to come around to make sure we are handling this . . . relationship . . . properly," Amanda said with a smirk.

"All I am asking is for you to let the good citizens of Vamoose know we are going together," Nick muttered in exasperation.

"And if I do, am I going to get to wear your high school ring around my neck?" She batted her eyes at him.

"Just answer the question, Hazard," Nick snapped. "Are we an *item* or aren't we?"

Amanda inhaled a deep breath and thought it over. She was really sticking her neck out here. If she made a commitment, it could blow up in her face like her first marriage. And if she didn't, she'd lose Thorn. "Okay, Thorn. We are an *item*, as you prefer to call it. But that means you'll have to stop fooling around with Ms. Bosom."

"I never did fool around with Ms. Bo—Jenny. She was doing the chasing and—"

"You let her catch you a couple of times while we were quarreling," Amanda finished on a sour note.

"Jenny brought me supper. I ate it. She offered dessert and I declined. End of story. No hanky-panky, no groping, no nothing. Despite your sweeping condemnation of the male population, I have done nothing to warrant your suspicions. I'm one of the good guys."

"That's what they all say," Amanda grumbled cynically.

"One of these days I'm going to destroy each and every one of your hang-ups, Hazard. Then you will be fresh out of excuses as to why you can't admit you love me."

Amanda's eyes widened in alarm. "Who said anything about love?"

"I did. Something wrong with *your* hearing, Hazard?"

"Thorn, your colossal confidence is exceeded only by your enormous ego."

Nick grinned outrageously as he pulled into the parking lot of Last Chance Cafe. "I think you might be in love with me, but you refuse to accept the fact."

"And *I* think *you* have rocks in your head." Damn the man. He was too perceptive by half, and he obviously knew her better than she thought he did. He wasn't fooled by the aloof sarcasm she utilized to protect her once-broken heart.

"I must have rocks in my head to fall for a cynical

woman like you. But every once in awhile I catch a glimpse of your good qualities and that keeps me going."

Amanda's jaw dropped off its hinges. "Are you saying—?"

"Come on, Hazard. Let's have lunch. I'm buying."

Amanda wobbled out of the car, her mind reeling with what Thorn *had not* said. Dazedly, she walked into the crowded cafe. Vamoosians were out in full force and every pair of eyes zeroed in on her and Thorn as they parked themselves in the corner.

Ms. Bosom looked none too happy to see Amanda by Thorn's side. But Amanda did admit that Ms. Bosom rose admirably to the challenge of female rivalry. Indeed, she used her outstanding attributes and her low-cut tank top to their best advantage when she leaned over to fill Thorn's coffee cup. The view of twin peaks capped with pink cotton knit were impossible to miss when they were staring in Thorn's face—literally. In fact, Ms. Bosom purposely brushed her chest against Thorn's cheek.

When Jenny sashayed down the aisle, Amanda drummed her well-manicured fingers on the table. "Well, Thorn? Aren't you going to tell Ms. Bosom that we're *going together?*"

Nick grinned at Amanda from over the rim of his coffee cup. "I thought you should be the one to tell her. After all, *you* are the reason our affair has been the best-kept secret in Vamoose."

"Coward," she muttered.

"Sticks and stones, Hazard."

"I'd like to get my hands on a few sticks and stones. You find this vastly amusing, don't you, Thorn?"

"You're the real coward here." His expression sobered as he eased back in the booth and stretched his legs out in front of him. He stared at the contents of his cup. "I want to see you fight for what you want for a change without backing away, clinging to old hang-ups. Loosen up a little, Hazard. In case you are too blind to notice, it's you I want, not Ms. Bo—Jenny."

Amanda decided to employ Thorn's tactic. Sporting a blinding smile, she leaned across the table toward him. "You're crazy about me, aren't you, Thorn? Despite all my flaws, and I will admit I am rife with them, there is something about me that intrigues you. I'm curious to know what it is."

Ms. Bosom intruded to spoil the moment.

"What can I get you, Nicky?" Jenny purred, bending down to give Thorn another display of her hilly terrain.

"I'll take the *chicken* sandwich with all the trimmings." Dancing onyx eyes darted to Amanda in silent challenge.

Nobody called *her* chicken and got away with it!

"And what about you, Amanda?" Jenny never took her eyes off the handsome object of her admiration.

"I'll have the chili dog and onions rings with all the cholesterol."

"Anything else?"

"Yes. Thorn is mine."

Jenny recoiled as if she had been socked in the mouth. "I beg your pardon?"

"You're forgiven," Amanda said sweetly.

"Nicky?" Jenny turned to him with vivid green eyes, compliments of colored contacts.

Damn it, leave it to Hazard to cut her way to the heart of the matter without beating around bushes.

"Hazard and I had *this thing* going before you came back to Vamoose," Nick explained as delicately as he knew how.

"I see."

"It has to do with previous commitments made and honored," Amanda inserted, holding Thorn's direct stare. "I never did believe in playing the field. Maybe that's why I never appreciated baseball, either," she added in afterthought.

"Baseball?" Ms. Bosom repeated blankly, her voice matching the expression on her face.

Amanda glanced up at the buxom brunette. Damn, the poor woman's brain voltage must have been all of three watts! "Could I have more coffee?"

Big mistake.

Jenny poured the scalding liquid on Amanda's fingertips.

"Oh, how clumsy of me!" Jenny cooed while Amanda hissed in pain.

When Jenny stomped off, Nick inspected Hazard's singed fingers. "Jenny took the news well, considering you shoved it down her throat."

"You have to be blunt when dealing with individuals who have the mentality of a tablecloth ..." A thought soared across her brain and stuck like an arrow— somewhere in the creases of gray matter—but Amanda didn't have time to assimilate the facts while battling her female rival. "Gawd, Thorn, I wonder what you see in that woman. . . . Never mind, I know the answer to that."

"For God's sake, Hazard, I was eighteen and my hormones were rioting. You know how teenagers are. To them, sex is like football. Everybody wants to score a touchdown, just to say he has—"

Before Amanda could respond, Abner Hendershot lumbered over to park himself beside her. "So, what's the word on the Jolly estate? We need to get this settled. As soon as wheat harvest is over, it will be time to renew agreements for leased ground. Will I be planting on Jolly soil or do I need to find another landlord to rent me cultivation land?"

"Is there some reason that leads you to think the agreement you had with Jolly would not be honored by his benefactor?" Nick inquired. "I took Ms. Hazard's suggestion and did some checking on both sides of the stories I heard. According to the director at the ASCS office, you failed to comply with the agriculture program. You altered the wheat base on the quarter section you rented from Elmer. It seems you took it upon yourself to harvest wheat on allotted layout ground. Elmer received a notice from the Department of Agriculture, informing him that he would be ineligible for farm subsidy if he and his renter continued the illegal practices."

"Now hold on, Nick. That was all a mistake," Abner snapped.

"Yeah, and you made it. If I were Elmer, I wouldn't rent to you again. You grazed so many cattle on his wheat pasture that it has caused a reduction in harvest yield. Elmer had agreed to accept one third of the crop as rent, so naturally his payment dropped while you fattened your steers until they damaged the wheat. You sold the cattle for a tidy profit and you made money at Elmer's expense. Knowing Elmer, he had a few things to say about your underhanded tactics."

Abner's face turned the color of stewed chicken.

Amanda was impressed. Thorn had been doing his homework. Bless the darling man!

Nick pressed even harder. "Elmer confronted you, didn't he? Did you threaten to have him declared incompetent and stashed in a home if he backed out of your agreement?"

Abner hauled himself out of the booth and stalked off without admitting or denying the allegation.

"And *you* call *me* blunt?" Amanda smirked.

"It must be contagious."

Amanda glanced up to see Randel Thompson and Jerry Jolly entering the cafe. That particular association was one that aroused Amanda's suspicious nature. Her trepidation intensified when Randel flashed her an annoyed glance and then directed his hostility toward Thorn. Amanda could not read the motive in the expression that hardened Randel's face, but whatever its source, the cowboy was not pleased to see Amanda and Thorn together.

"Now it's my turn," Nick announced.

Amanda grabbed his arm before he could stand up. "Don't, Thorn."

"Why the hell not? You told Ms. Bo—Jenny that we have a thing going. Romeo needs to know."

"Not while he is a suspect," Amanda insisted.

Nick dropped back into his chair. "Oh fine, run off my female admirers and keep your beau on a string. Damn it, Hazard, you don't even play by *your* own rules. You keep changing them as you go along."

Amanda shot Thorn a withering glance. "Don't get your feathers ruffled for nothing. I don't want Randel on a string. I already told you Randel has frog lips."

"But you let him see you naked," Nick accused.

"I was wearing a towel. And I did not invite Randel in my home. He came in to make sure I was all right."

Nick snorted derisively. "A likely story—" He snapped his jaw shut when Jenny set his meal under his nose and slung Amanda's plate across the table.

"No hard feelings." Amanda offered Ms. Bosom a peace-treaty smile which was not returned.

"Do keep that in mind," was all Jenny said before she turned around and walked off.

Amanda stared at that chili that oozed from the bun which had been haphazardly slapped on the raw hot dog. The onion rings were soaked with grease and heavily salted. No doubt, Ms. Bosom was getting even. Damn, now Amanda had more than one person who would have liked to see her dead. . . . Or could it have been one and the same?

Nick watched Hazard stare ponderously at her plate. "Afraid to eat?"

"Your old flame didn't waste her culinary talents on me."

"If Ms. Bo—Jenny did poison your food, you're lucky that you have me to rush you to the hospital with sirens screaming."

Amanda took a cautious bite and wheezed to catch her breath. There was so much cayenne pepper in the chili that it would have choked a horse. Nick reached over to whack her between the shoulder blades to revive her.

"No hard feelings, I believe you said," Nick prompted with a scampish grin.

"Ah, the price I have to pay for your love," Amanda croaked.

"I never said I loved you, Hazard. But if you want to offer me your *dying* confession, I'm all ears."

He grinned; she sputtered.

"All I want to know is what Ms. Bosom's name was before she married?" she choked in question.

Nick frowned at the unexpected question and then replied, "Long is her maiden name. That's what she goes by now, just like you use Hazard."

"And what was Jenny's mother's maiden name?" Amanda managed to get out in a strangled voice.

"Ogelbee."

Amanda digested that tidbit of information and nodded musingly. "Harry's sister, I suppose."

"Right." Nick frowned again. "What has that got to do with anything?"

Ms. Bosom sauntered down the aisle, smiling in spiteful satisfaction at the purple hue of Amanda's skin and her insatiable need to gulp water.

Amanda's watery eyes drilled into Thorn. "Has it occurred to you, Thorn, that Ms. Bosom arrived in town the same week Elmer died—the same week I started meeting with calamity?"

Nick turned as pale as a dark-complected man could get.

Amanda shoved her plate aside and helped herself to Thorn's French fries, her analytical mind sorting through a variety of facts she had acquired the past two weeks. She was beginning to have a few doubts about the top-heavy waitress.

Needless to say, Amanda did not leave a tip on the table when they left the cafe. She did not allow Thorn to leave one, either.

* * *

Amanda had just chewed her last Rolaids tablet when Billie Jane Baxter swanned into the office in her sequined blouse and painted-on jeans. The country singer looked as if she had just stepped off stage. Amanda did not know where Billie Jane found the strength to lift her arms or hold herself upright with all that gawdy turquoise and silver jewelry strapped around her wrists, fingers, and neck.

"Hi, Mandy," said the human gong. "I hope you'll overlook this getup. I was signing autographs at one of the music stores in the city and I didn't have time to change. There must have been a thousand fans lined up in the mall."

"Your fans must love you."

"Too true. Tooo true—oooo . . ."

Amanda feared Billie Jane was going to burst into a chorus of one of her country hits. God spare her!

Billie Jane dumped a boot box full of cancelled checks on Amanda's neatly arranged desk. "I hope you don't mind if I brought along the checks from my account in Nashville. I fired my financial adviser and I am just no good whatsoever with a checkbook. It never balances any better than the one from Vamoose Bank. And I have had to write so many checks to contractors for the construction of my new house that I simply lost track of them all. And with my hectic touring schedule, I have a devil of a time keeping up. And then the storm wreaked havoc on my new house." Billie Jane dropped into her chair and sighed audibly.

Amanda waited for the seams of Billie Jane's jeans to split. Miraculously, they didn't.

"Now I have to replace the *new* roof with a *new* roof. And two windows were broken by hail. And how am I supposed to know what kind of fixtures I want in those five bathrooms? I don't have the slightest idea which walls should have phone jacks installed. I swear I will never build another house again!"

When Billie Jane—rising country music star—unloaded, she really unloaded! Amanda was not a counselor. She was an accountant who occasionally turned detective. And Thorn could attest to the fact that Amanda did not always say the right thing at the right moment.

"You've got to help me out, Mandy." Jewelry jingled as Billie Jane threw up her hands. "You can't imagine the grueling schedule I keep. I want you to be my accountant *and* financial advisor."

Amanda kept her trap shut. She had pegged Billie Jane as a scatterbrain the first time the woman breezed into the office with her wild hair, her acrylic nails, fake eyelashes, and only God knew what else had not come as standard equipment in this souped-up model of feminine flesh.

"Can you straighten this mess out for me while I talk to the contractors? And there's my mother, of course. I need to stop by to see her. By the way, are you still living in my aunt's little rental house?"

"Yes." If Billie Jane threatened to use her clout with her aunt to raise the rent, Amanda would dump the cancelled checks on Billie's head, so help her she would!

"I hope you know what a good deal you got. Aunt Em is a tenderhearted softy."

"The vintage linoleum in the kitchen needs to be replaced. The carpet is threadbare, and the heating system is on its last leg," Amanda replied.

That changed the country singer's tune in a hurry.

"Is it? I haven't been in that old house since I was a kid, practicing my yodeling with my cousins." Billie glanced at her turquoise-studded watch. "I've got to run. Can you have both my checkbooks balanced in a couple of hours? I have a plane to catch. My band is meeting me in Dallas for a performance. The concert sold out in two days."

Amanda watched Billie Jane jingle-jangle out the door. Inhaling a fortifying breath, Amanda began sorting the checks in chronological order. She noted that Billie Jane could not spell worth a damn. It was a good thing the woman had stumbled into music. She would have made a terrible secretary.

Chapter Thirteen

Amanda stopped by Watt's Body Shop to check on her Toyota while she was waiting for Thorn to pick her up. As expected, Cleatus was no closer to beginning the repairs than he had been the day Amanda delivered the car. And since her jalopy truck had been dragged from Deep Creek by Cecil Watt's Towing Service and was also awaiting automotive repair, all Amanda had as a mode of transportation was Elmer's battered pickup with its weak battery. She ought to sell her vehicles and purchase an army tank. Then the deplorable county roads wouldn't be able to slow her down!

With Cleatus' assurance that he "would get right to" her Toyota, Amanda stepped outside to see Thorn pulling in the driveway. Without ado, she sank down on the seat and fired her question.

"What did you find out from Jerry Jolly?"

"Not much. Jerry has an alibi for the afternoon Elmer died, as well as for every day when you flirted with disaster. The man has an amazing memory."

"And who can validate his alibis?" Amanda wanted to know.

"Randel, for the most part."

"My, my. those two seem to be spending a great deal of time together. What an intriguing coincidence"

"I also find it an intriguing coincidence that when Benny hauled Clive home last night, Patricia was nowhere to be found."

Amanda digested that information and frowned ponderously.

"I went by Elmer's farm and nosed around for a few minutes," Nick said as he drove home.

"And?"

"Nothing. With the continuous rain it's impossible to identify tracks. But I did note that the crates of silver and China are missing."

"I'm not surprised. I expect Odie Mae and Eula Bell are trying to cover their own set of tracks." Amanda was silent for a moment before adding, "I would love to interrogate Bertie Ann. I would also like to write that woman's biography. She must have led an interesting life."

"Speaking of interesting, I was congratulated on my taste in women earlier this afternoon," Nick commented. "Velma flagged me down to tell me that it was all over town that you and I were seeing each other on a regular basis."

"Thorn?"

"Yeah, Hazard?"

"I realize we have passed a milestone in our . . . relationship . . . but let's keep it respectable, shall we?"

"Getting cold feet already?" Nick taunted. "Maybe I should propose—all for the sake of propriety, of course."

"Propose?" Amanda howled. "We just became an official *item.*"

"Oh, right." Nick back a grin. The thought of marriage had put Hazard in a tailspin. "I suppose we should *go together* for a couple of years."

"Good idea, Thorn. I'm too old to subject myself to the rumor that I *had* to get married."

"Yes, extremely bad for our images. Me—the chief of police—and you—the impeccable crime-solving accountant. My God, the things people might say!"

Amanda glared laser beams at Thorn's shoulders which were shaking with barely restrained amusement. "You know, Thorn, sometimes, you can be a real jerk."

Nick barked a laugh, but it transformed into a curse when he topped the hill and had to slam on the brakes. The squad car slid sideways, scraping the line of weeds and ridge of gravel that skirted the muddy road.

"Damn it to hell!" Nick muttered.

Amanda braced herself as the car careened and cattle scattered like quail. She didn't realize she had been holding her breath until the car ground to a halt— missing a startled calf by mere inches. Nick leaped out of the car, wading through the mud and flapping his arms like a duck taking flight. Amanda glanced down at her shiny navy blue pumps, shrugged, and climbed out to lend assistance. Mud gathered around her ankles and her shoes became twice their normal size.

"My cattle must have gotten through the fence at the creek," Nick speculated. "Rushing water sometimes washes out the posts and metal panels. I didn't take the time to check this morning." He gestured for Amanda to walk toward the opposite bar ditch. "We'll herd the cattle down the hill and into my driveway. I don't want someone sailing over the hill and running into the livestock the way we almost did—"

The sound of another vehicle slopping down the road put another curse on Nick's lips. He dashed back to move the squad car before the oncoming vehicle smashed into it. Meanwhile, Amanda clomped toward the edge of the road, herding cattle along the fence. A shocked gasp erupted from her lips when Elmer's battered truck—the one that was supposed to be parked on the hill beside *her* driveway, while the key was safely tucked in her purse!—crested the hill.

Amanda heard Thorn's bellow of alarm, but she stood frozen to the spot, staring at the driver who was barely distinguishable through the muddy windshield. The truck accelerated and swerved toward her. Amanda felt as if she were moving in slow motion. She knew instantaneously that she was the proposed target of a hit and run. But the knowledge did little to impel her flight into the ditch. Her feet were buried in mud.

The scream left her lips at the exact moment that she flew out of her shoes and launched herself toward a clump of weeds. All Amanda heard the next second was the roar of the engine and the slosh of mud. A moment later she was sprawled facedown, her heart beating against her rib cage like a deranged drummer.

"Hazard!"

The smell of burning rubber and exhaust fumes filled her senses. Amanda panted for breath while the truck zoomed off, hitting a calf before speeding away from the scene of the crime. Amanda heard the thrashing of weeds and glanced up through mud-caked lashes to see Thorn skidding down on his knees, his dark eyes as wide as salad plates.

"Hazard?"

The concern in his wobbly voice was damned touching. Amanda would have fully appreciated it if she had not been suffering the aftershock of near death.

"Good God Almighty!" Nick yanked her against him and squeezed what little stuffing she had left in her. Amanda couldn't breathe, what with her pulse exploding through her veins and Thorn crushing her in a bear hug that could shatter bones. The man did not know his own strength!

"Thorn," Amanda chirped, her voice two octaves higher than normal. "You're squooshing me."

Nick abruptly released her and began examining her for injury. "Are you okay? Did he hit you? I was sure he hit you. I—"

"Shut up, Thorn. You're bordering on hysterics," Amanda croaked. "I thought cops were always cool, calm, and collected in the face of adversity."

"Calm? Calm! How can I be calm? I had to watch you mowed down and practically run over. Damn that son of a bitch!"

Amanda crawled to her knees and then to her feet. She cursed at the pathetic sight of the calf sprawled in the middle of the road. The driver of the truck knew exactly what he was doing, Amanda decided. He knew Thorn couldn't pursue him while one victim was lying in the ditch and the other had been run down on the road.

While Amanda stood there watching the mother cow bawling over her injured calf, Nick jogged to the squad car to contact Deputy Sykes.

"Sykes," he blared over the two-way radio. "Hightail it over to Hazard's house."

"Hazard's house, right," Benny repeated.

While Nick explained what had happened and de-

manded that the driver of Elmer's truck be apprehended
and hanged on the spot, Amanda stared at the pitiful
calf. She didn't have to be a veterinarian to make a
prognosis. Before sunset, the size of Thorn's cattle herd
would decrease by one. And it was all *her* fault.

"Hazard, get your butt in the car!" Nick railed at her.

Amanda slogged numbly toward the patrol car and
collapsed on the seat. She said not one word while Nick
sped toward the driveway. Within minutes, he had gotten in his four-wheel drive pickup and backed it beside
the downed calf, hooked up the chain, and dragged the
animal off the road. Grimly, Nick ran his fingers down
the calf's spine. His gaze darted to Amanda, assuring
her that her diagnosis was correct. The calf's back was
broken. Without a word, Nick retrieved his pistol to put
the calf out of its misery.

Amanda blanched when two shots barked in the air.
But the ordeal was far from over. Cattle still lined the
ditches. Under Nick's instruction, Amanda circled behind the herd that had paused to graze. Four calves
broke and ran and had to be rounded up a second time
before the procession of livestock finally trotted through
the driveway and into the corral.

"You go take a shower while I mend the fence," Nick
commanded.

"I'll help."

"No!" Nick glowered at her. "The way your luck has
been running, you'll be shot down by a damned sniper.
Now get the hell in the house. We have a barbecue to
attend tonight and I have a fence to fix. I am not going
to stand here arguing with you and wind up being late!"

"You don't have to shout at me, Thorn," Amanda
blared at him.

"Damn it, Hazard. You scared twenty years off my life. I can damn well shout if I want to."

It went against the Hazard grain to be ordered around by the male of the species. It was one of her worst faults, according to Thorn. Rebelliously, Amanda climbed into the truck, tilted her muddy chin, and waited for Thorn to join her.

"Hazard, I am positively certain that if I told you *not* to dash off a cliff, you would do it just to spite me," Nick grumbled.

Amanda employed that age-old tactic that had been the downfall of men since time immemorial. She sent him one of those sweet, adoring smiles that buttered the bread of a man's ego.

"I'm not trying to be spiteful, Thorn. I just prefer to be with you, especially after such an unnerving ordeal."

The strategy worked superbly. The irritation drained clean out of him. Amanda rather expected it would. Thorn reached over to squeeze her hand and she squeezed back. It was a tender moment . . . as long as it lasted. . . .

"Okay, Hazard, I'm giving you your way, but don't think I don't know when I've been manipulated. That out-of-character comment and that mushy little smile were a dead giveaway."

"You are such a perceptive man. I'm glad I have you on my side."

"I'd rather have you on your back."

"Don't spoil the moment with ribald remarks, Thorn. We were supposed to be bonding on a nobler plane."

"Nonetheless, that's what you get for sweet-talking me." Nick shifted gears and switched the topic of conversation. "Did you get a look at the driver?"

Amanda nodded her muddy blonde head. "I saw curly black hair, sunglasses, and a camouflaged rain poncho that made it impossible to describe the suspect's physical size or distinguishing features. If I am not mistaken, and I doubt I am, he or she was wearing a wig. It could have been anybody. and I will not be the least bit surprised if your fence has been tampered with. I think that entire scene was deliberately planned and I'm really sorry about your calf."

"So am I, Hazard," he murmured. "But I'm glad it wasn't you."

Amanda's speculations proved correct. The wire that held the metal cattle panel in place over the creek had been snipped in two, and not by the force of raging water, either. Amanda was certain Thorn's metal panel had passed Mother Nature's test and failed at the hands of the stalker. Damn, she was going to have to sit herself down and analyze the facts before the attempts to scare her to death succeeded! It was bad enough that one of Thorn's calves had perished. Amanda shuddered at the thought of Thorn being sacrificed. She had developed a fond attachment for the man.

While Nick and Amanda dragged the panel back into place and fastened new wires, an owl hooted in the distance. Despite the most recent catastrophe, Amanda felt a sense of tranquility settling over her like a cozy quilt. For a city slicker, she was becoming very content with country living. She must have been a pioneer in a previous life.

By the time they returned to the house, Deputy Sykes was waiting for them.

"I checked out Ms. Hazard's home," Benny reported in his typical businesslike manner. "By the time I got there, the truck had been returned and there wasn't anyone in sight."

"No tracks?" Nick questioned irritably.

Benny shook his fuzzy brown head. "Whoever stole the truck must have hiked across the wheat field or pasture."

"Damn."

After Benny drove off, Nick stomped toward the barn to feed the sheep and return the cattle to the pasture. Amanda headed for the showers. Confound it, she had to get her hands on Elmer's will—and quickly! For some reason that document held the key that unlocked this mystery. It had to be linked to the attempts on her life, or to the thoroughly effective scare tactics—whichever. Where in the hell had Elmer stashed the damned thing?

While Amanda stood in the shower, she focused all her powers of thought and reasoning on the old hermit who had taken a liking to her. Amanda had no illusions about the cantankerous Elmer Jolly. He had been a bitter, suspicious man—a callus product of all the disappointments life had dealt him.

Elmer clung to the old ways and thumbed his nose at family intervention, and at acquaintances who tried to get on his good side for the benefits they might derive. Elmer had a tendency to stash things in the most unusual places. He had a tender regard for his "critters" and he had developed a fonder affection for livestock and research on wheat hybrids than humans. Amanda could understand why Elmer felt the way he had. His critters never betrayed him. And his research was a labor of love, produced by his own ambitious initiative.

Swell, Hazard. So you understand where Elmer was coming from. So where does that leave you? You still don't have the will. All you have is a dozen suspects, each of whom could have been provoked to anger and disposed of a frail old man who could not defend himself if he was caught with his guard down. . . .

The thought triggered visions of the stormy afternoon at Elmer's home. Distracted, Amanda grabbed a towel and dried herself off. Perhaps the will *had* been stashed under the house. She had not had the time to locate it before she was imprisoned in the foundation. Maybe Odie Mae and Eula Bell had confiscated all the goods and now had the will in their possession. . . .

"Here, Hazard. You'll need something to wear until we drive to your house so you can dress for the Hazard barbecue."

Amanda pulled up short in the hall, clutching her towel around her. She had been so immersed in thought that she hadn't heard Thorn return to the house. Dark eyes drifted over her towel-covered physique. She knew what Thorn was thinking. She could see him thinking it. He was fantasizing about encounters of the most intimate nature. Amanda was harboring a few of those fantasies herself. Unfortunately, they were working on a tight time schedule. "Later, Thorn. You are the main course for dinner tonight." She knew Thorn was to be sized up, interrogated, and stamped with the Hazard seal of approval, *if* he met all the necessary qualifications. "We'll see what shape you're in after you've been barbecued."

Nick draped his T-shirt and sweatpants over Hazard's shoulder on his way to the shower. "If you think I'll be out of the mood tonight, you're kidding yourself."

Amanda donned the oversized clothes and wandered down the hall, concentrating on Elmer and his ritualistic habits. . . . Another thought struck her like a lightning bolt. Amanda froze in her tracks when the vision of Elmer's home expanded in her brain. Suddenly, her mind became a fertile seed bed of planted information that had begun to germinate. Realization sprouted in her brain. With everyone dwelling on the assumption that Elmer had been pushed down the steps to his death, Amanda had been sidetracked by the original clue that had aroused her suspicions. *The false teeth.* No one had shoved Elmer down the steps . . . because Elmer was already dead before he reached the cellar.

With absolute concentration, Amanda scrutinized the scene in her mind's eye. She remembered the lopsided tablecloth that almost touched the floor, the blaring television, the tangle of pillows and quilts in the bedroom. *That* was why Elmer's home had been burned down—to destroy evidence at the *actual* scene of the crime!

It all began to make sense. Elmer had been interrupted *during* his meal. Someone had entered the house while the television was blaring. Elmer might have been jerked from his chair, causing the tablecloth to shift off center. A struggle probably ensued with Elmer battling and spouting threats at the intruder. Elmer might even have disclosed or prefabricated the contents of the will in a fit of temper. That information could have, in turn, set the intruder off.

Amanda inhaled a steadying breath as the scene unfolded like a nightmare. The tangle of bed linens hinted that there might have been a struggle in the bedroom. It could very well have been that Elmer was suffocated with his own pillows. And *that* was the reason the house had been carefully rearranged when she returned to the farm.

The killer was covering his or her tracks—the tracks at the *real* scene of the crime.

Elmer must've been killed in the bedroom, not in the cellar—as the killer wanted the rest of the world to believe. The threatening storm had worked to the killer's advantage, giving him, her, or them the perfect excuse to stash the body in the cellar. Indeed, who had questioned the possibility of murder except her? All of Vamoose was prepared to write Elmer's death off as an accident precipitated by the thunderstorm.

If that were so, why had Amanda become the target of attack? She recalled what Melvin Jolly had said to her twice—in seething anger. Amanda swallowed hard. She *had* to find that will.

Her pensive gaze circled the bedroom Thorn had converted into a den. She stared ponderously at the crate of jars that contained Elmer's notes. If Elmer stuffed his research data in glass canning jars for safekeeping, where would he stash his last will and testament?

The answer hit Amanda like a ton of jars—*canning jars!*

Amanda raced toward the kitchen counter to grab Thorn's keys. Damn, how could she have been such an imbecile not to have linked the obvious together? Checking her watch, Amanda scurried toward the front door. If she hurried, she could drive to Elmer's farm, retrieve what she was looking for, and be back in ten minutes. Fifteen minutes tops. Thorn was still in the shower. He would barely have time to miss her. . . .

Another thought struck Amanda as she twisted the door knob. As a precautionary measure, she should leave Thorn a note. She doubted that she would need rescuing, but one never knew.

Thrilled with the prospect of locating the long lost will, Amanda hopped in the four-wheel drive truck and sped off. Finding Elmer's will would go a long way in improving her attitude toward the upcoming barbecue at Uncle Dean's. It would also provide answers to questions that had hounded her to no end.

By damned, Hazard, I think you're really onto something here!

Nick stuck his head under the pulsating shower and scrubbed himself until he was squeaky-clean. Tonight was his grand debut. He was going to meet the Hazards. Mother would pump him full of questions and pass judgement. Nick was anxious to meet Mother in person, as well as the other Hazards. He was going to make a good impression.

Should he wear his traditional navy blue suit—the one and only suit he had to his name? Or should he stick to his usual attire of dress jeans, western shirt, and Roper boots? That really was more his style. He was a no-frills kind of man who was country born and country bred and damned proud of it. And besides, Mother said this was an informal affair. Nick had no intention of giving false impressions or overdressing for backyard barbecues.

Definitely boots and jeans, he decided as he stepped out of the shower. Nick grabbed the shaving cream and patted it on his face. He shaved slowly and carefully. It would never do a nick himself and arrive at Uncle Dean's with patches of Kleenex stuck over the chunks he had cut out of his skin.

Having scraped off his five o'clock shadow, Nick

reached for the toothbrush and dental floss. Mother had a fetish about oral hygiene. Tonight, his pearly whites would be gleaming to such extremes that Mother would need sunglasses to deflect the glare of his one-hundred-fifty watt smile.

Nick slapped on a little extra cologne for this monumental occasion. He tied the towel around his hips and padded to his bedroom. Within a few minutes, he was dressed and striding toward the living room to receive—what he hoped would be—Hazard's nod of approval.

No Hazard.

Nick frowned at the silence that greeted him. He veered around the corner to the kitchen to find it empty. His gaze landed on the hastily scribbled note where his keys should have been. An explosive curse resounded around the house. His eyes blazed over her message.

I went to Elmer's farm. Be back soon.
Hazard

Hazard had picked one hell of an inconvenient time to go romping off on another of her wild goose chases. They were due in the city in less than two hours. Damn it to hell!

Still swearing at regular intervals, Nick stormed out to the squad car. For a woman who was supposed to be intelligent and reasonable, there were times when Hazard displayed not one lick of sense. She seemed to think she was invincible, charmed. Just because she had escaped disaster a few times the past two weeks did not make her Superwoman! And if she got herself killed the very night he was scheduled to meet Mother and the rest of the Hazards, Nick was never going to speak to her again! What could that woman have possibly been thinking?

She *wasn't* thinking; she was *investigating*.

Scowling and cursing, Nick zoomed off. His hands clenched around the steering wheel, pretending it was Hazard's neck. *Damn the woman!* Nick repeated that epithet faithfully as he blazed over the muddy roads at speeds that were nowhere near reasonable and prudent for the existing conditions.

This time Hazard was going to pay—and pay dearly—for worrying him to death. And Nick was definitely worried. He had a bad feeling about this impulsive trip Hazard had taken to Elmer's farm.

A very bad feeling indeed!

Chapter Fourteen

Amanda parked Thorn's truck and grabbed the flashlight. Anxious anticipation was gnawing at her as she hurried toward the cellar. The creak of the door drowned out the gusty wind that whipped through the elm and cottonwood trees. Amanda shined the light on the rotten steps and descended carefully. The stench of stagnant water filled her senses and glistened in the light. Amanda took another tentative step down, searching for signs of snakes. Her gaze circled the gloomy cellar, remembering the scene that awaited her the day of the storm. Amanda shivered uncontrollably as the cold damp air clung to her skin. With grim determination, she shined the light around the corner.

Canning jars lay half submerged in the ground water that seeped into the cellar. Amanda was reasonably certain that somewhere amid this clutter was Elmer's will—sealed and stashed in a place most folks wouldn't think to look. But Amanda had focused on Elmer's customary pattern of behavior because something Thorn had said the previous day had finally clicked into her brain—a brain that had been jammed by too many conflicting facts.

Thorn had suggested Elmer might have stashed the will in the same place he stashed his research notes. Amanda was certain now that Elmer had hidden the will in the same *container,* not in the same *place.* The old man had stuffed money in canning jars and hid them all over his house. He sealed years of meticulous research data in Ball and Kerr jars and deposited them in his foundation. His last will and testament—witnessed by the banker and his secretary—had to be somewhere in this cellar.

Amanda braced her free arm against the wall and stepped onto the fallen shelves that protruded from the water. Like a gymnast on a balance beam, she made her way toward the submerged jars, hoping the one that might contain Elmer's will hadn't shattered when the shelves came tumbling down. Amanda plucked up a canning jar and shined her light on it. Pickles. Damn.

Systematically, Amanda set aside the jars of beets, pickles, jelly, and peaches. She couldn't help but wonder if these were the Christmas gifts Millicent Patch had mentioned that were given by the Methodist Women's Society. Whatever the case, Elmer had been well-stocked with fruits and vegetables. No doubt, he ate the contents and stored his treasure in the jars.

After several minutes of stacking the strewn jars, Amanda checked her watch. She was running short on time. She had to drive back to Thorn's farm and then stop by her own house to dress for dinner. More than likely, Thorn would be out of the shower by now and cursing her up one side and down the other. . . .

The flashlight reflected off a floating jar on the far

side of the cellar. None of the other jars were floating. Amanda felt her anticipation escalate as she tiptoed across the slick shelving. Balancing on her two-inch beam, she leaned out to retrieve the jar.

Eureka! The jar contained an envelope from Ed McMahon's million dollar sweepstakes. Amanda twisted the lid open and extracted the paper inside the envelop. Here, Amanda thought with a huge sigh of relief, was Elmer's long lost will. A rueful smile pursued her lips as she read the opening sentence.

Although there are those who consider me incompetent and would see me institutionalized for trying to protect what is mine, I, Elmer Wayne Jolly, am of sound mind and body.

Elmer had managed to get off one last parting shot. Amanda had expected as much from the feisty old man.

To the school district of Vamoose, I leave a certificate of deposit for one hundred thousand dollars to be used as a scholarship fund for the most deserving college-bound students.

"Damned decent of you, Elmer," Amanda complimented the dear, departed soul.

To the Methodist Women's Society, I bequeath five thousand dollars. A good jar of pickles is hard to come by these days. The Christmas pickles were worth at least that much.

Amanda chuckled. "Nice touch, Elmer."

To my brothers, Melvin and Claud, I leave my research notes which are stored under the trap door of my bedroom. I want to see amber waves of Jolly wheat blowing in the wind when I look down from the pearly gates. The profit from the sale of certified wheat should make my brothers' retirement much easier.

"That is kind of you, Elmer, but I'm not sure your brothers deserve such consideration."

I'm not sure my brothers deserve such consideration.

Amanda smiled to herself when she realized she and Elmer were on the same wave length. No wonder she felt an unexplainable bond with the old man.

But family is still family, and we have all done what we could through the years to protect the name and the traditions.

Here, Amanda decided, was the reference to his attempt to protect the woman he loved and lost to his own brother those many years ago.

And for that reason, I leave the property and the mineral rights from the land that once belonged to my brother Leroy to his widow Bertie Ann Jolly and their son Wally. Leroy's son, despite what Wally might say to the contrary.

Amanda frowned. An uneasy feeling trickled through her. She had been right all along. This last will and testament held a valuable clue that answered Amanda's questions. She knew who her mysterious stalker was, and she intended to look him up, just as soon as she finished reading the contents of the will.

Though it was impossible to forgive and, we could never go back to the way it had been, I have never been able to forget those few months of happiness in the springtime of my years. They came and went like the seasons, but the memories lasted a lifetime.

Amanda felt moisture fogging her eyes, pitying an old man who had generously given his heart away, only to have it broken. And through the bitterness and betrayal, Elmer had secretly cherished the memories of one, bright, shining moment before it was stolen from him.

"Hurry up, Hazard," Amanda ordered herself. "You're running out of time."

And to my accountant, Amanda Hazard, I leave my critters. Amanda Hazard has always come each time I called, no matter how insignificant my request. She never once charged me for consultation when I wanted advice. And never once did she expect anything from me. She accepted me for what I was, the way I was, and asked only what she could do for me each time I called. That kind of loyalty should be rewarded. Amanda Hazard called me her friend and when she makes a promise and commitment, she honors it for life. In that, we are a lot alike—or at least I could have been like her if I had not been betrayed by the one to whom I would have given a lifelong commitment.

Another mist of sentiment clouded Amanda's eyes. "Thanks, Elmer, you tough, sweet ole rascal you."

The cantankerous old man touched that soft core that Amanda usually concealed from the rest of the world. Yes, indeed. She and Elmer were alike in many ways— lots of bluster and fuss to protect that vulnerable spot that had callused over through the years.

I also bequeath the rest of my property to Amanda Hazard. She will be far better at dealing with renters than I ever was. And I do want a new renter, someone who will care for the land and protect it in ways my last renters refused to do. They took from the land without giving anything back, draining the nutrients and cutting corners every chance they had. I cut them no slack because they gave nothing to the land itself. Make sure your renter does better next time around, Missy. The land is forever. Take care of it.

Amanda wobbled on her legs and braced her arm against the wall before she fell, knocked off balance by the old man's generosity. "Oh, Elmer, you shouldn't have."

"You're right, lady, he damned sure shouldn't have."

Amanda very nearly leaped out of her skin when a gruff voice echoed around the musty walls of the cellar. While her heart pounded against her ribs, Amanda swiveled her head to see the incongruous form of a man in a rain poncho glaring down the barrel of a gun. Wally Jolly, no doubt. Amanda had wanted to confront him at her convenience. She was not offered a choice.

"Come up here, *now.*"

Before turning around, Amanda tucked the will in the band of her jeans and then faced the bewigged Jolly in sunglasses.

Wally gestured toward Thorn's truck. "You're driving."

"I'd rather not—" Amanda winced when Wally leaped down to ram the pistol in her chest. Arguing with a loaded gun wasn't the smartest thing to do. It ranked right in front of making a spur of the moment jaunt to Elmer's farm without dragging Thorn with her.

"Hurry up," came the brusque command.

Amanda danced to the tune of the loaded gun. With sickening dread, she slid beneath the steering wheel. Her mind reeled with imaginative, untimely endings to her life. Damn it, get a grip, will you, Hazard? You can't devise a plan of escape to this latest disaster if you have a panic attack. Use your brains before your friend here decides to blow them away.

"I assume you weren't happy to learn Elmer deeded his property over to me. Maybe we can settle for a compromise."

A mocking snort erupted from curled lips. "There will be no compromise. That land belongs to me—all of it. It is mine by right of birth."

Amanda backed out of the driveway. She had not understood the command Elmer had given her on the phone the day of his death, but she understood it now. Elmer had instructed Amanda not to believe the lies, no matter what. This was the lie that was waiting to be voiced and not to be believed.

Wally Jolly removed his wig and glasses, revealing hard blue eyes and thin brown hair. "Elmer refused to claim me because he never forgave my mother for running off and leaving him. Even my uncle—who raised me as his own—never knew the truth. Only my mother did, and she didn't tell me until after Leroy died."

Amanda's mind cranked as she eased the truck onto the road and headed in the direction her companion indicated. She remembered Velma telling her that Bertie Ann had set up housekeeping with Elmer until she began her affair with Leroy when he returned from his tour of duty. It would be difficult to contest the claim of Elmer's child. Who would question Bertie Ann and Wally's claims? For certain, the Jolly family resemblance could have been handed down by either Leroy or Elmer. No one would be the wiser.

"After Leroy died, Elmer refused to accept me as his son so I could inherit what was rightfully mine."

Amanda nodded, assimilating the facts she had gathered. "Elmer saw to it that Leroy was disinherited. That was why the land changed hands for the baffling price of one dollar an acre."

"Elmer cut out his own brother and refused to let Leroy and Bertie Ann anywhere near him. Only Odie Mae and Eula Bell kept in touch all these years."

"So you came to see Elmer the day of the storm, to persuade him to write you into his will," Amanda speculated.

Amanda cruised along at ten miles an hour, hoping beyond hope that Thorn had found her note and had come tearing after her. Thorn was to have been her insurance, just in case she met with trouble—which she had. So where the hell was her knight in shining police car when she needed him? Damn it, the one time Amanda had let herself count on Thorn he wasn't around!

"You suffocated Elmer, didn't you?" she questioned. "That's why you went back to straighten up the house. You wanted everybody to think Elmer died in the cellar. It was your car I saw driving off in a cloud of dust the day of the storm. You're also the one who called the ambulance before I could summon the proper authorities to investigate."

Wally muttered sourly. "You're too nosy for your own good."

Amanda ignored the remark. "You're the one who told Melvin I was to inherit everything, weren't you? Of course, I doubt that you told Melvin what you did to his brother. Melvin kept silent to protect his family because that has become a Jolly tradition."

"I knew you were going to be a problem," Wally grumbled. "How did you figure it all out? Nobody else had a clue."

"His teeth."

"What?"

"Elmer's store-bought teeth," Amanda explained. "Elmer only wore dentures to eat. After a meal, he rinsed them off and tucked them in his shirt pocket. That's how I knew Elmer hadn't accidentally stumbled down the steps."

Wally muttered something foul under his breath. Amanda did not ask him to repeat it. Mother, after all, did not approve of such offensive language, especially in front of a lady—or rather a woman Mother *wanted* to behave like a lady.

"So, Wally, are you going to fill me in on all the details?" Amanda asked boldly. "I think I have a right to know after all the times you tried to scare me to death."

"What difference is it going to make now?" he snorted sardonically.

"My inquiring mind wants to know."

"Drive a little faster and I might tell you," Wally Jolly baited her.

Amanda speeded up one mile an hour.

"Elmer had tried to run me off with his shotgun when I went to see him three weeks ago. But the last time I caught him unaware. He had the TV volume turned so loud that he didn't know I was in the house until I was standing behind him at the table. He went into one of his rages and ordered me out of the house, swearing he wasn't going to give me anything and that he was leaving *everything* to his accountant."

"And then you killed him, all for nothing." Amanda stared at Wally in disgust. "Elmer lied to you. If you had known him better, you would have realized that he always became contrary and spouted like a tea kettle when he was angry. The truth is, he left Bertie Ann and you the land and mineral rights that once belonged to Leroy. It would have eventually been yours."

Another raft of curses floated from curled lips. "Damn that old bastard. Did he think that giving back the land that should have been Leroy's and my mother's compensates for banishing them from the family? I deserved to have it all, not just one lousy section of land and the mineral rights!"

Damn, talk about a bastard, thought Amanda. This broken branch on the Jolly family tree was a greedy, spiteful excuse of a man.

"And if not for you—" he continued in a resentful tone, "everything would have turned out just fine."

Amanda applied the brake and bought herself a little time. "So you *were* trying to kill me? Why bother? You obviously knew I hadn't found the will, either. You tore my house upside down, looking for the will and then returned everything to its place so I couldn't claim my home had been demolished because of Elmer's murder—"

The pistol jabbed Amanda in the ribs. "Keep driving."

She begrudgingly complied. Curse it, where was Thorn? What was he doing? Primping and sprucing up for his debut with the Hazards?

"I tore the place upside down trying to find that damned will so I could destroy it. When I realized you hadn't located the will either, I burned down Elmer's house, hoping the will was in it. Soon, you and the will will be out of the way and I can take my case to court. I will have what should have been mine years ago—"

Amanda had been waiting for Wally to distract himself while she was wringing a confession out of him.

Now was her golden opportunity. Amanda put the pedal to the metal and the truck fishtailed in the mud, flinging her companion against the passenger door. She put a hatchet chop to his wrist, knocking the pistol to the floor.

Hallelujah! Now she had a fighting chance!

It was at that moment that a siren screamed and flashing lights lit up the darkness. Another round of nasty curses that would have offended Mother's sensitive ears exploded in the cab of the truck. Wally lunged at Amanda while she was trying to maintain control of the truck. The vehicle swerved toward the ditch and bounced over the clump of weeds and gravel that skirted the road.

Bless Commissioner Brown's heart. This unmoved bulwark of debris prevented Amanda from plunging down the steep slope at sixty miles per hour. She could envision herself wrapped around a fence post. Thorn would be none too happy if she scratched his prize possession—his shiny black truck with the hay fork protruding from the back bumper, looking to all the world like a gigantic bumblebee.

A pained yelp burst from Amanda's lips when her head collided with the window and an elbow caught her in the solar plexus. She couldn't breathe to save her life. She needed an unhindered flow of oxygen to her stunned brain and she needed it now!

A meaty hand shot past her, fumbling with the door latch as the truck veered toward the middle of the road. Amanda attempted another karate chop, but she caught another elbow in the chin. Her senses reeled and her teeth vibrated like a harp string.

If her would-be murderer knocked out her teeth, Mother was going to be *extremely* upset!

Cold air whipped around Amanda as the door swung open, leaving her dangling half in and half out of the speeding truck. To her stunned disbelief, her assailant snarled a few more obscenities, yanked on her hair, and bit down on her hand until she unclamped it from the steering wheel. Boy! Talk about fighting dirty!

Amanda felt herself launched into space by a blow to the cheek. Her nose was bleeding. She was reasonably sure of that, and her lip must have split. She tasted her own blood the instant before she rolled through the mud and gravel like a rag doll that had been tossed from a speeding car. Amanda clawed the mop of damp hair from her face in time to see the truck spinning sideways. A bloodcurdling screech leaped free when the truck broadsided her, sending her cartwheeling into the ditch.

The last sound to penetrate her dazed mind was the squeal of sirens that assured her that Thorn was hot on the trail of her assassin. She knew Thorn would come through—eventually. After all, Magnum P.I. had nothing on Thorn. Nick Thorn was Vamoose's personification of truth, justice, and the American Way—Amanda's Superman in cowboy boots, her hero.

Of course, Thorn was going to be mad as hell at her. He never did appreciate the fact that she dabbled in detective investigation and courted catastrophe for a hobby. This time, Amanda decided, she had courted catastrophe a little too closely. She was feeling dreadfully nauseous. Her entire body throbbed in rhythm with her pulse and she couldn't tell where she hurt the worst. . . .

The world turned darker than the inside of a cow. Amanda collapsed in an oblivious heap as the patrol car

topped the hill and sped past the spot where she lay—
unnoticed.

Nick cursed at the same speed at which he drove. He
was too far behind his black truck to see exactly what
was going on, but he knew Hazard was in trouble when
the truck fishtailed all over the road. Nick had surged
down the hill and cruised over the rise of the terrain too
late to see Hazard tossed out and left for dead. All he
saw was his truck speeding off, flinging mud in all directions.

He had immediately called for a back-up from Deputy Sykes and radioed the county sheriff's department
for further assistance. He expected to find a hostage situation awaiting him when he and the other law enforce-
ment officers managed to set up a roadblock. This night
was not turning out as Nick had anticipated. Hazard was
damned sure going to regret this latest shenanigan—*if*
she survived. Nick fully intended to raise all kinds of
hell with her.

"Benny, take the road to Abner Hendershot's farm
and set up a roadblock at the intersection a half mile
west," Nick ordered.

"A half mile west," Benny repeated. "10–4."

Nick radioed the dispatcher, requesting a back-up to
block the roads east and north of said intersection. That
done, he floorboarded the accelerator. Nick cursed the
driver of his truck when the cylinder-operated hay fork
lowered like a lance. Nick slammed on the brake and
swerved before his own hay fork speared through the ra-
diator of his patrol car. Damn it, he could see himself
having a collision with his own truck—his pride and

joy. If that truck sustained so much as a scratch, he was going to take a hammer to Hazard's head!

"Nick?" Benny Sykes' gung-ho professionalism failed him when he saw Thorn's truck speeding straight toward the roadblock. "That's *your* truck I'm blocking!"

"No shit, Benny," Nick muttered.

The driver of the black farm truck spotted the patrol car ahead of him and swerved toward the ditch, shifting into four-wheel drive on the move. The vehicle did indeed resemble a bumblebee in flight as it soared off the road and splashed down in the ditch. Benny's squad car darted forward to block the improvised escape route. More sirens screamed and lights flashed as the back-up patrols closed in at Nick's command. The black truck buzzed and spun in the mud, trying to reverse direction. Six officers appeared, pistols aimed and ready. The truck ground to a halt—up to its fenders in mud.

Nick followed proper procedure, ordering the driver out with his hands above his head. When the driver emerged without a hostage in tow, a puzzled frown furrowed Nick's brow. Where the hell was Hazard? Lying on the floorboard of his truck with a bullet hole draining the life out of her?

While the other officers latched onto the suspect and read him his rights, Nick sloshed toward his truck, imagining the worst. Bewildered, he stared inside his truck, seeing only the discarded weapon. He wheeled toward the man who lay spread-eagle on the hood while he was being frisked with swift, practiced efficiency.

"Where is she?" Nick demanded.

"Where's who?" came the sarcastic reply.

Nick wheeled toward his patrol car and radioed for am ambulance to meet him at Elmer Jolly's farm. He was reasonably certain Hazard had been in the truck when he first spotted it fishtailing on the road. She had to be somewhere within two miles of Jolly Farm, Nick deduced.

Wary dread gnawed at him as he retraced his path. He wasn't certain he wanted to be the one to locate Hazard.

Still swearing a blue streak, Nick stopped the patrol car at the location where the tracks swerved from one side of the muddy road to the other. With flashlight in hand, he paced the north ditch before crossing the road to inspect the south side.

And then he saw her. He wanted to shoot Hazard a couple of times for putting him through hell again, but he suspected she had already taken a direct hit. And all for what? he asked himself bitterly. Nick sure hoped Elmer Jolly appreciated the extremes to which Hazard had gone to serve as the executor of his estate. Hazard may be joining Elmer at the pearly gates real soon.

"Damn it, Hazard. You go to incredible lengths to stand me up, don't you?" Nick scowled as he sidestepped down the ditch. "If you didn't want me to meet Mother, why didn't you just say so!"

When the ambulance siren filtered through his tormented mind, Nick stopped in his tracks. He wasn't going to venture any closer to the sprawled body this time. He would let the paramedics do their duty. He wasn't even going to watch them examine Hazard for wounds. He was simply going to stand there and sweat blood.

Nick didn't even remember how he had responded to the questions the paramedics posed. He was in a daze, remembering other nights he would have preferred to forget. . . .

"Hey, Thorn, isn't this the same lady you pulled out

of Whatsit River a few months ago?" the red-haired paramedic questioned.

Nick inhaled a fortifying breath. "Yes."

"Thought so."

Nick gulped hard. "Is she—?"

"Still alive? Yes," the paramedic confirmed before he and his partner settled Amanda on the stretcher. "It looks like a few bruises and scrapes. Maybe a fracture."

Nick half collapsed in relief.

"Here. I found this tucked in the band of her jeans."

Nick accepted the folded paper with shaking hands and stuffed it in his pocket.

"You want me to call Dr. Simms again? I'll have him meet us at the hospital."

Nick nodded agreeably. His vocal apparatus wasn't functioning all that well at the moment. But he had damned well better get his act together—and quickly. He had phone calls to make. Mother needed to know that he and Hazard wouldn't be coming for dinner. He also had a criminal to interrogate. It was going to be a long night.

And this time, by damned, Hazard was on her own, Nick promised himself. Last time she nearly got herself killed trying to be a one-woman police squad, he had sat beside her hospital bed like a faithful puppy. But not this time! She could call Romeo the rodeo clown to hold her hand. Nick Thorn was *not* going to be there, no siree. He was really going to call it quits this time. Hazard had gone too far in her attempt to solve this crime. She had also broken her promise to confide in him and to let him assist her.

Jenny Long was looking better to Thorn by the minute. At least Ms. Bo—Jenny didn't stew in her own juice. Maybe what Nick needed was a good cook who fawned all over him. That beat the hell out of Hazard's daring heroics! Nick didn't need a born crusader, he needed a fawning cook.

Nick Thorn was officially washing his hands of Hazard—for good, forever! The affair was over. Hazard was a hazard to her own health and to Nick's mental well-being. She had chopped his emotions to bite-size bits for the very last time!

Amanda awoke to see a familiar face bending over her.

Dr. Simms smiled kindly as he laid the stethoscope against her chest. "So we meet again, Ms. Hazard. You seem to have a knack of landing in difficulty." He checked the dilation of her eyes. "I assume you plan to make a habit of this. Perhaps we should reserve you a room so we don't have to waste time with the paperwork of readmittance." His Reeboks squeaked on the waxed floor as he pivoted to examine her left leg— the one that felt as if the hide had been scraped off it.

"The last time you were here—in January, I believe—you tried to check yourself out of the hospital the same night you arrived. This time you will be an overnight guest. We have a small matter of a broken arm with which to contend."

Her eyes widened in alarm.

"Nothing too serious," he assured her. "Your left arm won't require surgery or insert pins to hold you together. This is just a standard, run-of-the-mill fracture."

"Where's Thorn?" she managed to ask, though her mouth felt as if it was stuffed with cotton.

"I haven't seen him. From what the paramedics told me, he had a few loose ends to wrap up in the case."

So Thorn really was steamed about his truck. He wasn't speaking to her. And furthermore, he wasn't coming around to see if she was in one piece. She would make it up to him somehow—just as soon as she was back on her feet. Her gaze—gleaming with determination—drilled into the gray-haired physician.

"No," Dr. Simms declared. "Don't even think I'm going to let you out of here tonight, and that is that. I'm not making any exceptions the way I did last time. I am not signing your clean bill of health until your arm is set in plaster and all your vital signs deserve my recommendation." He patted her good arm—the one that had only sustained a few bruises and scrapes. "Cheer up. Hospital food isn't all that bad."

Amanda resigned herself to her hospital stay since Thorn wasn't here to bail her out. She was dying to know—Well, not exactly *dying,* she amended. She was *curious* to know if Thorn had wrung the entire story out of Elmer's supposed son.

It just wasn't fair. She had done all the legwork in this case and Thorn was getting to do the final wrap-up. He would probably keep her in suspense about the outcome, just to punish her.

She thought she deserved praise rather than punishment.

Thorn obviously did not agree. . . .

Chapter Fifteen

The following morning Velma Hertzog, chomping and popping her gum, breezed into Amanda's hospital room to report all the details of the chase, roadblock, and the results of the interrogation.

"Wally Jolly was jailed and Nick threw the book at him." Crackle, snap. "Nick also found out that Wally was the one who burglarized Chester Korn's home and used the stolen goods to set up his headquarters at his grandparents' old homestead. It was all so exciting! Nick's picture is splashed all over the front page of the *Vamoose Gazette*. Here, see for yourself."

Amanda stretched the paper out on her lap to see Officer Thorn's handsome mug staring back at her. Thorn had received glowing accolades for the capture and arrest of the murder suspect whose photo was included at the bottom of the page. Amanda frowned as she read the article. Officer Thorn said *this* and Officer Thorn said *that*. She had busted her butt, stuck her neck out, and broke her arm to solve this case! and all she got was a bouquet of bug-infested irises from Velma's garden. The sheriff's department had pinned so many medals of recognition on Thorn's chest that the man wouldn't be able to walk upright with all that heavy weight dangling off him.

"Was Thorn's truck damaged in the chase?" Amanda questioned, struggling to keep the irritation from seeping into her voice.

"Yep." Snap, crack. "Cecil Watt towed the truck over to Cleatus's auto body shop for repairs. Nick's truck got moved up to first in line since he has become the hero of the week." Chomp, chomp. "It was amazing how Nick put two and two together and figured out how and why Elmer was killed."

Velma sank her overweight body onto the edge of the bed and eyed the lunch tray. "You gonna eat that piece of cake?"

"No. Go ahead."

Velma removed the wad of gum and placed it on the edge of the saucer. "I guess Thorn went looking for Bertie Ann Jolly last night after the fiasco with her son," she said around chunks of white cake. "Bertie Ann claimed Wally had been a real pain in the ass the last few years. He must have paid her back for all the hell she raised in her younger days. It seems none of us around Vamoose knew much about Wally since the family moved away so long ago. But we've got the scoop on Wally now. He has been married and divorced four times. He moves in and out of his mother's house in the city while he is between women and jobs. According to Bertie Ann, Wally had dreamed up some kind of scam to inherit the Jolly property. When the estate went to probate, he was going to claim to be Elmer's son."

Wally had said as much to Amanda. He had also said a lot of naughty things that would have had Mother sputtering for breath! Amanda had the feeling that even Bertie Ann had no idea that Wally had killed Elmer. That weasel had only told the Jolly family what he wanted them to know.

"Nick demanded the truth, and nothing but the truth, from Bertie Ann. I guess he must have put the fear of God in her with talk of being an accomplice to murder, burglary, and attempted murder. She broke into tears and swore that Wally was Leroy's son, even though Wally was ready to testify in court that he was the direct descendant of Elmer Jolly. I guess Wally's finances were in a state of disaster and he was looking for some quick cash—what with all those ex-wives to support."

Velma wiped the chocolate icing off her mouth and grinned. "I also hear you are now a property owner. Nick turned Elmer's will over to the court to be processed. Of course, Melvin and Claud are none too happy, but Elmer had his say and that is the end of it. You can bet it came as a blow to all the widows around Vamoose who tried to butter Elmer up the past few years. They tried to pay him calls to get on his good side. He shooed them all away—none too politely. But who would have thought old Elmer would have taken such a liking to you that he left you his property."

"I don't want his land," Amanda murmured.

Velma stuffed her gum back in her mouth and chomped on it. "Well, it's yours nonetheless. And after all you've been through, I'd say you deserve it—"

"I see our patient is recovering nicely." Dr. Simms observed as he squeaked into the room in his Reeboks. "How is the arm feeling?"

"Like a tree trunk. Do you happen to have a chain saw with you?"

Dr. Simms laughed and his stethescope bounced on his chest. "Sorry, but you and that cast are going to be inseparable for six weeks. Maybe that will keep you out of trouble ... or at least slow you down. I advise against getting thrown from speeding pickups for awhile, unless you want to come back to see me sooner than usual."

The physician gave her chart a thorough perusal. "You can check out whenever you're ready."

"I was *ready* last night," Amanda muttered crankily.

Dr. Simms grinned and left. Amanda flung her legs over the edge of the bed and reached for the clothes Velma had brought for her.

"Um ... hon? There is something you need to know before you're released." Velma failed to make eye contact. She was staring at Nick's photo on page one of the *Vamoose Gazette*. "Nick and Jenny Long were seen together late last night and again this morning. He dropped her off at work."

Amanda felt as if Velma had stuffed a knotted fist in her midsection.

"I ... uh ... thought you and Nick were going together."

So did Amanda. Apparently Thorn was more than a little peeved about the incident that landed her in the hospital and his truck in the body shop. Amanda recalled what Thorn had once said about fighting for what she wanted—*if* she wanted it badly enough—instead of tangling herself in her hang-ups. But maybe she didn't want a fair-weather friend who made himself scarce when the going got a little rough. How much could Thorn really care if he turned to Ms. Bosom after

Amanda got caught in a minor scrape with a murderer? A fine friend Thorn turned out to be!

If Thorn wanted a cook who was long on body and short on brains, a kowtowing female who kept his ego stroked and well fed, then fine and dandy. Amanda didn't need that big ape hanging around anyway. There was always Romeo the rodeo clown. Now that Randel was off the list of suspects, maybe Amanda would do a little courting of her own. How bad could ole frog lips be?

Despite her silent pep talk, Amanda didn't feel a damned bit better after Velma dropped her on her doorstep. To Amanda's surprise, Randel had appointed himself keeper of her critters. The livestock had been fed and Randel swaggered toward her with a basket of eggs and a countrified smile.

"Feeling better, 'Manda honey?"

Obviously Randel had heard that Thorn and Ms. Bosom were keeping company. Randel was in the courtship mode again.

"I wanted to stop by and see you before Jerry Jolly and I headed to Texas. We're going to look at a stud colt and some mares we're thinking of buying. Jerry and I are going into business together."

"What about your employer, Buddy Hampton?"

"I quit. I decided to train and show my own stock for a change. And I'm going to open a Mr. Fix-it shop in Vamoose to tide me over until the horse ranch is established."

Amanda imagined the fix-it business would go great guns in Vamoose. There were scads of senior citizens who needed chores and repairs done around their homes and farms by an able-bodied man. Amanda was in need of a few repairs herself from time to time.

"I'll be back to see you after my trip," Randel handed her the basket of eggs and dropped a kiss to her lips.

Amanda amended her declaration that frog lips weren't all that bad to kiss. There was no spark, no sizzle, no nothing. Damn, she missed Thorn's full, sensuous lips. Too bad he was wearing them out on Ms. Bosom these days.

When Randel sauntered to his flashy yellow short-bed pickup. Amanda stared at the basket of eggs. "As long as I've waited for these, they should have been gold," she grumbled before she stamped into the house.

While she stood in the empty silence of her home, Amanda recalled the words Miss Scarlett had uttered when Rhett Butler had gone the same way as the wind. Amanda really was going to be miserable if she didn't find a way to get Thorn back. And tomorrow may have been another day for Miss Scarlett, but Ms. Hazard was not into procrastination. Amanda almost never put off until tomorrow what she could get in trouble doing today.

With Thorn on her mind, Amanda set about to improve her appearance and whip up a meal to rival Ms. Bosom's chicken casserole. Ms. Bosom may have had the chicken, but Amanda had the farm-fresh eggs. All she had to do was wipe the dust off her cookbook and get to work. Amanda hoped Ms. Bosom hadn't completely satisfied Thorn's appetite before Amanda could deliver her magnificent dinner.

* * *

The incessant chiming of the door bell pealed through the house. Nick stepped out of the shower and tied a towel around his hips. The door bell clanged again, and again.

"I'm coming already! Don't blow a gasket, damn it."

Nick jerked open the door to find Hazard poised before him. There was a purple bruise on her jaw, no skin on her right elbow, and a cast on her left arm. Sympathy welled up inside him, but he forcefully hammered it down.

His gaze caught and hung on the red cotton tank top that testified to the fact that Hazard's anatomical architecture was better designed than Ms. Bo—Jenny's could ever be without surgical implants. Hazard's jeans fit like denim gloves and her boots had been polished to a shine. Her form-fitting attire was clearly an attack on his male senses and his willpower.

Her hair had that breezy look about it, as if she had hurriedly blown it dry. In her good arm she balanced a casserole dish that had peace-treaty written all over it. Well, tough. Nick had said his last goodbye. It was finished. Kaput.

"Good evening, Thorn," she said, the epitome of cheerfulness.

"You're here, so what's good about it?" he said snidely.

Amanda braced herself against the cold wind of rejection and sailed toward the kitchen to unload her casserole. "I brought you supper."

"I'm not hungry."

"I made it myself." She had spent hours on this damned soufflé. The first two had fallen flat. The hogs, however, had gobbled them up.

"If you made it yourself, I'm *really* not hungry!"

Nick propped himself negligently against the door-jamb and crossed his arms over his bare chest. "You look like the one who needs dinner catered. In fact, I'm surprised Dr. Simms signed your release. You should be under observation in the psychiatric ward. You really need to do something about your suicidal tendencies, Hazard."

So that's what this cold shoulder routine was all about, she reasoned. Thorn was in a huff because she had gotten herself into a teensy-weensy little scrape. That had to be it. He hadn't even mentioned his dented truck yet. Amanda smiled to herself. The fact that Thorn was annoyed indicated he still cared. There was hope.

Amanda sauntered back to Thorn, imitating Ms. Bosom's famous drumroll walk. His obsidian eyes dropped to the low-cut tank top. His nostrils flared with the scent of her perfume—his favorite—but he made no move toward her. Thorn was going to be difficult, Amanda realized.

"You're really ticked off at me, aren't you, Thorn?"

"You could say that, Hazard. Or you could say that I have watched you flirt with disaster one too many times and that I have had all I am going to take!"

Nick exhaled a harsh breath and raked his fingers through his dark hair. "You just don't get it, Hazard. Detective investigation isn't just a game. It's a dangerous profession. There are some ruthless kooks out there. You seem to think you can involve yourself in a case and all your suspects will line up like ducks in a row for you to interrogate. Well, it doesn't always work that way! Sometimes killers come out of the woodwork for reasons you can't even imagine—as in this case. They stalk you for motives you can't figure out—also as in this case. Wally Jolly was desperate for money and he was determined to get it—over your dead body, and it very nearly came to that!" Nick's eyes blazed with frustration. "Damn it, Hazard! Finding you sprawled in that ditch was the last straw. You are not tearing my emotions out by the taproot ever again!"

Boy, he really *was* pissed! This called for drastic measures. Amanda was on the verge of losing the one man she had allowed herself to depend on in the last seven years. And that was saying a lot for a card-carrying feminist who waved her flag of independence in every male face. Thorn's had been no exception.

"So you really want to call it quits, Thorn?"

Nick gave his raven head a decisive nodd. Valiantly, he fought the erotic sensations that surged through his body—and with the same success, he was sorry to say, as General Custer at the Battle of Little Bighorn. His male body instinctively reacted to the sexy female who paraded toward him. It was an inevitable as sunrise. But that was beside the point. Sex wasn't everything. Hell, lately it wasn't anything!

"Quits, Hazard. You scared the best years off my life."

"I see." Amanda nodded pensively and paused directly in front of Thorn. "So I would be wasting my.breath *if*— and this is all hypothetically speaking, of course—I told you that I might have fallen in love with you." She glanced speculatively up at him from beneath a fringe of long curly lashes. "And you wouldn't care *if* I told you that you were the last thought on my mind while I was fighting for my life, *if* I admitted I was counting on you to save me from my own foolishness. And I don't suppose you would want to hear that there has been no one but you since my divorce and there probably won't be anyone else, even *if* you and Ms. Bosom have decided to set up housekeeping together—"

"Hazard—"

"And I don't suppose it would do one smidgen of good *if* I told you that I need you to protect me from myself when I become overly involved in murder cases that I can't seem to avoid when one of my clients is needlessly killed." Amanda paced back and forth in front of Thorn, head downcast, eyes monitoring her booted feet. "You see, Thorn, I have this troublesome hang-up about unswerving loyalty to my clients and my friends. Elmer made mention of it—"

"I know. I read the will—"

"And of course, I don't imagine you would give a hoot *if* I told you that I spent the entire afternoon in the kitchen trying to emulate Ms. Bosom's fine culinary talents, just to impress you. My hens started laying, you see, and—"

"Hazard—"

"And I thought with all those farm-fresh eggs I could whip up a mouth-watering delicacy to tantalize your taste buds—"

"Shut up, Hazard. You're yammering like Mother."

Amanda's head snapped up and her blue eyes flashed fire. "I really wish you hadn't said that, Thorn."

A faint smile twitched his lips as he reached over to uplift the turn-down corners of her mouth. "Would you have been happier *if*—and this is hypothetically speaking, of course—I told you I suffered all the torments of the damned when I found you in that ditch, *if* I said I had every intention of taking what Ms. Bo—Jenny offered and wound up turning her down—again, *if* I would have said that I *might* have fallen in love with you, even if you make me so damned mad with your wild escapades that I'd like to wring your neck?"

Amanda regarded him for a long moment. *"Do* you, Thorn?"

"Do I what? Want to wring your neck? Yes, most definitely."

"No, do you—?"

The phone blared. Nick smiled wryly while Hazard hung on tenterhooks. "Excuse me. My public calls. I have received scads of praise for solving this intriguing case. I made all the local and area papers, did you know?"

"Yes, I know. And all at my expense," Amanda grumbled. "You haven't been very appreciative about all the trouble I endured to make you the hero of the week—"

"Hello?"

"Nick? I'm worried about Amanda," said Mother. "I tried to phone her last night after you called to say you had a case working and you couldn't come to dinner. All I get at Amanda's house is that confounded answering machine. Good heavens! Amanda wasn't in any danger last night, was she? She isn't cut out for police work."

Nick shot Hazard a quick glance. It was obvious that Mother did not know her darling daughter as well as she thought she did. Hazard thrived on the thrills of crime solving. She was addicted to the challenge of the chase and capture. There were kleptomaniacs, pyromaniacs, and there were *detect*imaniacs. Hazard fell into the latter category. She simply could not keep from poking her nose in dangerous places. Solving crimes had become the driving obsession in her life.

"Not to worry, Mother. Your daughter is fine. In fact, she's cooking supper for me this evening."

"Amanda? Cooking? Are you *sure* she is okay?"

"Yes." With the exception of a broken arm, skinned knees, and a number of bruises, she is in splendid shape, Nick silently added.

Mother cleared her throat. "Is she there now?"

"Yes. Hold on a minute." Nick extended the phone to Hazard.

Amanda frowned at Thorn. "I can't talk now. I broke my arm."

Nick shoved the receiver into her good hand. "You're damned lucky it wasn't your neck. Be a good girl and talk to Mother. Tell her to what daring extremes you went last night to keep me from meeting her and the rest of the Hazards."

"Doll, are you there?"

Amanda clamped her hand over the receiver as if it were Mother's mouth. "I didn't do that on purpose, Thorn."

"You'll never convince me of that, Hazard. You are obviously ashamed of me."

"That is the most ridicu—"

"Doll?"

Amanda lifted the receiver and glared sharp thorns at Thorn. "Hi, Mother. Sorry we couldn't make it last night."

"Well, you missed a fine dinner. We were all so disappointed that we didn't get to meet your man friend." Mother cleared her throat and plunged on, asking and then answering her own questions.

Nick dropped his towel and stood there wearing nothing but a rakish smile. Amanda's appreciative gaze flooded over his well-sculpted physique, not missing the slightest detail. She, of course, had always been a stickler for details.

"Sorry, Mother, I hate to interrupt you, but I'm going to have to get back to you later. Something has come up." She stared deliberately at the "something that had come up."

"But—"

Amanda dropped the receiver in its cradle and smiled impishly. "I'll say one thing for you, Thorn, you do have a most fascinating way of getting attention. Does this mean I've been forgiven for all my stupid stunts?"

"No." He swaggered toward her, lifting her up into his arms. "It will take you all night to work your way back into my good graces."

"What about my soufflé?"

He grinned again, showing off his pearly whites. "I've got news for you, Hazard, I'm not in love with your cooking."

She grinned back. "So you're saying you're in love with *me*—period?"

"I didn't say that, either. I am only playing up to you because I want to rent the farm ground you inherited from Elmer."

"And I only made you a soufflé because I wanted to practice for the Betty-Crocker Bake-Off," she flung back just as flippantly.

Nick tumbled with her onto his bed. "Damn it, Hazard, just what *am* I going to do about you? I'm not sure I can live *with* you and I can't make myself do *without* you."

Her good hand ventured off on a journey of rediscovery, altering Thorn's heartbeat in one second flat. However, Nick was determined to lay down a few ground rules before he lost the ability to form rational thought.

"No more wild heroics, Hazard. I really mean it this time. I don't handle crisis as well as I used to."

"Whatever you say, Thorn," Amanda murmured. Her hand drifted down the washboarded muscles of his belly . . . and beyond. . . .

"And from now on, I want you to confide all your suspicions and information to me," he demanded, his voice dropping an octave with the downward descent of her hand. "No more striking off on your own to satisfy your craving for detective investigation. I'll handle the dirty work if any other cases arise."

"Right, Thorn, and I'll be in charge of the firearms," she volunteered with great enthusiasm. Her hand closed around the pistol he was packing and he gasped for breath. "Loaded weapons will be my specialty."

"Hazard—" he said in a strangled voice.

"What, Thorn?"

"If I ever do come right out and say how I feel about you, would you tell me how you honestly feel about me?"

Her eyes darted from the weapon in her possession to his handsome face and she smiled mischievously. "Maybe we should say it simultaneously so neither of us has to stick our necks out too far. On the count of three. One . . . two—"

Nick soundly cursed Alexander Graham Bell and his grand invention. The telephone, Nick was sure, was solely responsible for the ruination of man's love life. He really was going to have to invest in an answering machine.

Rolling sideways, Nick pushed Hazard to her back and reached over her to answer the phone that set on his antique oak nightstand. "Hello?"

"Nick?" Chomp, crack. "It's Velma. I just wanted to let you know I brought Amanda home this afternoon." Snap, pop. "She seemed kind of down to me."

Nick cast Hazard a wry smile. Hazard looked *down* to him, too. Flat on her back, as a matter of fact. If everybody would leave him the hell alone, he might be able to do something about it.

"I know this isn't any of my business." Snap, crackle.

You got that right, Velma, Nick silently replied.

"But Amanda could use some company right about now. Vamoose's hero of the week, for instance."

Hazard would have all the company she needed—and then some—if you would hang up the damned phone, Velma!

"Thanks for calling, Velma. I'll see what I can do about lifting Hazard's spirits—" His voice evaporated when Hazard's hand and lips slid down his body, wandering to places that could endure no more stimulation than they had already received.

"You won't be sorry, Nick," Chomp, snap. "Bye."

"Hazard, cut it out," Nick groaned as he fumbled to toss the phone in its cradle. "I'm setting a short fuse here."

"I've got news for you, Thorn, there is nothing short about your fuse."

"Now I suppose you're going to tell me you're a demolition expert, Hazard."

Blue eyes gleamed up at him. "Trust me on this one, Thorn. I damned well know a lighted stick of dynamite when I see one."

When Thorn smiled at her in pure male anticipation, Amanda was positively certain that her meticulously labored-over soufflé would fall—long before they got around to eating it.

Amanda Hazard's keen intellect, unerring instincts, and reliable intuition proved her right—as usual.

Note To Readers

I hope you enjoyed the second book in the continuing series set in small-town America. Amanda Hazard will soon be back with Thorn at her side, faithfully serving her clients in Vamoose. Velma, the gum-chewing beautician, the "Snail Brothers," and the overenthusiastic Deputy Sykes will reappear from time to time. You will also meet a cast of other lively characters—or dead ones, as the case might be.

Until we meet again in Vamoose,

WHO DUNNIT? JUST TRY AND FIGURE IT OUT!

THE MYSTERIES OF MARY ROBERTS RINEHART

THE AFTER HOUSE	(2821-0, $3.50/$4.50)
THE ALBUM	(2334-0, $3.50/$4.50)
ALIBI FOR ISRAEL AND OTHER STORIES	(2764-8, $3.50/$4.50)
THE BAT	(2627-7, $3.50/$4.50)
THE CASE OF JENNIE BRICE	(2193-3, $2.95/$3.95)
THE CIRCULAR STAIRCASE	(3528-4, $3.95/$4.95)
THE CONFESSION AND SIGHT UNSEEN	(2707-9, $3.50/$4.50)
THE DOOR	(1895-5, $3.50/$4.50)
EPISODE OF THE WANDERING KNIFE	(2874-1, $3.50/$4.50)
THE FRIGHTENED WIFE	(3494-6, $3.95/$4.95)
THE GREAT MISTAKE	(2122-4, $3.50/$4.50)
THE HAUNTED LADY	(3680-9, $3.95/$4.95)
A LIGHT IN THE WINDOW	(1952-1, $3.50/$4.50)
LOST ECSTASY	(1791-X, $3.50/$4.50)
THE MAN IN LOWER TEN	(3104-1, $3.50/$4.50)
MISS PINKERTON	(1847-9, $3.50/$4.50)
THE RED LAMP	(2017-1, $3.50/$4.95)
THE STATE V. ELINOR NORTON	(2412-6, $3.50/$4.50)
THE SWIMMING POOL	(3679-5, $3.95/$4.95)
THE WALL	(2560-2, $3.50/$4.50)
THE YELLOW ROOM	(3493-8, $3.95/$4.95)

Available wherever paperbacks are sold, or order direct from the Publisher. Send cover price plus 50¢ per copy for mailing and handling to Penguin USA, P.O. Box 999, c/o Dept. 17109, Bergenfield, NJ 07621. Residents of New York and Tennessee must include sales tax. DO NOT SEND CASH.

"MIND-BOGGLING . . . THE SUSPENSE IS UNBEARABLE . . .
DORIS MILES DISNEY WILL KEEP YOU
ON THE EDGE OF YOUR SEAT . . ."

THE MYSTERIES OF DORIS MILES DISNEY